"Only stunned.   **job of it!"**

Hilary didn't know the voice at all, and it had no meaning for her. She knew that she had a pain in her head, nothing more. That was the whole world.

Something else came into this world. Grit—cold, wet grit against her mouth. Horrid. She wasn't being lifted any more. She was lying on her face in the road. She remembered the bicycle, and thought it was all smashed up, and how was she going to get into Ledlington now?

All these thoughts really took no time at all. Consciousness came back and they were there, waiting for the light to touch them. She became aware of two things simultaneously, and then a third. The car with its engine running, and its lights shining on her—those two things first. And then the slam of a door. Someone had slammed the door of the car.

The man at the wheel put the car into bottom gear and jammed his foot down hard on the accelerator.

Hilary heard the sudden roar of the engine. It came to her as sound, as danger, as terror itself. . .

Also by Patricia Wentworth

The Clock Strikes Twelve
Lonesome Road
Pilgrim's Rest

Published by
WARNER BOOKS

PATRICIA WENTWORTH

THE CASE IS CLOSED

WARNER BOOKS

A Warner Communications Company

The characters and situations in this book are entirely imaginary and bear no relation to any real person or actual happening

WARNER BOOKS EDITION

Copyright © 1937 by Patricia Wentworth
All rights reserved.

This Warner Books Edition is published by arrangement with Harper & Row, Publishers, Inc., 10 E. 53rd St., New York, N.Y. 10022

First published in Great Britain by Hodder and Stoughton.

Warner Books, Inc.
666 Fifth Avenue
New York, N.Y. 10103

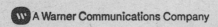 A Warner Communications Company

Printed in the United States of America

First Warner Books Printing: January, 1986

10 9 8 7 6 5 4 3 2 1

CHAPTER ONE

Hilary Carew sat in the wrong train and thought bitterly about Henry. It was Henry's fault that she was in the wrong train – indisputably, incontrovertibly, and absolutely Henry's fault, because if she hadn't seen him stalking along the platform with that air, so peculiarly Henryish, of having bought it and being firmly determined to see that it behaved itself, she wouldn't have lost her nerve and bolted into the nearest carriage. The nearest carriage happened to be a third-class compartment in the train on her right. It was now perfectly obvious that she ought to have got into the train on the other side. Instead of being in the local train for Winsley Grove, stopping every five minutes and eventually arriving at 20 Myrtle Terrace in time to have tea and rock cakes with Aunt Emmeline, she was in a corridor train which was going faster every minute and didn't seem to have any intention of stopping for hours.

Hilary stared out of the window and saw Henry's face there. It was a horrible wet, foggy afternoon. Henry glared back at her out of the fog. No, glared wasn't the right word, because you don't glare unless you've lost your temper, and Henry didn't lose his temper, he only looked at you as if you were a crawling black beetle or a frightfully naughty small child. It was more effective losing your temper of course, only you couldn't do it unless you were made that way. Hilary's own temper was the sort that kicks up its heels and bolts joyously into the

5

heart of the fray. She sizzled with rage when she remembered the Row — the great Breaking-off-of-the-Engagement Row — and Henry's atrocious calm. He had looked at her exactly as he had looked at the station just now. Superior, that was what Henry was — damned superior. If he had *asked* her not to go hiking with Basil, she might have given way, but to tell her she wasn't to go, and on the top of that to inform her that Basil was this, that, and the other, all of which was none of Henry's business, had naturally made her boil right over.

The really enraging part was that Henry had proved to be right — *after* the Row, and when she had begun to hike with Basil and hadn't got very far. Only by that time she had told Henry exactly what she thought about him and his proprietary airs, and had finished up by throwing his engagement ring at him — very hard.

If he had lost his temper even then, they might have made it up, flashed into understanding, melted again into tenderness. But he had been *calm* — calm when she was breaking their engagement! A ribald rhyme bobbed up in Hilary's mind. She had a private imp who was always ready with irreverent doggerel at what ought to have been solemn moments. He had got her into dreadful trouble when she was six years old with a verse about Aunt Arabella, now deceased:

> 'Aunt Arabella has a very long nose.
> Nobody knows
> Why it grows
> So long and so sharp and as red as a rose.'

She hadn't ever been very fond of Aunt Arabella, and after the rhyme Aunt Arabella had never been very fond of her.

The imp now produced the following gem:

> 'If only Henry could get in a rage,
> We shouldn't have had to disengage.'

This was most sadly true.

6

The disengagement was now a whole month old.

It is very difficult to go on being angry for a whole month. Hilary could get angry with the greatest of ease, but she couldn't stay angry, not for very long. About half-way through the month she had begun to feel that it was about time Henry wrote and apologised. In the third week she had taken to watching for the post. For the last few days the cold and dreadful prospect of a future devoid of rows with Henry had begun to weigh upon her a good deal. It was therefore very heartening to be able to feel angry again.

And then imagination played her one of its really low tricks. Henry's eyes looking back at her out of the fog, looking back at her out of her own mind, ceased to look scornfully, ceased to look haughtily into hers. They changed, they smiled, they looked at her with love — 'And they won't again ever — not ever any more. Oh, *Henry!*' It was jut as if someone had suddenly jabbed a knife into her. It hurt just like that. One moment there she was, quite comfortably angry with Henry, and the next all stabbed and defenceless, with the anger running away and a horrid cold sinking feeling inside her. The back of her eyes stung sharply — 'If you think you're going to cry in a public railway carriage — '

She blinked hard and turned back from the window. Better not look out any more. The mist played tricks — made you feel as if you were alone, made you think about things that you simply were not going to think about, and all the time instead of being such a mutt, what you'd got to do was to find out where the blighted train was going and when it was likely to stop.

There had been two other people in the carriage when she got in. They were occupying the inside corner seats, and they had made no more impression on her than if they had been two suit-cases. Now, as she turned round, she saw that one of them, a man, had pushed back the sliding door and was going out into the corridor. He passed along it and out of sight, and almost immediately the woman who had been sitting opposite him moved in her seat and leaned a little forward, looking hard at Hilary. She was an elderly woman, and Hilary thought she looked very ill. She had on a black felt hat and a grey coat with a black fur collar — the neat inconspicuous clothes of a respectable woman who has stopped bothering about her appearance, but is tidy from habit and training. Under the dark brim her hair, face, and eyes were of a uniform greyish tint.

Hilary said, 'I've got into the wrong train. It sounds awfully stupid, but if you could tell me where we're going — I don't even know that.'

A curious little catch came up in the woman's throat. She put up her hand to the collar of her coat and pulled at it.

'Ledlington,' she said. 'First stop Ledlington.' And then, with the catch breaking her voice, 'Oh, miss, I knew you at once. Thank God he didn't! And he'll be back any minute — he'd never have gone — not if he'd recognised you. Oh, *miss*!'

Hilary felt something between pity and repulsion. She had never seen the woman before. Or had she? She didn't know. She began to think she had, but she didn't know where. No, it was nonsense — she didn't know her, and the poor creature must be mad. She began to wish that the man would come back, because if the woman was really mad she was between her and the corridor —

'I'm afraid,' she began in a little polite voice, and at once the woman interrupted her, leaning right forward.

'Oh, miss, you don't know me — I saw that the way you looked at me. But I knew you directly you got in, and I've been hoping and praying I'd get the chance to speak to you.'

Her black gloved hands were gripping one another, the kid stretched across the knuckles, the finger ends sticking out because they were too long. The fingers inside them twisted, plucked, and strained. Hilary watched them with a sort of horror. It was like watching something with pain.

She said, '*Please* —'

The woman's voice went on, urgent, toneless, with the catch, not quite a cough, breaking it.

'I saw you in the court when the trial was on. You come in with Mrs. Grey, and I asked who you was, and they told me you was her cousin Miss Carew, and then I minded I'd heard speak of you — Miss Hilary Carew.'

The fear went out of Hilary and a cold anger stiffened her. As if it wasn't enough to live through a nightmare like Geoffrey Grey's trial, this woman, one of the horrible morbid crowd who had flocked to watch his torture and Marion's agony — this damned woman, because she had recognised her, thought she had an opportunity to pry, and poke, and ask questions. *How dare she?*

She didn't know how white she had turned, or how her eyes blazed, but the woman unlocked those twisting hands and held them up as if to ward a blow.

'Oh, miss — *don't*! Oh, for God's sake don't look at me like that!'

Hilary got up. She would have to find another carriage. If the woman wasn't mad, she was hysterical. She didn't much like the idea of passing her, but anything was better than having a scene.

As she put her hand on the sliding door, the woman caught at the skirt of her coat and held it.

'Oh, miss, it was Mrs. Grey I wanted to ask about. I thought you'd know.'

Hilary looked down at her. The light colourless eyes stared back straining. The hand on her coat shook so that she could feel it. She wanted most dreadfully to get away. But this was something more than curiosity. Though she was only twenty-two, she knew what people looked like when they were in trouble — Geoffrey Grey's trial had taught her that. This woman was in trouble. She let her hand drop from the door and said,

'What do you want to know about Mrs. Grey?'

At once the woman released her and sat back. She made a great effort and contrived a calmer, more conventional tone.

'It was just to know how she is — how she's keeping. It's not curiosity, miss. She'd remember me, and I've thought about her — oh, my God, many's the time I've waked in the night and thought about her!'

The moment of self-control was over. With a shuddering sob, she leaned forward again.

'Oh, miss — if you only knew!'

Hilary sat down. If the poor thing wanted news of Marion, she must have it. She looked frightfully ill. There was no doubt that the distress was real. She said in her kindest voice,

'I'm sorry I was angry. I thought you were just one of the people who came to look on, but if you *knew* Marion, that's different. She — she's awfully brave.'

'It's haunted me the way she looked — it has, indeed, miss. The last day I didn't know how to bear it — I didn't indeed. And I tried to see her. Miss, if I never spoke another word, it's true as I tried to see her. I give him the slip and I got out and round to where she was staying, and they wouldn't let me in — said she wasn't seeing anyone — said she was resting — ' She broke off suddenly with her mouth half open and stayed like that, not seeming to breathe for a dragging moment. Then, in a whisper, hardly moving her lips, 'If she'd ha' seen me — ' She fixed her light wild eyes on Hilary and said, her tone quickened with horror, 'She didn't see me. Resting — that's what they told me. And then *he* come, and I never got another chance — he saw to that.'

Hilary made nothing of this, but it left her with the feeling that she ought to be able to make something of it. She spoke again in the same kind voice as before.

'Will you tell me your name? Mrs. Grey will like to know that you were asking after her.'

The woman put one of the black-gloved hands to her head.

'I forgot you didn't know me. I've let myself run on. I shouldn't have done it, but when I see you it come over me. I always liked Mrs. Grey, and I've wanted to know all the year how she was, and about the baby. It's all right, isn't it?'

Hilary shook her head. Poor Marion — and the baby that never breathed at all.

'No,' she said — 'she lost the baby. It came too soon and she lost it.'

The black hands took hold of one another again.

'I didn't know. There wasn't no one I could ask.'

'You haven't told me your name.'

'No,' she said, and drew a quick gasping breath.

'Oh, he'll be coming back in a minute! Oh, miss — Mr. Geoffrey — if you could tell me if there's any news — '

'He's well,' said Hilary. 'He writes when he's allowed to. She's gone to see him today. I shall hear when I get back.'

As she spoke, she had stopped seeing the woman or remembering her. Her eyes dazzled and her heart was so full of trouble that there was no room for anything else. Geoff in prison for life — Marion struggling through one of those terrible visits which took every ounce of strength and courage out of her ... She couldn't bear it. Geoff, who had been so terribly full of life, and Marion, who loved him and had to go on living in a world which believed he was a murderer and had shut him up out of harm's way . . . What was the good of saying, 'I can't bear it,' when it was going on, and must go on, and you had to bear it, whether you wanted to or not?

A man came down the corridor and pushed at the sliding door. Hilary got up, and he stood aside to let her pass. She went as far down the corridor as she could and stood there looking out at the trees and fields and hedges going by in the mist.

CHAPTER TWO

'You look dreadfully tired,' said Hilary.

'Do I?' said Marion Grey indifferently.

'You do — *and* cold. And the soup's good — it truly is. It was all jelly till I hotted it, but if you don't drink it quickly it won't stay hot, and lukewarm things are frightful.' Hilary's voice was softly urgent.

Marion shivered, took a mouthful or two of the soup, and then put down the spoon. It was as if she had roused from her thoughts for a moment and then sunk back into them again. She was still in her outdoor things — the brown tweed coat which she had had in her trousseau, and the brown wool beret which Aunt Emmeline had crocheted for her. The coat was getting very shabby now, but anything that Marion wore took the lines of her long graceful body. She was much, much too thin, but if she walked about in her bones she would still be graceful. With her dark hair damp from the fog, the beret pushed back, the grey eyes fixed in a daze of grief and fatigue, she had still the distinction which heightens beauty and survives it.

'Finish it, darling,' said Hilary.

Marion took a little more of the soup. It warmed her. She finished it and leaned back. Hilary was a kind child — kind to have a fire waiting for her — and hot soup — and scrambled eggs. She ate the eggs because you have to eat, and because Hilary was kind and would be unhappy if she didn't.

'And the water's hot, darling, so you can have a really boiling bath and go straight to bed if you want to.'

'Presently,' said Marion. She lay back in the chintz-covered arm-chair and looked at the small, steady glow of the fire.

Hilary was clearing the plates, coming and going between the living-room and the little kitchen of the flat. The bright chintz curtains were drawn across the windows. There was a row of china birds on the shelf above the glowing fire — blue, green, yellow, and brown, and the rose-coloured one with the darting beak which Geoff had christened Sophy. They all had names. Geoff always had to find a name for a thing as soon as he bought it. His last car was Samuel, and the birds were Octavius, Leonora, Ermengarde, Sophy, and Erasmus.

Hilary came back with a tray.

'Will you have tea now, or later when you're in bed?'

Marion roused herself.

'Later. And you're doing all the work.'

Hilary heaved a deep sigh of relief. This meant Marion was coming round. You couldn't really reach her in that deep mood of grief and pain. You could only walk round on tiptoe, and try and get her warmed and fed, and love her with all your heart. But if she was coming out of it she would begin to talk, and that would do her good. Relief brought the colour back into Hilary's cheeks and the sparkle into her eyes. She had one of those faces which change continually. A moment ago she had

13

looked a little pale thing with insignificant features and the eyes of a forlorn child who is trying very hard to be good and brave. Now she flashed into colour and charm. She said,

'I love doing it — you know I do.'

Marion smiled at her.

'What have you been doing with yourself? Did you go and see Aunt Emmeline?'

'No, I didn't. I started, but I never got there. Darling, I *am* a fool. I got into the wrong train, and it was an express, and I couldn't get out until it got to Ledlington, so of course it took me hours to get back again, and I didn't dare risk going down to Winsley Grove for fear of not being home before you were.'

'Nice child,' said Marion speaking out her thought. And then, 'Aunt Emmeline will be in a fuss.'

'I rang her up.'

Hilary came and sat down on the hearth-rug with her hands locked round her knees. Her short brown hair stood up all over her head in little curls. She was lightly and childishly built. The hands locked about her knees were small, hard, and capable. Her mouth was very red, with a curving upper lip and rather a full lower one. Her skin was brown, her nose a good deal like a baby's, and her eyes very bright but of no particular colour. When she was excited, pleased, or angry a vivid carnation came up under the clear brown skin. She had a pretty voice and a pretty turn of the head. A nice child, with a warm heart and a hot temper. She would have cut off her head for Marion Grey, and she loved Geoffrey like the brother she had never had. She set herself to thaw Marion out and make her talk.

'I had an adventure in my wrong train. First of all I thought I'd got shut in with a perfectly mad lunatic, and then she turned out to be a friend of yours, darling.'

Marion actually smiled, and Hilary felt a throb of triumph. She *was* coming out of it, she *was*. She proceeded to make her adventure as thrilling as possible.

'Well, you know, I just rushed into the train because of seeing Henry—'

'Oh—' said Marion.

Hilary nodded with vigour.

'Looking about eleven feet high and too purposeful for *words*. I should think he'd just been seeing his mother and she'd been telling him what an escape he'd had, and how she'd been quite sure from the very beginning that I wasn't at all suitable and would never have made him the sort of wife *she* had been to his father.'

Marion shook her head reprovingly. Hilary made a face and hurried on.

'When I think that I might have had Mrs. Cunningham for a mother-in-law it gives me a creep all down my spine. *What* an escape! I expect my guardian angel arranged the Row on purpose to save me.'

Marion shook her head again.

'Henry won't expect you to see very much of her.'

Hilary flushed scarlet and stuck her chin in the air.

'*Henry* won't?' she said. 'How do you mean, Henry won't? We're absolutely, finally, and completely disengaged, and I don't care what he expects or doesn't expect. And you're *not* letting me get on with my story, which is most adventurous and exciting. And the only reason I said anything at all about Henry was because I've got a nice open nature and I had to explain why I bolted into a completely wrong train and didn't notice where I was until we were well on the way, and then I found it was a corridor train, so I knew I'd done something silly. And when I asked the woman in the corridor corner where we were going, first she said Ledlington, and then she clasped her hands and said she'd recognised me the minute I got into the train.'

'Who was she?'

'Darling, I don't know. But you ought to be able to place her, because it was you she really wanted to ask about. And at first I thought it was just curiosity, because she let on that she'd seen me with you in court – it must have been the afternoon Aunt Emmeline crocked up, because that was the only time I was there — and of course I just boiled, and got up to go and find another carriage, because ghouls make me perfectly sick. And then I saw she wasn't a *ghoul*.'

'How?' Marion's voice was strained.

'She caught my coat, and I could feel her shaking. She looked most frightfully unhappy and sort of desperate — not gloating like a *ghoul*. And she said she only wanted to know how you were, because she'd always liked you, and — and things like that.'

It came over Hilary rather late in the day that it would really have been better to stick to Henry as a topic. She had bolted for the second time with a rather similar result. The story of her adventure wasn't really calculated to bring Marion out of her mood, but she would have to go through with it now, because Marion was asking insistently,

'Who was she?'

'I don't know, darling — I told you I didn't. I really do think she was a bit batty, because she talked in the oddest way. There was a man with her. He went along the corridor just about the time I came to — after seeing Henry, you know. And she said awfully queer things about him, like thanking God he'd gone, because she'd been hoping and praying she'd get a chance of speaking to me. She was most frightfully worked up, you know, twisting her hands about and clutching at her collar as if she couldn't breathe.'

'What was he like?' said Marion slowly. She was leaning her head upon her hand, and the long fingers hid her eyes.

'Well — rather like Aunt Emmeline's Mrs. Tidmarsh — you know, the one who comes in and obliges when Eliza has a holiday. Not *really*, but a sort of family likeness — that all-overish look and awfully respectable — and the way she called me miss all the time. I've known Mrs. Tidmarsh do it twice in a sentence, and I'm not at all sure this poor thing didn't too.'

'Middle-aged?'

'Born that way. You know how it is with Mrs. Tidmarsh — you simply couldn't think of her being a baby, or young. Like her clothes — they never get any older, and you can't imagine their ever being new.'

'I don't suppose it matters,' said Marion Grey. And then, 'What did she want to know?'

'About you — how you were — whether you were all right — and — and about Geoff — ' She hesitated. 'Marion, she did say one awfully queer thing. I don't know whether I ought — '

'Yes — tell me.'

Hilary looked at her doubtfully. That was the worst of getting into a wrong train, you never knew where it was going to take you.

'Well, I expect she's balmy really. She said she'd tried to see you whilst the Case was going on. She said she gave *him* the slip and went round to where you were staying, but of course they didn't let her in. But she said something like "If they had" under her breath — I didn't quite catch it, because she was all choky and shaky, but that's what it sounded like. No, it was, "I didn't see her," and then, "If I had," or something like that. She was so worked up that I can't be sure.'

Hilary's voice became uncertain and faded away. Something had happened to the atmosphere. It had become strange, and the strangeness came from Marion, who had not moved and who did not speak. She sat there with her hand over her eyes, and the strangeness flowed from her and filled the room.

Hilary bore it as long as she could. Then she unlocked her hands and scrambled up on to her knees, and at the same moment Marion got up and went over to the window. There was an oak chest which made a window-seat, the deeply panelled front towards the room, the top littered with green and blue cushions. Marion swept them to the floor, opened the lid, and came back with a photograph-album in her hand. She did not speak, but sat down and began to turn the leaves.

Presently she found what she was looking for, and held the page for Hilary to see. It was a snapshot taken in a garden. A rose arch, a bed of lilies with sharply recurved petals, a tea-table, people having tea. Marion smiling out of the picture — an elderly man with a heavy moustache.

Hilary had never seen James Everton, but every line of his face was most sickeningly familiar. All the news-papers in England had been full of him and his photograph a year ago when Geoffrey Grey was being tried for his murder.

Geoffrey wasn't in the picture. That was because he was taking it, and Marion's smile was for him. But there was a third person, a woman leaning over the tea-table setting down a plate of scones. Like Marion, she faced the camera. She had a plate in her right hand, and she looked as if someone had just spoken to her or called her name.

Hilary gave a little gasp and said,

'Oh, yes — that's her!'

CHAPTER THREE

There was a pause. Hilary looked at the photograph, and Marion looked at Hilary with a faint bitter smile.

'That is Mrs. Mercer,' she said — 'James' housekeeper.' She took the book back and laid it open on her knee. 'Geoffrey might have got off if it hadn't been for her. Her evidence tipped the scale. She cried, you know, all the time she was giving it, and of course that went down with the jury. If she'd been vindictive or hard, it wouldn't have hurt Geoff half as much, but when she swore with sobs that she'd heard him quarrelling with James about the will, she damned him. There was just a chance they'd believe he'd found James dead, but she finished that.' Marion's voice left off on the edge of a break. After a moment she said in a curious, wondering tone, 'I always thought she was such a nice woman. She gave me the recipe for those scones. She seemed to like me.'

Hilary was sitting back on her heels.

'She said she'd always liked you.'

'Then why did she do it? Why did she do it? I've thought myself blind and stupid, and I can't get a glimmer of why she should have done it.'

'Yes — why?' said Hilary.

'She was lying. But why should she have lied? She *liked* Geoff. She gave that evidence against him as if she was on the rack — that's what made it so damning. But why did she give it at all? That's what I can't, can't get any answer to. James was dead when Geoff got there. We went over and over it together. It was eight o'clock when James rang him up. We had just finished dinner, and he went straight off — Oh, you've heard it a hundred times, but what matters is that it's true. James *did* ring him up.

He *did* go down to Putney just as he said in his evidence. He stood over there and hung up the receiver, and said "James wants to see me at once. He sounds in a most awful stew." He kissed me and ran down the stairs. And when he got there James was dead — fallen down across his writing-table, and the pistol lying there. And Geoff picked it up. Oh, if he only hadn't picked it up! He said he didn't know he had until he saw it in his hand. He came in by the garden door, and he didn't see anyone till he saw James, and James was dead, and the pistol was there and he picked it up. And then Mercer came knocking at the door, and it was locked. Hilary — who locked it? It was locked on the inside and the key in the door, and only Geoff's finger-prints on the key and on the handle, because he went and tried the door when Mercer knocked. And then he turned the key and let him in, and there was Mercer and Mrs. Mercer, and Mercer said, "Oh, my God, Mr. Geoff! What have you done?" '

'*Don't!*' said Hilary. 'Don't go over it, darling — it doesn't do any good.'

'Do you think I'd sit here and talk if there was anything I could do?' said Marion in a low, exhausted voice. 'Mercer said he hadn't heard anything except what he took to be a burst tyre or a motor-bike backfiring about a minute before. He was in the pantry cleaning the glass and silver and putting it away. And he *was* — his cleaning things were all spread about, and the stuff was on his hands. But Mrs. Mercer had been upstairs to turn down James' bed, and she said when she came through the hall she heard voices very loud in the study. And she said she went and listened because she was frightened, and she swore she heard Geoffrey in there quarrelling with James. And then she swore she heard the shot, and screamed and ran for Mercer.' She got up, and the photograph-album fell sprawling against Hilary's knees.

With an abrupt but graceful movement Marion

pushed back the chair and began to walk up and down. She was so pale that Hilary was frightened. Her air of exhaustion had changed into one of restless pain.

'I've gone over it, and over it, and over it. I've gone over it until I can say it in my sleep and it doesn't mean anything at all. None of it means anything. It got to be like that in court.— just a noise — just words. And that woman crying and swearing Geoff's life away, and no reason for it, no motive anywhere — no motive for anyone to kill James. Except Geoff if he'd lost his head and done it in a rage when James told him about the new will and cutting him out of everything. Hilary, he didn't do it — he didn't! I swear he didn't! They made a lot of his hot temper, but I'll swear he didn't do it! James brought him up to be his heir, and he'd no right to change like that. He'd no right to take him into the office and promise him a partnership, and then go back on it, if that's what he meant to do. But Geoff wouldn't have touched him — I know he wouldn't. He wouldn't even have hit him, and it simply isn't possible that he shot him.' She stopped her restless pacing by the window and stood with her back to the room for a silent moment. Then she said, 'It isn't possible — except in a nightmare — but this has been a nightmare so long, and — sometimes — I — feel — that — I — may — begin— to — believe — in — it.'

Hilary said 'No!' with a quick sob.

Marion turned round.

'Why did James destroy his will and make another one? Why did he leave everything to Bertie Everton? He never had a good word to say about him, and he was fond of Geoff. They were together all the day before. There wasn't any quarrel — there wasn't anything. And next day he destroyed his will and made another one, and at eight o'clock that night he sent for Geoff, and Geoff found him dead.'

'You don't think — ' said Hilary.

'I've done nothing but think — I'm nearly mad with thinking.'

Hilary was shaken with excitement. She had lived with Marion for nearly a year, and never, never, never had Marion discussed the Case before. She kept it shut up in a horrible secret place inside her, and she never forgot it for a moment waking or sleeping, but she never, never, never spoke about it.

And Hilary had always seethed with bright ideas about the Case. If Marion would only talk about it, open her horrid secret place and let the darkness ou⁺ and Hilary's bright ideas in, well, she felt quite, quite sure she would be able to pounce on something which had been overlooked and the whole thing would be cleared up.

'No — no — darling, do listen. Marion, *please*. You don't think somebody forged the will?'

Marion stood by the chest, half turned from the room. She gave a laugh that was a good deal like a sob.

'Oh, Hilary, what a child you are! Do you suppose that wasn't thought of? Do you suppose everything wasn't thought of? He drove down to the bank, and it was witnessed by the manager and one of the clerks.'

'Why?' said Hilary. 'I mean, why didn't he get the Mercers to do it? You don't generally go to a bank to sign your will.'

'I don't know,' said Marion wearily. 'He did, anyhow. The Mercers couldn't sign because they had a legacy. James sent for his solicitor and destroyed the old will in his presence. Then he got him to make the new one, and they went down to the bank together and James signed it there.'

'Where was Bertie Everton?' said Hilary.

'In Edinburgh. He went up by the night train.'

'Then he *was* here the day before?'

'Oh, yes — he went down to Putney and he saw

James — dined with him as a matter of fact. But you can't make anything out of that, except that obviously something was said or done which made James change his mind — and his will. He had always loathed Bertie, but something happened all in about an hour and a half to make him decide to leave him every penny he'd got. I was down for a thousand in the old will, and he even cut that out. Bertie's brother Frank, who'd always had an allowance from him and can't keep a job to save his life, he was cut out, too. Under the old will the allowance was to continue. He's a bad hat and a rolling stone, but he was just as much James' nephew as Bertie or Geoff, and James always meant to provide for him. He used to say he'd got a screw loose, but he didn't loathe him like he loathed Bertie. Bertie was everything he detested — and he left him every penny.'

Hilary put her hands on the floor behind her and leaned on them.

'Why did he detest him? What's the matter with Bertie?'

Marion gave an odd, quick shrug.

'Nothing. That's what enraged James. He used to say that Bertie had never done a stroke of work in his life nor wanted to. He's got some money, you know, and he just floats round gracefully, collecting china, playing the piano, dancing with all the girls, and being very agreeable to their mothers and aunts and grandmothers — you never see him speaking to a man. And when James heard he was embroidering chair-covers for a set of Louis Quinze chairs he'd picked up at a sale — well, Geoff and I honestly thought he was going to have a fit.'

'Marion, how do you know this Bertie creature was in Scotland when James — died?'

'He went up by the night train. He was staying at the Caledonian Hotel in Edinburgh. He'd been there for some days when he came down to see James, no one knows why. Well, he saw him and he went back again. His waiter said he had breakfast and lunch in the hotel, and after lunch he made a complaint about the bell in his room being out of order, and at four o'clock he was worrying about a telephone call he was expecting.' She lifted her hand and let it fall on the lid of the chest. 'You see — he couldn't have been at Putney. James was dead by a quarter past eight. Besides — Bertie — if you knew him —'

'I'm thinking about the other one,' said Hilary — 'Frank, the rolling-stone bad-lot one.'

'It's no good, I'm afraid,' said Marion. 'Frank was in Glasgow. He's got the best alibi of anyone, because he was actually having his allowance paid over to him just before six o'clock. James paid it through a Glasgow solicitor weekly because Frank never could make any money last for more than a week whatever it was. He called to collect it just before six that day, and he didn't leave the office till getting on for a quarter past six, so I'm afraid he couldn't possibly have murdered James. It would have been so nice and simple if he had, but — he didn't.'

'Who did?' said Hilary before she could stop to think.

Marion was standing still. At Hilary's question she seemed to become something more than still. Where there is life there is breath, and where there is breath there is always some movement. Marion seemed to have stopped breathing. There was a long, frightening minute when it seemed to Hilary that she had stopped breathing. She stared at her with round, terrified eyes, and it came to her that Marion wasn't sure — wasn't sure about Geoff. She loved Geoff terribly, but she wasn't sure that he hadn't killed James Everton. That seemed so shocking to Hilary that she couldn't think of anything to say or anything to do. She leaned back upon her hands and felt them go numb.

Marion's stillness broke. She turned suddenly, and suddenly all the self-control of that year of misery and iron broke, too. She said,

'I don't know — nobody knows — nobody will ever know. We shall just go on, and on, and on, and we shall never know. I'm twenty-five and Geoff is twenty-eight. Perhaps we shall have to go on for another fifty years. *Fifty years.*' Her voice went down into some cold depth.

Hilary took her weight off her numb hands and scrambled up.

'Marion — darling — *don't*! It's not really for life — you know — they let them out.'

'Twenty-five years,' said Marion in a tormented voice. 'Twenty-five years, and something off for good conduct. Say it's twenty years — twenty *years*. You don't know what one year has done to him. It would have been better if they had killed him at once. They're killing him now, a little at a time, a little bit every day, and long before the twenty years are up he'll be dead. There won't be any-thing left that I knew or loved. There'll be a body called Geoffrey Grey, because his body won't die. He's strong, and they say it's a very healthy life, so his body won't die. Only my Geoff is dying — now — now — whilst we're talking.'

'*Marion!*'

Marion pushed her away.

'You don't know what it's like. Every time I go I think, "Now I'm going to reach him, really reach him — I won't let anything stop me reaching him this time. It doesn't matter about the warder, it doesn't matter about any-thing — we'll be together again — that's the only thing that matters." But when I get there — ' she made a ges-ture of despair — 'we're not together. I can't get near him — I can't touch him — they won't let me touch him — they won't let me kiss him. If I could put my arms round him I could call him back. He's going away from me all the time — dying away from me — and I can't do anything about it.' She took hold of the back of the armchair and leaned on it, trembling. 'Think of him coming out after twenty years, quite dead! What can you do for a dead man? He'll be quite dead by then. And what shall I be like? Perhaps I shall be dead, too.'

'Marion — Marion — *please*!'

Marion shuddered from head to foot.

'No, it's no good — is it? One just has got to go on. If my baby hadn't died — ' She stopped, straightened up, and put her hands over her face. 'I shall never have children now. They're killing Geoff, and they've killed my children. Oh, God — why, why did it happen? We were so happy!'

CHAPTER FOUR

Hilary woke from something that wasn't quite sleep, and heard the clock in the living-room strike twelve. She hadn't meant to go to sleep until she was sure that Marion was asleep, and she felt rather despising towards herself because she had fallen into a doze. It felt rather like running away to go off into a dream and leave Marion awake and unhappy. But perhaps Marion was asleep.

She slipped out of bed and went barefoot into the bathroom. Marion's window and the bathroom window were side by side. If you hung on to the towel-rail with your left hand and leaned right out of the bathroom window, you could reach Marion's window-sill with your right hand, and then if you craned your neck until it felt as if it was going to crack, you could get one ear just far enough into the room to hear whether Marion was asleep or not. Hilary had done it times without number and never been caught. The fall of the curtain hid her from the bed. She had listened a hundred times, and heard Marion sigh and heard her weep, and had not dared to go to her, but had stayed awake for company's sake, and to think loving, pitiful thoughts of her and Geoff.

But tonight Marion slept. The faint, even sound of her breathing just stirred the stillness of the room.

Hilary drew back with the acrobatic twist which practice had made perfect. A light chill shiver of relief ran over her as she dived back into bed and snuggled the clothes up round her. Now she could go to sleep with a good conscience.

From the time she was quite a little girl she had had a perfectly clear picture in her own mind of this process of going to sleep. There was a sleep country, just as there was an awake country. The sleep country had a very high wall round it. You couldn't get in unless you could find a door, and you were never sure what door you were going to find, so every going to sleep was an adventure. Sometimes, of course, you opened a very dull door and got into an empty room with nothing inside it. Sometimes, like poor Marion, you couldn't find a door at all, and just wandered groping along the wall getting more and more tired with every step. Hilary had very little personal experience of this. Doors sprang open to her before her fingers fumbled for the latch.

But tonight she couldn't get to sleep. She was cold after hanging out of the bathroom window, so she buried herself up to the eyes in blankets. Then all of a sudden she was in a raging heat and pushing them away. Her pillow was too high — too low — too soft — too hard. Then, just as she thought she had settled herself, her nose began to tickle.

And all the time something went round and round in

her head like a gramophone record. Only it was like a record which someone is playing next door — you can hear it enough to be driven nearly crazy, but strain as you will, you can't quite make out the tune. Round, and round, and round, and round went the gramophone record in Hilary's head — round, and round, and round, and round. But she couldn't make sense of it. It was all the little bits of things which she had heard and known about the Everton murder and about Geoffrey Grey's trial, but they didn't hang together and they didn't make sense. That was because you can't make sense out of nonsense — and she didn't care what anyone said, it *was* nonsense to believe that Geoff had shot his uncle.

Hilary straightened her pillow for the umpteenth time and promised herself not to move until she had counted a hundred, but long before she got there her nose was tickling again, and a hair had got into her ear, and the arm she was lying on had pins and needles in it. She flung the bedclothes off and sat up. It wasn't any use, she had much better get up and do something. And all of a sudden it came to her that she would go into the living-room and dig out the file about the trial and read it right through. She knew where it was — down at the bottom of the oak chest — and with Marion asleep, and hours and hours of the night before her, she could go right through the file from beginning to end. She wanted to read the inquest, because she had missed that altogether through being in the Tyrol with Henry's cousins, and meeting Henry, and getting practically engaged to him but not quite.

She put on her dressing-gown and slippers, tiptoed across the passage, and shut the living-room door. She turned on both lights and got out the file. Then she sat down in the big armchair and began to read all about the Everton Case.

James Everton was shot somewhere between eight

o'clock and twenty minutes past eight on the evening of Tuesday, July 16th. He was alive at eight o'clock, for that was when he telephoned to Geoffrey Grey, but he was dead twenty minutes later, because that was when Geoffrey opened the door and the Mercers rushed into the study. Mrs. Mercer said she had only just heard the shot. She said on her oath, 'I had been up to turn down Mr. Everton's bed, and when I was coming through the hall I heard the sound of voices in the study. It sounded as if there was a quarrel going on. I didn't know of anyone being there with Mr. Everton, so I was frightened and I went to the door to listen. I recognised Mr. Geoffrey Grey's voice, and I was coming away, because I thought that if it was Mr. Geoffrey it was all right. Then I heard the sound of a shot. I screamed out and Mercer came running from his pantry, where he was cleaning the silver. He shook the door, but it was locked. And then Mr. Geoffrey opened it, and he had a pistol in his hand and Mr. Everton was fallen down across his desk.'

Pressed by the Coroner as to whether she had heard what Mr. Grey was saying when she recognised his voice, Mrs. Mercer became very agitated and said she would rather not say. She was told she must answer the question, whereupon she burst into tears and said it was something about a will.

The Coroner: 'Tell us exactly what you heard.'

Mrs. Mercer, in tears: 'I can't say any more than what I heard.'

The Coroner: 'No one wants you to. I only want you to tell us what you did hear.'

Mrs. Mercer: 'Nothing that I could put words to — only their voices, and something about a will.'

The Coroner: 'Something about a will, but you don't know what?'

Mrs Mercer, sobbing hysterically: 'No, sir.'

The Coroner: 'Give the witness a glass of water. Now, Mrs. Mercer, you say you heard the sound of voices in the study, and that you thought there was a quarrel going on. You have said that you recognised Mr. Geoffrey Grey's voice. You are quite certain that it *was* Mr. Grey's voice?'

Mrs. Mercer: 'Oh, sir — oh, sir, I don't want to tell on Mr. Geoffrey.'

The Coroner: 'You are sure it was his voice?'

Mrs. Mercer, with renewed sobs: 'Oh, yes, sir. Oh, sir, I don't know why I didn't faint — the shot went off that loud on the other side of the door. And I screamed, and Mercer came running from his pantry.'

Horribly damning evidence of Mrs. Mercer, corroborated by Alfred Mercer to the extent of his having heard the shot and his wife's scream. He had tried the door and found it locked, and when Mr. Grey opened it he had a pistol in his hand, and Mr. Everton had been shot dead and was lying half across the desk.

The Coroner: 'Is this the pistol?'

Mercer: 'Yes, sir.'

The Coroner: 'Had you ever seen it before?'

Mercer: 'Yes, sir — it belongs to Mr. Grey.'

Hilary's heart beat hard with anger as she read. How was it possible for things to look so black against an innocent man? What must Geoff have felt like, having to sit there and see this black, black evidence piling up against him? At first he wouldn't think it possible that anyone could believe it, and then he would begin to see them believing it. He would see them looking at him with a kind of horror in their eyes because they were believing that he had killed his own uncle in an angry quarrel over money.

For a moment the horror touched Hilary. It *wasn't* true. If everyone else in the world believed it, Hilary wouldn't believe it. The Mercers were lying. Why? What motive could they possibly have? They had a good place, and good wages. Why should Mercer kill his master? Because that was what it came to. If they were lying about Geoffrey Grey, it must be to cover themselves. And there was no motive at all. There was no motive. They had a soft job which they had done nothing to forfeit. James Everton's new will, signed the very morning of his death, made this perfectly clear. They had the same legacies as under the old will, ten pounds apiece for each year of service. And they had been there something under two years — the second ten pounds was not yet due. Does a man throw away a good job, and good prospects and commit murder into the bargain, for the sake of twenty pounds in hand between him and his wife?

Hilary sat and thought about that ... He might. Money and comfort are not everything. The dark motives of jealousy, hate, and revenge run counter to them, and in that clash security and self-interest may go down. But there would have to be such a motive. It had been looked for — it must have been looked for — but it had not been found. Hilary put it away to think about.

She read Geoffrey's evidence, and found it heart-breaking. His uncle had rung him up at eight o'clock. The other people who gave evidence kept saying 'the deceased', or 'Mr. Everton', but Geoffrey said 'My uncle'. All through his evidence he said my uncle — 'My uncle rang me up at eight o'clock. He said, "That you, Geoffrey? I want you to come down here at once — at once, my boy." He sounded very much upset.'

The Coroner: 'Angry?'
Geoffrey Grey: 'No — not with me — I don't know. He sounded all worked up, but certainly not with me, or

he wouldn't have called me "my boy". I said, "Is anything the matter?" And he said, "I can't talk about it on the telephone. I want you to come down here — as quickly as you can." And then he hung up.'

The Coroner: 'You went down?'

Geoffrey Grey: 'At once. It takes me about a quarter of an hour from door to door. I get a bus at the end of my road which takes me to within a quarter of a mile of his gate.'

The Coroner: 'Mr. and Mrs. Mercer have said that you did not ring the bell. They say that the front door was locked. You did not, therefore, go in that way?'

Geoffrey Grey: 'It was a fine warm evening, and I knew the study window would be open — it's a glass door really, opening into the garden. I should always go in that way if my uncle was at home and I wanted to see him.'

The Coroner: 'You were in the habit of going to see him?'

Geoffrey Grey: 'Constantly.'

The Coroner: 'You lived with him at Solway Lodge until the time of your marriage?'

Geoffrey Grey: 'Yes.'

The Coroner: 'I must ask you, Mr. Grey, whether your relations with your uncle were of a cordial nature?'

At this point the witness appeared distressed. He said in a low voice,

'Very cordial — affectionate.'

The Coroner: 'And there had been no quarrel?'

Geoffrey Grey: 'No — none.'

The Coroner: 'Then how do you account for his destroying the will under which you benefited and making a new will in which your name does not appear?'

Geoffrey Grey: 'I can't account for it.'

The Coroner: 'You know that he made a new will on the morning of July 16th?'

Geoffrey Grey: 'I know it now — I didn't know it then.'

The Coroner: 'You didn't know it when you went to see him?'

Geoffrey Grey: 'No.'

The Coroner: 'Or that he had destroyed the will under which you benefited? You are on oath, Mr. Grey. Do you still say that you did not know of any change in his will?'

Geoffrey Grey: 'I had no idea.'

The Coroner: 'He did not tell you about it over the telephone?'

Geoffrey Grey: 'No.'

The Coroner: 'Or after you got down to Putney?'

Geoffrey Grey: 'When I got down to Putney he was dead.'

The Coroner: 'You say you reached Solway Lodge at twenty minutes past eight?'

Geoffrey Grey: 'It would be about that. I didn't look at the time.'

The Coroner: 'The house stands by itself in about two acres of ground, and is approached by a short drive?'

Geoffrey Grey: 'Yes.'

The Coroner: 'Will you tell us how you approached the house?'

Geoffrey Grey: 'I came up the drive which leads to the front door, but I didn't go up to the door — I turned to the right and skirted the house. The study is at the back, with a glass door leading into the garden. The door was wide open, as I expected it to be.'

A Juryman: 'Were the curtains drawn?'

Geoffrey Grey: 'Oh, no. It was broad daylight — very fine and warm.'

The Coroner: 'Go on, Mr. Grey. You entered the study —'

33

Geoffrey Grey: 'I went in. I was expecting my uncle to meet me. I didn't see him at once. It was much darker in the room than it was outside. I stumbled over something, and saw the pistol lying on the ground at my feet. I picked it up without thinking what I was doing. And then I saw my uncle.'

The Juryman: 'First you said it was broad daylight, and now you say it was dark in the room. We'd like to hear something more about that.'

Geoffrey Grey: 'I didn't say it was dark in the room — I said it was darker than it was outside. It was very bright outside, and I'd had the sun in my eyes coming round the house.'

The Coroner: 'Go, on, Mr. Grey. You say you saw Mr. Everton — '

Geoffrey Grey: 'He had fallen across his desk. I thought he had fainted. I went nearer, and I saw that he was dead. I touched him — he was quite dead. Then I heard a scream, and someone tried the door. I found it was locked, with the key on the inside. I unlocked it. The Mercers were there. They seemed to think I had shot my uncle.'

The Coroner: 'The pistol was still in your hand?'

Geoffrey Grey: 'Yes — I had forgotten about it.'

The Coroner: 'This is the pistol?'

Geoffrey Grey: 'Yes.'

The Coroner: 'It has been identified as your property. Have you anything to say about that?'

Geoffrey Grey: 'It belongs to me, but it has not been in my possession for a year. I left it at Solway Lodge when I got married. I left a lot of my things there. We were taking a flat, and there was no room for anything that was not in use.'

The Juryman: 'We would like to know why you had a pistol.'

Geoffrey Grey: 'My uncle gave it to me about two years

ago. I was going on a holiday trip in eastern Europe. There was some talk of brigands, and he wanted me to take a pistol. I never had any occasion to use it.'

The Coroner: 'Are you a good shot?'

Geoffrey Grey: 'I am a fair shot.'

The Coroner: 'At a target?'

Geoffrey Grey: 'At a target.'

The Coroner: 'You could hit a man across a room?'

Geoffrey Grey: 'I have never tried.'

The Coroner: 'Mr. Grey — when you were coming up the drive and skirting the house, did you meet anyone?'

Geoffrey Grey: 'No.'

The Coroner: 'Did you hear the sound of a shot?'

Geoffrey Grey: 'No.'

The Coroner: 'You saw nothing and heard nothing as you approached the study?'

Geoffrey Grey: 'Nothing.'

Why couldn't he have heard someone or seen someone as he came up to the house on that fine warm evening? The murderer couldn't have been very far away. Why couldn't Geoff have come across him, or at least have caught a glimpse of him as he ran? . . . Why? Because he had taken very good care that Geoff shouldn't see him. Because he knew that Geoff shouldn't see him. Because he knew that Geoff was coming. Because he knew that James Everton had rung him up, and that it would take him a quarter of an hour to get to Solway Lodge, so that the murderer had a quarter of an hour in which to shoot James Everton and get clear away. Of course Geoff hadn't heard anything or seen anyone — the murderer would take very good care of that. But the Mercers must have heard the shot. Long before Mrs. Mercer came down the stairs and screamed in the hall, and Mercer came running from the pantry where he was cleaning the silver. Marion had *said* he was cleaning it — the stuff

35

was all over his hands. But he didn't leave his silver, and Mrs. Mercer didn't scream, until Geoff was in the study with the pistol in his hand.

There was a lot of technical evidence about the pistol. The bullet that killed James Everton had certainly been fired from it. Geoff's finger-prints were on it. Of course they were. He picked it up, didn't he? But there were no other finger-prints. *There were no other finger-prints.* So it couldn't be suicide. Even if Geoff hadn't stuck to that awkward bit of evidence about stumbling over the pistol just inside the window. They made a lot of that at the trial, she remembered, because the glass door was eight or nine feet from the desk and James Everton must have died at once. So that even apart from the finger-prints, on Geoff's own evidence, suicide was out of the question.

Hilary drew a long sighing breath.

The Mercers must be lying, because it was a choice between them and Geoff. But the jury had believed them, both at the inquest and at the trial.

She read Marion's evidence . . . Nothing there. Just a few questions and answers. But Hilary had a heart-wringing picture of Marion standing up and taking the oath and giving those answers. She and Geoff had been so utterly, absolutely happy. Their happiness was like a shining light which they took with them wherever they went, and it made everyone else happy, too. And in that dark, crowded court-room the light was going out. It was a hot sunny day outside — the papers kept on referring to the heat — but in that horrible crowded room Marion and Geoffrey were watching the light go out.

The Coroner: 'You were present when your husband was rung up on the evening of the sixteenth?'
Marion Grey: 'Yes.'
The Coroner: 'Did you notice the time?'
Marion Grey: 'Yes — the clock was striking eight. He

36

waited for it to finish striking before he lifted the receiver.'

The Coroner: 'What did you hear?'

Marion Grey: 'I heard Mr. Everton asking my husband to come down to Solway Lodge.'

The Coroner: 'Do you mean that you could actually hear what Mr. Everton was saying?'

Marion Grey: 'Oh yes, I could hear him quite plainly. He wanted him to come down and see him at once. He repeated that — "At once, my boy." And when my husband asked if anything was the matter he said, "I can't talk about it on the telephone. I want you to come down here as quickly as you can." Then my husband hung up the receiver and said, "That's James. He wants me to go down there at once." And I said, "I know — I heard him." My husband said, "He sounds properly upset. I can't think why." '

After that she was asked about the pistol. She said she had never seen it before.

The Coroner: 'You never saw it in your husband's possession?'

Marion Grey: 'No.'

The Coroner: 'How long have you been married?'

Marion Grey: 'A year and a week.'

The Coroner: 'You never saw the pistol during that time?'

Marion Grey: 'No.'

The Coroner: 'You live in a flat in Maudslay Road?'

Marion Grey: 'Yes.'

The Coroner: 'You have lived there ever since your marriage?'

Marion Grey: 'Yes.'

The Coroner: 'It is not a large flat?'

Marion Grey: 'No, quite small — four rooms.'

The Coroner: 'If the pistol had been there, you would have seen it?'

Marion Grey: 'It couldn't possibly have been there without my seeing it.'

The Coroner: 'There were no locked cupboards or boxes?'

Marion Grey: 'No.'

The Coroner: 'And you did not see the pistol at all?'

Marion Grey: 'I have never seen it before — anywhere.'

The Coroner let her go after that.

Hilary turned a page.

CHAPTER FIVE

Bertie Everton was called.

The Coroner: 'You are Bertram Everton?'

Bertram Everton: 'Oh, yes, certainly.'

The Coroner: 'You are a nephew of the deceased?'

Bertram Everton: 'Oh, yes.'

The Coroner: 'When did you see him last?'

Bertram Everton: 'Well, you know, I dined with him the very night before it happened. Most extraordinary thing, you know, because we weren't in the way of seeing one another what you might call constantly. But there it is — '

The Coroner: 'Do you mean that you were not on good terms with your uncle?'

Bertram Everton: 'Oh, well, I don't know that I should go as far as that, you know. Just happier apart and all that sort of thing.'

The Coroner: 'Was there any quarrel between you?'

Bertram Everton: 'Not at all. I don't quarrel with people, you know.'

The Coroner: 'You disagreed perhaps?'

Bertram Everton: 'Just about life and that sort of thing. My uncle was a business man. Earnest, hard-working fellows business men. Personally I collect china. We didn't see eye to eye about it at all.'

The Coroner: 'But you dined with him on the evening of Monday the fifteenth?'

Bertram Everton: 'Yes — as I told you.'

The Coroner: 'You had been staying in Scotland?'

Bertram Everton: 'In Edinburgh.'

The Coroner: 'You came all the way down from Scotland to dine with an uncle with whom you were not on particularly friendly terms?'

Bertram Everton: 'Oh, come — that's a bit rough! It wasn't quite like that.'

The Coroner: 'Perhaps you will tell us what it *was* like, Mr. Everton.'

Bertram Everton: 'Well, it was this way. I collect china, and when I'm in a place like Edinburgh I go nosing about, you know. You don't always find anything, but sometimes you do, and you might find something, and you never know, don't you know? Well, I didn't find anything I wanted for myself, but there's a fellow I know in town who collects jugs — name of White.'

The Coroner: 'Is this relevant, Mr. Everton?'

Bertram Everton: 'Well, I shouldn't have said it was, but you seemed to want to know, don't you know.'

The Coroner: 'Perhaps you will tell us as shortly as possible why you came down from Edinburgh to see your uncle.'

Bertram Everton: 'Well, that's just the point, you know — I didn't really come down to see my uncle. I came down to see this fellow who collects jugs — did I tell you his name was White? — because, you see, I'd come across a set of jugs in the Toby style featuring all the generals in what's usually called the World War, don't you know — the only set ever made, and very interesting and all that if that's the sort of thing you're interested in, don't you know? And the fellow that's got them wants to sell them to the Castle Museum, so I thought my fellow had better get an offer in quickly, you know, and I came down to see him, don't you know?'

The Coroner: 'And did you see him?'

Bertram Everton: 'Well, I didn't, don't you know. He'd flown over to Paris, on the spur of the moment, as you might say, so I rang up Uncle James and suggested dining with him.'

The Coroner: 'You said just now you were better apart. What made you suggest dining with him on this occasion?'

Bertram Everton: 'Well, there I was, at a loose end as you might say. A free meal, a little family chit-chat, and all that sort of thing, don't you know.'

The Coroner: 'Had you any special business that you wished to discuss with the deceased?'

Bertram Everton: 'Well, there was the matter of my brother's allowance, don't you know. He was by way of giving him an allowance, and there seemed to be a sort of idea that it would brighten the landscape if he could be induced to make it a bit larger, so I said I would see what could be done — if I got a chance and all that sort of thing.'

The Coroner: 'Well, you dined with your uncle. Did you discuss the question of your brother's allowance with him?'

Bertram Everton: 'Well, it wasn't what I should have called a discussion. I said, "In the matter of old Frank's allowance, Uncle James — " And he said — I suppose I've got to repeat all this?'

The Coroner: 'If it has any bearing on the question of why he altered his will.'

Bertram Everton: 'Well, I suppose you might say that it had, because he damned poor old Frank to me, don't you know, and said he'd better hurry up and find himself a job, because if anything happened to him — that's my uncle — poor old Frank would find he'd been left without a penny, because he — my uncle, you know — was damn well going to alter his will and cut out all the damned sucking-up hypocrites who thought they were going to make a good thing out of him and were going to find out their mistake before they were twenty-four hours older. Well, that did take me a bit aback, don't you know, and I said, "Draw it mild, Uncle! Poor old Frank's worst enemy couldn't say he was a hypocrite." And he gave me a most unpleasant sort of look and said, "I wasn't talking about your brother Frank."'

The Coroner: 'In fact he told you he was going to alter his will?'

Bertram Everton: 'Well, it seemed to kind of point that way, don't you know?'

The Coroner: 'Did he tell you he was going to alter it in your favour?'

The witness hesitated.

The Coroner: 'I must ask you to answer that question.'

Bertram Everton: 'Well, it's really very awkward answering that sort of question, don't you know.'

The Coroner: 'I am afraid I must ask you to answer it. Did he tell you he was making a will in your favour?'

Bertram Everton: 'Well, not exactly, don't you know.'

The Coroner: 'What did he say?'

Bertram Everton: 'Well, if you really want to know, he

said that if he'd got to choose between a smooth-tongued hypocrite and a damned tomfool, he'd choose the fool, don't you know.'

(Laughter in the Court.)

The Coroner: 'And you took that reference to yourself?'

Bertram Everton: 'Well, it seemed to point that way, don't you know.'

The Coroner: 'You took him to mean that he was about to execute a will in your favour?'

Bertram Everton: 'Well, I didn't think he'd do it, don't you know. I just thought he'd had a row with Geoffrey.'

The Coroner: 'Did he tell you so?'

Bertram Everton: 'No — I just got the impression, don't you know.'

Hilary's cheeks burned with anger. If it had been a proper trial, he wouldn't have been allowed to say those things. You can say anything in a Coroner's court, and this Bertie creature had got across with his suggestion of a quarrel between Geoff and his uncle. From first to last there was never a shred of evidence that there had ever been such a quarrel, but from first to last the suggestion was believed by the public. They read Bertie Everton's evidence at the inquest, and they believed that Geoffrey Grey had quarrelled with his uncle — that James Everton had found him out in something discreditable, and that that was why he had altered his will. And the jury which afterwards tried Geoffrey Grey for his uncle's murder was drawn from that same public. Once a suggestion has entered the general atmosphere of human thought, it is very difficult to neutralise it. Bertie Everton's unsubstantiated suggestion of a quarrel undoubtedly helped to set the black cap on the judge's head.

Hilary turned a page. What she had been reading was

partly a newspaper report and partly a transcription into type of shorthand notes. As she turned the leaf, she saw before her a photograph of Bertie Everton — 'Mr. Bertram Everton leaving the court.' She had seen him once at the trial of course, but that was like remembering a nightmare. Hilary looked with all her eyes, but she couldn't make very much of what she saw. Not very tall, not very short. Irregular features and longish hair. The picture was rather blurred, and of course no photograph gave you the colouring. She remembered that Bertie Everton had red hair. He seemed to have rather a lot of it, and it was certainly much too long.

She went on reading his evidence.

He said he had taken the ten o'clock non-stop from Edinburgh to King's Cross, arriving at half past five on the afternoon of the 15th, and after dining with James Everton he had caught the 1.5 from King's Cross, arriving in Edinburgh at 9.36 on the morning of the 16th. He had gone straight to the Caledonian Hotel, where he had a late breakfast and then put in some arrears of sleep. He explained at considerable length that he could never sleep properly in a train. He lunched in the hotel at half past one, after which he wrote letters, one to his brother and one to the Mr. White who had been mentioned in connection with the set of Toby jugs. He had had occasion to complain about the bell in his room being out of order. He went out for a walk some time after four o'clock, and on his way out he went into the office to enquire if there had been any telephone message for him. He thought there might have been one from the man who had the jugs. On his return to the hotel he went to bed. He was still very short of sleep, and he wasn't feeling very well. He did not go into the dining-room, because he did not want any dinner. He went straight up to his room and rang for some biscuits. He had a biscuit or two and a drink out of his flask, and went to bed. He couldn't say what time it was — somewhere round about eight o'clock. He wasn't noticing the time. He wasn't feeling at all well. He only wanted to go to sleep. The next thing he knew was the chambermaid knocking on the door with his tea next morning. He had asked to be called at nine. Asked where he had been during the time that he was absent from the hotel, he replied that he couldn't really say. He had done a bit of nosing about and a bit of walking, and he had had a drink or two.

And that was the end of Bertie Everton.

The next thing was the typed copy of a statement by Annie Robertson, a chambermaid at the Caledonian Hotel. There was nothing to show whether it had been put in at the inquest or not. It was just a statement.

Annie Robertson said Mr. Bertram Everton had been staying in the hotel for three or four days before July 16th. He might have come on the 12th, or the 11th, or the 13th. She couldn't say for certain, but they would know in the office. He had room No. 35. She remembered Tuesday, July 16th. She remembered Mr. Everton complaining about the bell in his room. He said it was out of order, but it seemed all right. She said she would have it looked at, because Mr. Everton said sometimes it rang and sometimes it didn't. It was about three o'clock in the afternoon when Mr. Everton complained about the bell. He was writing letters at the time. Later that evening, at about half past eight, his bell rang and she answered it. Mr. Everton told her he wanted some biscuits. He said he didn't feel well and was going to bed. She brought him the biscuits. She thought he was the worse for drink. She brought his tea next morning, Wednesday, July 17th, at nine o'clock. He seemed all right then and quite himself.

Hilary read this statement twice. Then she read Bertie Everton's evidence all over again. He had been out of the hotel between four o'clock and getting on for half past eight. He *might* have flown to Croydon and reached

Putney by eight o'clock, or at least she supposed he might. But he couldn't possibly have been back in his room at the Caledonian Hotel ordering biscuits and complaining about not feeling well by half past eight. James Everton was alive and talking to Geoff at eight o'clock. Whoever shot him, it couldn't have been his nephew Bertie, who was ordering biscuits in Edinburgh at half past eight.

Hilary wrenched her mind regretfully away from Bertie. He would have done so beautifully, and he wouldn't do at all.

The other nephew, Frank Everton, hadn't been called at the inquest. Marion's statement that he had been collecting his weekly allowance from a solicitor in Glasgow between a quarter to six and a quarter past on the evening of the 16th was borne out by another of those typewritten sheets. Mr. Robert Johnstone, of the firm of Johnstone, Johnstone and McCandlish, declared that he had been in conversation with Mr. Francis Everton, with whom he was well acquainted, between the hours of five-forty-five and six-fifteen on Tuesday, July 16th, when he had paid over to him the sum of £2 10s. 0d. (two pounds ten shillings), for which sum he held Mr. Francis Everton's dated receipt.

Exit Frank Everton. With even deeper regret Hilary let him go. Bad hat, rolling stone, family ne'er-do-well, but definitely not First Murderer. Even with a private aeroplane — and what would the family skeleton be doing with a private aeroplane — he couldn't have done it. He would need a private aerodrome — no, two private aerodromes, one at each end. She toyed with the idea of the black sheep getting into his private aeroplane at Messrs. Johnstone, Johnstone and McCandlish's front doorstep, taxi-ing down a busy Glasgow thoroughfare, flying all out to Putney, vol-planing down into James Everton's back garden — all without attracting the slightest attention. It was a highly tempting picture, but it belonged to an Arabian Nights entertainment — the Tale of the Tenth Calendar, or some such fantasy. It couldn't be sufficiently materialized to deflect the finding of a court of law.

It all came down to the Mercers again. If Geoff was speaking the truth, then the Mercers were lying. Of course Geoff was speaking the truth. She believed in Geoff with all her heart. If he said James Everton was dead when he arrived at twenty minutes past eight, then he was dead, and Mrs. Mercer's evidence about the quarrel and the shot was a lie. She couldn't have heard Geoff quarrelling with his uncle, and she couldn't have heard the shot when she said she heard it if Mr. Everton was already dead when Geoff arrived. No, Mrs. Mercer was telling lies, and that was why she had come over all gasping and frightened in the train — she'd got a bad conscience and it wouldn't let her alone because of what she'd done to Marion and Geoff.

But why had she done it?

That was quite easy. Mercer must have shot his master, and Mrs. Mercer had lied to save his neck. It was frightfully wicked of her, but it was the sort of wickedness you could understand. She had lied to save her husband, and in saving him she had damned Geoffrey.

She had certainly done that very completely. Hilary had a feeling that she needn't have done it quite so completely. The very badness of her conscience had made the thing worse. How could you help believing the evidence of a woman who seemed so heartbroken at having to give it? Well, that was the explanation — Alfred Mercer had shot James Everton, and Mrs. Mercer had lied to cover it up.

She turned the next page, and there, staring her in the face, was the evidence of Mrs. Thompson. She had forgotten all about Mrs. Thompson. It wasn't only Bertie

46

and Frank Everton who had alibis — beautiful watertight alibis — the Mercers had one, too. Mrs. Thompson exonerated them. There was a picture of her which might almost have been a picture of Mrs. Grundy — large, solemn, massive, and as solid as the British Constitution. She was the housekeeper from next door, Sir John Blakeney's housekeeper and twenty-five years in his service. She was supping by invitation with the Mercers, Sir John being away from home. She was in the kitchen from half past seven until the alarm was given. During all that time Mercer was in the pantry cleaning his silver, or else in the kitchen with her and Mrs. Mercer. The house was an old-fashioned one, and the pantry opened out of the kitchen. She could swear he never went through into the house until the alarm was given. He ran through the kitchen then, and seeing something was wrong, she went after him into the hall, where she saw the study door standing open, and Mrs. Mercer crying, and Mr. Grey with a pistol in his hand.

The Coroner: 'Did you hear the shot?'

Mrs. Thompson: 'No sir — I'm very deaf, sir.'

The Coroner: 'Did you hear Mrs. Mercer scream?'

Mrs. Thompson: 'No, sir, I wouldn't hear anything like that, not with two doors shut between.'

The Coroner: 'There were two doors between the kitchen and the hall?'

Mrs. Thompson: 'Yes, sir — the kitchen door and the baize door.'

The Coroner: 'Mrs. Mercer had been with you in the kitchen?'

Mrs. Thompson: 'Yes, sir.'

The Coroner: 'She says she went upstairs to turn down Mr. Everton's bed. How long had she been gone when the alarm was given?'

Mrs. Thompson: 'I should say it was the best part of five minutes, sir — not any longer.'

The Coroner: 'There is a point which I would like to have cleared up. Is Alfred Mercer in the court? I would like to recall him for a moment.'

Alfred Mercer recalled.

The Coroner: 'In all this evidence there has been no mention of Mr. Everton's dinner hour. What was his dinner hour?'

Mercer: 'Eight to half past, sir.'

The Coroner: 'You mean that the hour varied from day to day?'

Mercer: 'Yes, sir. If it was a fine evening he didn't like to come in from the garden.'

The Coroner: 'On this particular evening had he dined?'

Mercer: 'No, sir. It was ordered for half past eight.'

The Coroner: 'I would like to recall Mrs. Mercer.'

Mrs. Mercer recalled.

The Coroner: 'On July 16th Mr. Everton had ordered his dinner for half past eight?'

Mrs. Mercer: 'Yes, sir.'

The Coroner: 'You are the cook?'

Mrs. Mercer: 'Yes, sir.'

The Coroner: 'Dinner was ordered for half past eight, yet at a quarter-past eight you went upstairs to turn down his bed. Isn't that a little unusual?'

Mrs. Mercer: 'Yes, sir. Everything was cold, sir.'

The Coroner: 'You mean you had no cooking to do?'

Mrs. Mercer: 'No, sir. Everything was ready in the dining-room except for my pudding, which I was keeping on the ice.'

The Coroner: 'I see. Thank you, Mrs. Mercer, that will do. Now, Mrs. Thompson, let us get this quite clear.

You have sworn that Alfred Mercer was in the kitchen or in the pantry between half past seven and twenty minutes past eight, which was the time that the alarm was given as near as we can fix it?'

Mrs. Thompson: 'Yes, sir.'

The Coroner: 'I have here a plan of the house. It bears out your statement that there is no way out of the pantry except through the kitchen. The pantry window, I am told, is barred, so that there would be no egress that way. You swear that you did not leave the kitchen yourself between seven-thirty and eight-twenty?'

Mrs. Thompson: 'Yes, sir.'

The Coroner: 'You swear that Alfred Mercer did not pass through the kitchen during that time?'

Mrs. Thompson: 'He come into the kitchen, sir. Me being so deaf, he had to come right up to me before I could hear what he said, but he never went through anywhere except back to his pantry.'

The Coroner: 'I see — you were talking?'

Mrs. Thompson: 'Yes, sir.'

The Coroner: 'And Mrs. Mercer was there all the time until she went to turn down the bed?'

Mrs. Thompson: 'I think she went through to the dining-room once, sir.'

The Coroner: 'What time was that?'

Mrs. Thompson: 'Somewhere about eight o'clock, sir.'

The Coroner: 'How long was she away?'

Mrs. Thompson: 'Not above a few minutes, sir.'

The Coroner: 'Did she seem as usual?'

Mrs Thompson: 'Well, no sir, I can't say she did. Shocking bad she was with toothache, poor thing. That's what Mercer come in to talk to me about — said he couldn't get her to go to the dentist. "And what's the sense," he said, "crying your eyes out with pain instead of taking and having it out?" '

The Coroner: 'I see. And Mrs. Mercer was crying with her toothache?'
Mrs. Thompson: 'All the time, poor thing.'

That finished with Mrs. Thompson.

CHAPTER SIX

There was medical evidence, there was police evidence, there was evidence about the will. The medical evidence said that James Everton had died at once. He had been shot through the left temple. The police surgeon had arrived at a quarter to nine. He said that in his opinion Mr. Everton could not have moved after he was shot. He certainly could not have dropped the pistol where Mr. Grey said he had found it, neither could he have thrown it there. He must have fallen forward and died at once. The shot had been fired from a distance of at least a yard, probably more. This, together with the absence of his finger-marks on the pistol, made suicide out of the question. The exact time of death was always difficult to determine, but there was nothing to contradict the evidence of his having been alive at eight o'clock.

The Coroner: 'He might have been dead as long as three-quarters of an hour when you first saw him?'
    'It is possible.'
The Coroner: 'Not longer?'
    'I should say not longer, but it is difficult to place these things exactly.'

The Coroner: 'He might have been alive as late as twenty past eight?'
'Oh, yes.'

There was more of this sort of thing. In the upshot it seemed to Hilary that the medical evidence left them just where they were as far as the time question went. Medically speaking, James Everton might have been shot at twenty past eight, when the Mercers said they heard the shot, or at any time between then and eight o'clock when he had talked to Geoffrey on the telephone. The police said that the front door was locked and bolted when they arrived, and that all the windows on the ground floor were fastened with the exception of the dining-room windows, which were open at the top. They were very heavy sash windows not at all easy to move.

Mrs. Thompson, recalled, said that neither Mercer nor Mrs. Mercer went near any of the doors or windows after the alarm was given. Mercer went into the study, and when he had made sure that Mr. Everton was dead he went to the telephone, but Mr. Grey took the receiver from him and called up the police himself. Mrs. Mercer sat down on the bottom step of the stairs and cried 'something dreadful'. She was quite sure that nobody interfered with any doors or windows.

The Coroner addressed the jury, and from beginning to end it was perfectly clear that he believed that Geoffrey had shot his uncle.

'We have here a household like hundreds of other well-to-do households. Mr. James Everton was a chartered accountant, the sole partner in an old-established firm. His nephew, Mr. Geoffrey Grey, was associated with the business, and he has told us that he expected to be made a partner. Until his marriage a year ago he lived with his uncle at Solway Lodge, Putney. The domestic staff consisted of Alfred Mercer, and his wife and a daily help of the name of Ashley, who has not been called as it was her habit to leave at six o'clock. The Mercers agree that she left at this hour on the day in question. Mrs. Thompson, however, was in the house, having been invited to supper by the Mercers. Mrs. Thompson is Sir John Blakeney's housekeeper and lives at Sudbury House, which is the next house to Solway Lodge. She has lived there for twenty-five years. You have heard her evidence. I need not labour its importance. If you believe Mrs. Thompson — and there is no reason to disbelieve her — it is quite impossible for Alfred Mercer to have left the kitchen during the time under review. She says he came and went between the kitchen and the pantry, where he was cleaning silver, but that he never at any time left the kitchen premises. It is quite impossible that he should have done so without her seeing him. If, therefore, you believe Mrs. Thompson's evidence, no suspicion rests on Alfred Mercer. At twenty past eight, as he has told you, he heard the sound of a shot and his wife's scream. He then ran out into the hall, where he found Mrs. Mercer in a terrible state. He tried the study door and found it locked. Mr. Grey then opened it from the inside. He had a pistol in his hand, and Mr. Everton was lying dead across his desk. Mrs. Thompson, who followed Alfred Mercer, corroborates this, but as she is very deaf she did not hear either the shot or the scream. I think you may take it that no suspicion rests upon Alfred Mercer.

'We will now take Mrs. Thompson's evidence with regard to his wife. Mrs. Mercer did leave the kitchen twice, once "round about eight o'clock". Mrs. Thompson cannot put it nearer than that, and she says that the absence was not "above two or three minutes". Mr. and Mrs. Grey have both sworn to hearing Mr. Everton's voice on the telephone at eight o'clock. In this respect you can, I think receive their evidence. I see no reason to doubt that Mr. Grey came to Solway Lodge that evening in response to a telephone call from his uncle, or that that call was put through, as he states, at eight o'clock. I think you may, therefore, dismiss this absence of Mrs. Mercer's as immaterial. She says she went through the dining-room with some plates, and there is no reason to doubt what she says.

'I would like you now to pay particular attention to Mrs. Mercer's second absence. Shortly after a quarter past eight she again left the kitchen, with the avowed intention of arranging Mr. Everton's room for the night. This might at first sight appear a suspicious circumstance, since the cook is not usually free to attend to upstairs duties during the quarter of an hour immediately preceding what is the principal meal of the day for a business man. Her explanation that owing to the hot weather a cold supper had been ordered and was already set out in the dining-room is confirmed by the police. They also state that Mr. Everton's bed had in fact been turned down. Now I want you to notice the time element very carefully here. If you suspect Mrs. Mercer, you must suppose that she went upstairs, performed her duties there, and came down again, bringing with her the pistol which Mr. Grey swears he left behind when he moved from Solway Lodge a year ago, but of which she and her husband deny any knowledge. Well, you have to suppose that she has loaded that pistol and brought it downstairs, that she then enters the study and without further ado shoots her employer. You have to imagine her locking the door, wiping her finger-prints off the handle — *no prints were found upon it but those of Mr. Grey* — wiping her finger-prints off the pistol — *only Mr. Grey's finger-prints were found there* — and then making her escape by way of the glass door. To do all this she had under five minutes, and she had still to get back into the house. If you can believe that this nervous, hysterical woman could first plan and commit a cold-blooded murder, and then coolly remove all traces of her complicity, you are still faced with the problem of how she got back into the house. The front door was locked and bolted, and all the windows on the ground floor were fastened with the exception of the two in the dining-room, which were open at the top. The police report that it is impossible to raise the lower half of these windows from the outside. The back door was also locked. Mrs. Thompson is positive that the key was turned after she was admitted. The police found it locked. I have gone into all this in detail because I wish to make it quite clear that Mrs. Mercer is not under suspicion. In spite of her absence from the kitchen at the crucial time, it was, as I think I have shown you, a physical impossibility for her to have committed the crime and got back into the house. The study door remained locked until Mr. Grey opened it from the inside. He has himself testified that the key was sticking in the lock. Mrs. Mercer could not have come through that door and left it locked upon the inside.

'We will now turn to the evidence of Mr. Bertram Everton. I need not point out to you the importance of this evidence. Mr. Bertram Everton has sworn that when he dined with his uncle on the evening of Monday, July 16th, Mr. James Everton informed him that he was about to change his will. He conveyed this impression in terms which Mr. Bertram Everton understood to mean that he himself was to be a beneficiary. I will read you a transcript from the shorthand notes of this part of the evidence.

' "Did he tell you he was making a will in your favour?"
' "Well, not exactly."
' "What did he say?"
' "Well, if you really want to know, he said that if he'd

got to choose between a smooth-tongued hypocrite and a damned tomfool, he'd choose the fool."

' "And you took that reference to yourself?"

' "Well, it seemed to point that way."

' "You took it to mean that he was about to execute a will in your favour?"

' "Well, I didn't think he'd do it, don't you know. I just thought he'd had a row with Geoffrey."

' "Did he tell you so?"

' "No — I just got the impression."

'Now this evidence is borne out by the ascertained facts. It is a fact that on the morning of the sixteenth — that is, the morning after this conversation with Mr. Bertram Everton — Mr. James Everton sent for his solicitor and altered his will. You have had Mr. Blackett's evidence. He stated that he had received instructions on the telephone to bring Mr. Everton's will to Solway Lodge immediately. He found his client very far from well. In his view Mr. Everton had received some severe shock. He had described him to you as neither excited nor angry, but pale, subdued, and highly nervous. His hand was shaking, and he did not appear to have slept. Without explanation he tore the old will across and burned it in the open grate. The principal legatee under this old will was Mr. Geoffrey Grey. There were also legacies to Mrs. Grey, to Mr. Francis Everton, and to Mr. And Mrs. Mercer. Having burnt the will, Mr. Everton instructed Mr. Blackett to draw up a new one. In this new will Mr. Geoffrey Grey's name does not appear. Neither Mrs. Grey nor Mr. Francis Everton receive any legacy. The bequests to the Mercers are unaltered, and the remainder of the property goes to Mr. Bertram Everton. You will notice that this corresponds exactly with the impression conveyed to him by his uncle's remarks of the evening before.

'In a murder case suspicion is apt to attach to the person who benefits most largely by the death. In this case, however, no suspicion falls on Mr. Bertram Everton, who, perhaps fortunately for himself, was in Edinburgh at the time of the murder, and was moreover without a motive, because even if he understood his uncle to have the intention of making a will in his favour, he could not in fact have known that such a will had actually been signed. Statements of employees of the Caledonian Hotel, Edinburgh, confirm his presence there at a late breakfast, at lunch, at round about three o'clock, at something after four, at eight-thirty p.m. on the 16th, and at nine a.m. on the 17th. It is therefore quite impossible to connect him with the crime.

'We now come to Mr. Geoffrey Grey's evidence. He denies any quarrel with his uncle or any knowledge of any reason for the alteration of his uncle's will. Yet Mr. James Everton did alter his will. According to Mr. Blackett's evidence he altered it in deep distress of mind. When the new will had been drawn up he drove to his bank accompanied by Mr. Blackett. He signed his new will in the manager's room with the manager and one of the bank clerks as witnesses. I invite your attention to this point because it makes it quite clear that Mr. Everton was not under duress of any kind — he was acting of his own free will. He had cut one nephew out of his will, and had left all his property to another, yet the nephew who was cut out, Mr. Geoffrey Grey, has sworn that he knew of no reason for this. He has sworn that there was no break in his cordial relations with his uncle.

'Let us proceed with his evidence. He says his uncle rang him up on the evening of July 16th. Mrs. Grey confirms this. There is no reason to disbelieve either of them at this point. The telephone bell rang, and Mr. Grey was summoned to Solway Lodge. He says the terms of this summons were affectionate. Only a few hours had passed since Mr. Everton had in great trouble of mind cut him out of his will, yet he swears that the summons was an affectionate and friendly one. He swears that when he arrived at Solway Lodge he found his uncle dead, and the pistol which killed him lying by the open glass door. He picked it up, heard Mrs. Mercer scream, and going to the door, found it locked, with the key on the inside. He unlocked it, and saw the Mercers in the hall.'

Hilary stopped reading. Geoff — poor Geoff! It was so absolutely damning. What could you do with evidence like that? What could any jury do? They were only out of the room ten minutes, and not for one moment of those ten minutes could anyone have doubted what their verdict would be — Wilful murder against Geoffrey Grey.

Hilary closed the file. She hadn't the heart to read any more. The trial was only the same thing over again — the evidence more strictly controlled, but the same evidence; the speeches longer; the facts equally damning. She had read it all at the time. The jury had been out half an hour instead of ten minutes. They brought in the same verdict:

Wilful murder against Geoffrey Grey.

CHAPTER SEVEN

The sitting-room clock struck three. Hilary was asleep, her head tilted against the back of the chair, the file still heavy across her knees. The light stared down at her and took all the colour out of her face. The birds and flowers of Marion's chintz were bright, but Hilary was pale and very deeply asleep. The light shone on her closed eyelids without reaching her. One moment she was there, full of trouble for Geoffrey and for Marion, and then quite suddenly one of those doors in the long, smooth wall of her city of sleep had opened and let her through.

She came into a queer place. It was a very queer place indeed, a long dark passage running crooked all the way, and because she was in a dream the darkness did not prevent her from seeing the walls of the passage, and they were all made of black looking-glass. She could see herself reflected in them, and two Hilarys walking one on either side of her. In the dream that seemed quite natural and comforting, but when she had gone a little way the reflections began to change, not all at once, but slowly, slowly, slowly, until the two who walked with her were not Hilary, but two strangers. She could not see who they were, but she knew that they were strangers. If she could have turned her head she would have been able to see, but she couldn't turn her head. A cold fear gripped the back of her neck and held it rigid. Something in her began to feel lost child and not wanting to dream this dream any more. Something in her melted, and wept, and cried for Henry, because in her dream she had forgotten about Henry's Atrocious Behaviour and only remembered that he wouldn't let anything hurt her.

The light shone on her closed eyelids, and the tears of her dream welled up and ran down over her pale cheeks tear by tear. They wetted the bright pattern of the chintz, soaking into the blue bird-feathers and the rose-coloured paeony-petals. One of the tears wandered into the deep crinkle at the corner of her mouth. The salt taste of it came through into the dream.

In the next room Marion Grey lay in the dark and slept. She did not dream at all. All day long she turned a courageous mask upon the world. She had her living to earn. She earned it as a mannequin. All day long she

stood, walked, and postured in clothes that were sometimes beautiful and sometimes hideous, but always stag-
geringly expensive. The long graceful lines of her body
and the fact that she was Geoffrey Grey's wife gave her a
certain value. All day long she endured that knowledge.
She had got the job through a friend, and Harriet St. Just
had been completely frank. 'You will change your name
of course. Equally, of course, it will be known who you
are. I am taking a risk — it may be good for trade, it may
be bad. With my particular clientele, I think it will be
good. If it is bad, you will go. At once. I am taking a big
risk.' The risk had justified itself. She earned her living
and she earned it hard. Tomorrow she would be back at
Harriet's — she would be Vanya. Tonight she was not
even Marion Grey. She was sunk in so deep a trance of
fatigue that she had lost herself, lost Geoffrey, lost the
cold sorrow which lay always like ice upon her heart.

Geoffrey Grey slept, too. He lay on his narrow bed, as
his mother had seen him lie when he was a baby, as he
had lain on his almost equally hard school bed, as
Marion had watched him lie in the moonlight, in the
breaking dawn, one arm thrown over his head and the
hand of the other under his cheek. He was asleep and
dreaming with a furious zest of all those things from
which he was shut away. His body was in prison, but his
mind went free. He was running in his school sports, win-
ning the hundred yards again, breasting the tape, hearing the applause break out. And then all in a flash he was
flying with Elvery. A roar of sound — stars — cloud
underneath them as white as boiling milk — and the
wind going past. And then he was diving into the bluest
sea in the world — down into it, and down, and down,
and the blue getting bluer all the time. And then up
again crazily fast, and Marion waiting for him in the
sunshine. They took hands and ran over the sea together
hand in hand, just skimming the bright water. Once in a

way the crest of a wave came up at them in foam and hung them with rainbows. He saw Marion with a rainbow in her hair.

Captain Henry Cunningham was not asleep when the clock struck three. He had, in point of fact, given up trying to go to sleep. He had given it up some time before at, say, a quarter to two, when he had switched on the light and tried to concentrate upon an article about Chinese porcelain. He had made no hand at it at all. If he was really going to chuck the Service and carry on the antique business which his godfather, old Mr. Henry Eustatius, had so surprisingly bequeathed to him, he had a lot of arrears of knowledge to make up with regard to porcelain. He had not, of course, made up his mind about sending in his papers, but he would have to make up his mind before the month was out. The Morrises' offer couldn't be kept open much longer — it would have to be accepted or refused. His leave would be up at the end of the month.

Hilary was, of course, the disturbing factor. Hilary had been immensely keen about their running the antique business together. He had practically made up his mind then. But if Hilary was off, he felt like being off too — off to the ends of the earth as far as possible from Hilary Carew, and from his mother who never saw him without telling him what an escape he had had. With inward rage Henry was aware that he had not escaped, and that he had no desire to escape. Hilary had behaved atrociously — he used her own words — but he hadn't the slightest intention of letting her get away with it. He was leaving her alone because he was angry, and because she deserved to be left alone, and when she had been punished sufficiently and was properly humble and penitent he meant to forgive her. At least that is what it all looked like in the daytime, but at night it didn't seem quite so easy. Suppose Hilary wouldn't make it up.

Suppose she had got really entangled with that swine Basil Montague. Suppose — suppose — suppose he had lost her . . .

It was at these moments that sleep receded and porcelain lost its power to fix the mind. Henry sat miserably on the edge of his bed and wondered, undutifully and not for the first time, why his father had married his mother, and why his mother disliked Hilary so much. She hadn't stopped abusing her the whole afternoon, and it was the last afternoon which Henry meant to spend at Norwood for a good long time. Thank heaven and his queer old godfather for the four-roomed flat over the antique shop which provided such a good excuse for not spending his leave with his mother. He had planned to live in the flat with Hilary.

There he was, back at Hilary again. His rage turned against himself because he was letting a chance glimpse of her unbalance him. When you have mapped out a path you should be prepared to follow it, and he was letting an accidental glimpse of Hilary tempt him to leave the mapped-out path and go plunging across country with the one idea of reaching her as soon as possible, snatching her up and kissing her, carrying her away and marrying her out of hand. He had actually fallen so low as to write to her — not the sort of calm forgiving letter of the plan but an incoherent appeal to make it up, to love him again, to marry him quickly. Even superior young men have their moments of weakness. It is true that he had surmounted his. The ashes of that undignified appeal were choking the grate at this moment, the light draught from the chimney stirred them lightly. So perish all traitor thoughts.

Henry directed a most portentous frown upon the grate. He hadn't really *seen* Hilary this afternoon, he had only caught that one teasing, tantalising, unsatisfying glimpse. It had left him with the impression

that she was pale. His heart contracted at the thought of
Hilary pale, of Hilary ill. His brain instantly reminded
him that she never had very much colour on a cold day.
It was, of course, possible that she had caught sight of
him before he had caught sight of her, and that the
pallor was due to a smitten conscience. Henry's brain
here produced a sardonic 'I don't think!' He had no
reason to suppose that Hilary's conscience was taking a
hand in the affair at all. It had always struck him as a
very spritely and resilient conscience. He somehow
didn't see it being pale and remorseful over having dis-
regarded his wishes.

At this point two conflicting comments emerged as it
were from opposite sides of his mind. 'Little beast!' was
one. And the other, 'Oh, Hilary — *darling*!' Very disturbing to the feelings, to be so mixed up about a girl as
not to be able to think of her as the darling of your heart
without being irritatingly conscious that she *was* a little
beast, or to dismiss her as a little beast without the in-
stant and poignant reminder that she *was* the darling of
your heart. From this quite common dilemma there is no
escape alone. Two may sometimes find the way out hand-
in-hand. Henry had no hand to hold. He continued to
gloom at the grate, where the ash had settled into an
almost impalpable dust.

CHAPTER EIGHT

Hilary opened her eyes and blinked at the light. It was
very bright for London sun in November, and it was
surprisingly high over head. She blinked again. It wasn't

the sun, it was the electric light shining down on her from the bowl in the ceiling. And she wasn't in bed, she was in the living-room of the flat, in Geoff's big chair, with something heavy weighing her down. She sat up, the heavy thing fell off with a bang on the floor, and she saw that it was the file of the Everton Murder.

Of course — she had been reading it. She had read the inquest, and then she must have dropped asleep, because the clock was striking seven and a horrid cold, foggy light was seeping in through the curtains. She was cold, and stiff, and sleepy — not comfortably sleepy, but up-all-night, train-journey tired.

'Bath,' said Hilary to herself very firmly. She stretched, got out of the chair, and picked up the file, and as she did so the door opened and Marion stood looking at her with surprise and something else — anger.

'Hilary! What *are* you doing?'

Hilary clutched the file. Her funny short curls were all on end. She looked rather like a ghost that has forgotten how to vanish, a guilty and dishevelled ghost. She said in a casual, murmuring voice,

'I went to sleep.'

'Here?'

'Um.'

'You haven't been to bed?'

Hilary glanced down at her pyjamas. She couldn't remember whether she had been to bed or not. She had undressed, because here she was in her pyjamas. Then she began to remember.

'Um — I went to bed — but I couldn't sleep — so I came in here.' She shivered and pulled her dressing-gown round her. Marion had the frozen look again. It was enough to make anyone feel cold.

'Reading *that*?' said Marion, looking at the file.

'Yes. Don't look like that, Marion. I only wanted — I've never read — the inquest.'

'And you've only to read it for the whole thing to be cleared up!' Marion's voice had a sharp edge of anger on it.

Hilary came wide awake. It wasn't fair of Marion to talk like that when she was only trying to help. And then she was full of compunction. Poor darling, it was only because everything to do with the case just got her on the raw. She said with a quick rush of pity,

'Don't! I did want to help — I *did*. I'll put it away. I didn't mean you to see it, but I went to sleep.'

Marion went to the window and pulled back the curtains. The daylight showed beyond the glass, sickly with fog, sodden with moisture. She turned back and saw Hilary putting away the file. The Everton Case was closed. Geoff was in prison. Here was the new day that she had to meet. She said not unkindly,

'Run along and dress. I'll get breakfast.'

But Hilary hesitated in the doorway.

'If — if you didn't hate to talk about it so much, darling — '

'I *won't* talk about it!' said Marion, the edge on her voice again. She was dressed for the street and cleverly made up. She looked like an ultra-modern poster — incredibly thin, amazingly artificial, but graceful, always graceful.

Hilary said quickly. 'There are things — I wish you would — there are things I want to ask about.'

'I *won't* talk about it!' said Marion again.

Hilary had stopped looking like a ghost. She was brightly flushed and her eyes were wet. She saw Marion's queer poster colouring all blurred as if it was drowned in tears. But they were her tears, not Marion's — Marion wouldn't cry. She turned and ran into her own room and shut the door.

When Marion had gone to work Hilary washed up the breakfast things, made beds, and ran over the floors with a carpet-sweeper where there was a carpet and with a mop where there wasn't. The flat was very small, and it didn't take long. They had a woman once a week to do the heavy cleaning.

When she had finished Hilary sat down to think. She took a pencil and paper and wrote the things that came into her mind.

Mrs. Mercer — why did she cry such a lot? She cried at the inquest, and she cried at the trial, and she cried in the train. But it didn't stop her saying she heard Geoffrey quarrelling with his uncle. She needn't have said it. She cried, but she went on saying it.

That was the first thing that struck her.

Then — the daily help hadn't been called as a witness. She would like to ask her some questions. About that toothache of Mrs. Mercer's — it seemed funny that she should have had it that night. So convenient if you were all to bits with a bad conscience and felt you simply had to put your head in your hands and groan. You *could* with a toothache, and nobody would think anything about it.

Then Mrs. Thompson. Terribly respectable, terribly deaf. How convenient to have a deaf visitor if someone was going to be shot and you knew it. If you didn't know it, why have a deaf visitor?

There was of course no logic in this, but Hilary had not a very logical mind. She wasn't bothering about being logical, she was just putting down what came into her head. The deafness of the Mercers' visitor was one of these things. Another thing that struck her was what a lot of alibis everyone had. Looking back on what she had read last night, it seemed to her that all those people couldn't have had better alibis if they had sat down and thought them out beforehand. And bright as lightning there zigzagged through her mind the thought, '*Suppose they had.*'

Mercer — Bertie   Everton — Mrs.   Mercer — Frank Everton . . .

Mrs. Thompson to supper on just that one night. Mrs. Thompson so deaf that she couldn't hear a shot, but able to testify that Mercer hadn't left the kitchen and that Mrs. Mercer hadn't been gone long enough to shoot James Everton and get back into the house. Not that she thought that Mrs. Mercer had shot James Everton. She was a dithery dreep of a woman, and she wouldn't have the nerve to shoot a guinea-pig. Hilary simply couldn't believe in her firing a pistol at her employer. A dreep is and remains a dreep. It doesn't suddenly become a cool plotting assassin. Mrs. Mercer's weepy evidence might be, and probably was, a tissue of lies, but it wasn't she who had shot James Everton.

Well, that looked as if the Mercers were a wash-out. But the Evertons, Bertie and Frank, one in Edinburgh and the other in Glasgow — what about them? The answer to that was discouraging in the extreme. You could put it into one word — nothing. Nothing about the Evertons — nothing. Bertie was in Edinburgh, and Frank was in Glasgow, with solicitors vouching for them, and chambermaids bringing their early morning tea and answering their bells when they rang. There simply wasn't anything you could do about the Evertons. If they had been specialising in alibis for years they couldn't have come out of it better. It wasn't any good — it really *wasn't* any good. The case was closed. Geoff was in prison, and by the time he came out he'd be dead. And Marion would be dead, too. And these two dead people would have to go away and try to make a new life somewhere.

Hilary shivered. It was a most desperately bleak thought. No wonder Marion had that frozen look. Of course Geoffrey might have been really dead — he might have been hanged. After reading that evidence Hilary wondered why he hadn't been hanged. There had been an enormous petition. People had been most awfully sorry for Marion because she was going to have a baby, and she supposed the jury must have had some faint doubt in their minds, because they had recommended him to mercy. It must have been that. Or perhaps they, too, were sorry for Marion, whose baby might have been born on the very day fixed for the execution. It was born the day she heard about the reprieve. And the baby died, and Marion hung on the edge of death, and then came back like a ghost to haunt the place where she had been so happy.

Another shiver ran over Hilary, but this time it was a shiver of revulsion. However bad things were, you needn't sit down under them. If you looked at them too long they got you down. You mustn't go on looking at them — you must do something. There was always something to be done if you put your mind to it. Hilary began to put her mind to it, and at once she knew what she could do about the Everton Case. She could go down to Putney and rout out the daily help who hadn't been called as a witness.

She walked to the bottom of the road and caught a bus, just as Geoffrey Grey had done on the night of July 16th, sixteen months ago. It had taken him between a quarter of an hour and twenty minutes to reach Solway Lodge, getting off at the corner and making quick work of Holly Lane with his long stride. It took Hilary twenty-five minutes, because she didn't know the way and had to stop and ask, and she didn't go in by the garden gate, but round to the proper entrance, where she stood and looked through iron scroll-work at a leaf-strewn drive wept over by dripping half-denuded trees. She didn't go in — it wasn't any use going in. The house was shut up, and three boards in a row proclaimed Bertie Everton's desire to sell it. Houses which have figured in a murder case do not sell very easily, but it is of course permissible to hope.

Hilary passed the notice-boards and a second gate and came to the entrance of Sudbury House. Sudbury House belonged to Sir John Blakeney. Mrs. Thompson was Sir John Blakeney's housekeeper, and it was from Mrs. Thompson that Hilary hoped to extract the name and address of that uncalled witness. The gate stood open, and she walked in, and along a narrow winding drive. When Holly Lane was really a lane Sudbury House had been a desirable country residence. It stood square and dignified in Georgian brick, the dark red flush of Virginia creeper still clinging to the side that caught the sun.

Hilary went to the front door and rang the bell. She supposed she really ought to go the back door, but she just wasn't going to. If she let this thing get her down, it *would* get her down. She wasn't going to help it by having an inferiority complex and going round to back doors.

She waited for the front door to open. It was quite simple — she was going to ask for Mrs. Thompson. It was for whoever opened the door to do the rest. She had only got to stick her chin in the air, bite the inside corner of her lip rather hard, and tell herself not to be a rabbit.

And in the event she was quite right — it was perfectly simple. A most fat, benevolent butler opened the door. He had lovely manners and seemed to see nothing odd about her wanting to see Mrs. Thompson. He reminded Hilary of air balloons she had loved when she was a child — pink, smooth, and creaking a little if you blew them up too tightly. The butler's creak was partly a wheeze and partly starch. He showed her into a sort of morning-room and went away almost as lightly as a balloon would have done. Hilary did hope he wouldn't blow away or blow up before he got to Mrs. Thompson. Her balloons had been liable to these tragic fatalities.

After about five minutes Mrs. Thompson came in. She was much, much fatter than the butler, but she didn't in the least suggest a balloon. She was the most solid human being Hilary had ever beheld, and her tread shook the floor. She wore black cashmere, with white frilling at the throat and an onyx brooch like a bullseye set in plaited gold. Her neck bulged above the frilling, and her cheeks bulged above her neck. She wore no cap, but her masses of hair were tightly plaited and wound about her head in a monstrous braid which did not as yet show any sign of turning grey. The contrast between this shiny black hair and the deep habitual flush of the large face below it gave her a very decided look. Hilary saw at once that here was a person who knew her own mind — her yea would be yea, and her nay nay. The last faint hope that Mrs. Thompson might have been lying at the inquest faded away and died before the emphatic responsibility of her aspect. Hilary found her so alarming that she would have dithered if she had let herself stop to think. She said, 'Mrs. Thompson?' in a pretty, breathless voice, and Mrs. Thompson said, 'Yes, Miss.'

'I wondered,' said Hilary, and then she stuck, and Mrs. Thompson said 'Yes, miss' again, but this time her small, steady grey eyes took on a look of recognition — at least that was what Hilary thought. The colour came brightly into her cheeks and burned there. She said,

'Oh, Mrs. Thompson, I know you're busy, and I'm interrupting you, but if you would just let me ask you one or two questions — '

Mrs. Thompson stood there very large and portentous. The look of recognition was gone. Her face was like a brick wall. At last she said,

'I know your face, but I don't remember your name.'

'Hilary Carew. I'm Mrs. Grey's cousin — Mrs. Geoffrey Grey.'

Mrs. Thompson came a heavy step nearer and put up a hand to her ear.

'I'm very hard of hearing — I'll have to trouble you to speak up, miss.'

'Yes — I remember.' Hilary pitched her voice high and clear. Aunt Emmeline's Eliza was hard of hearing too, so she had had practice. 'Is that better?'

Mrs. Thompson nodded.

'People don't speak up as they used to do, but that will be all right. What did you want, miss?'

'It's about the Everton Case. You're the second person who remembers seeing me at the trial though I was only there one day. At least I suppose that's where you saw me.'

Mrs. Thompson nodded again.

'With Mrs. Grey, pore lady.'

'Yes,' said Hilary. 'Oh, Mrs. Thompson, he *didn't* do it — he really didn't.'

Mrs. Thompson shook her head.

'And that's what I should have said myself if I hadn't seen him with the pistol in his hand.'

'He didn't — he really didn't,' said Hilary very earnestly and very loud. 'But it's no good talking about that, and that's not what I came here to talk about. I only wanted to ask you if you know about the daily help, the woman who used to come in and help Mrs. Mercer at Solway Lodge, because they didn't call her either at the inquest or at the trial, and there's something I want to ask her most dreadfully badly.'

Mrs. Thompson didn't snort, because she had been very well brought up and knew her manners. It was, however, apparent that only a sense of what was due to herself prevented her from snorting.

'That Mrs. Ashley!'

'Was that her name?'

Mrs. Thompson nodded.

'And a good thing they didn't call her for a witness, for a poorer spirited, more Peter-grievous kind of a creature I never come across nor never want to!'

'And do you know where she lives?' said Hilary quickly.

Mrs. Thompson shook her head with heavy scorn. It was not for her to know the lurking-places of Peter-grievous females who went out by the day.

Hilary turned quite pale with disappointment.

'Oh, Mrs. Thompson — but I want to find her so frightfully badly.'

Mrs. Thompson considered.

'If she'd had anything to tell, the police 'ud have got it out of her, and she'd have been called for a witness and have had hysterics in the court as likely as not. People ought to be able to control themselves is what I say, but Mrs. Ashley never. And I can't give you her address, miss, only knowing about her through Mrs. Mercer, but you might hear of her at Smith the greengrocer's about three doors up from where you come into the High Street, because it was Mrs. Smith recommended her to Mrs. Mercer when she was looking for help. And I won't say she wasn't pretty fair at her work, though I couldn't have stood her about the house myself.'

Hilary came away quite bright and brisk. Mrs. Smith would be able to give her Mrs. Ashley's address, and she might be able to find out something that would help Geoff. She hadn't expected anything of Mrs. Thompson who must have been pumped completely dry between the inquest and the trial. If you don't expect anything you don't let yourself feel disappointed. Mrs. Thompson thought Geoffrey had done it, but then of course she didn't know Geoff. She could only repeat what she had said at the inquest and finish up with 'I saw him with the pistol in his hand.' Hilary wasn't going to let herself be damped and daunted by that.

She found the greengrocer's shop without difficulty, and was given Mrs. Ashley's address by the buxom fair-haired Mrs. Smith, who obviously thought that she was looking for daily help — 'And I'm sure, madam, you'll find Mrs. Ashley very nice about the house — very nice indeed. Ladies I've recommended her to have always been very well satisfied — 10 Pinman's Lane, and if you go round the corner and take the second on the left and the third on the right you can't miss it. And you'll find her in. She was here not half an hour ago, and she was going home then. The lady she's been working for is away, and all she's got to do is keep the house aired.'

Hilary thought Pinman's Lane a most depressing place. The houses were old and tottery, with tiny windows. She knocked at the door of No. 10. Nothing happened. She knocked again. Then someone began to come down the stairs, and the minute Hilary heard that footstep she knew why Mrs. Thompson had wanted to snort. It was one of those trailing footsteps, a hesitating, slow dreep of a footstep. James Everton must have had some fatal attraction for dreeps, because Mrs. Mercer had been one too. Or — a window opened brightly in Hilary's mind — was Mercer the kind of man who liked to lord it over a batch of spineless, subservient women? She was wondering about that when the door opened and Mrs. Ashley stood there putting back the faded hair from her faded eyes and peering at Hilary in a vaguely questioning manner. She had once been a very pretty girl. The faded hair had been a pale ash-blonde, and the faded eyes a very soft pale blue. Her features were regular and good, but the apple-blossom tints which had coloured them had long since departed, leaving her lined and sallow. She might have been thirty-five, she might have been fifty-five. There was no knowing.

Hilary said, 'May I come in?' and walked firmly past her and into the room on the right. She felt quite sure that it was no use waiting to be asked in, and she wasn't going to stand on the doorstep and talk about the Everton Case in the hearing of the neighbours.

The room was most dreadfully pathetic — very old linoleum on the floor with the pattern worn away and the edges frayed, a rug that looked as if it had been picked off a rubbish heap, and a sofa with broken springs and bulges of horsehair coming through the burst American cloth. There was a wooden chair and a sagging wicker one, and a table with a woollen table-cloth which had once been red.

Hilary stood by the table and waited for Mrs. Ashley to come in and shut the door.

CHAPTER NINE

Mrs. Ashley looked frightened to death. Hilary thought she had never seen anyone so ridiculously frightened in her life. Ridiculously because — well, really, there wasn't anything for her to be frightened about. You don't need to look like a rabbit in a trap just because you once worked in a house where there was a murder and someone comes to ask you a few quite harmless questions about it. All the same, there was Mrs. Ashley with her mouth open in a pale O and her eyes staring with terror.

'I'm Mrs Grey's cousin,' repeated Hilary firmly.

Some kind of a sound came out of the pale O, but it didn't make any sense.

Hilary tapped with her foot. She really could have shaken the creature.

'Mrs. Geoffrey Grey — Geoffrey Grey's wife. I'm her

cousin. I only wanted to ask you one or two questions — Mrs. Ashley, why are you so frightened?'

Mrs. Ashley caught her breath. Her chin trembled. She put up a hand to cover her mouth.

'I don't know anything — I can't say anything.'

Hilary restrained herself. If she lost her temper, it would be all up. She said in the careful, gentle voice which she would have used to someone who was not quite right in the head:

'There's nothing to be frightened about. I really only wanted to ask you something about Mrs. Mercer.'

This seemed to have a soothing effect. Mrs. Ashley took her hand away from her mouth, moistened her lips with a pale tongue, and said in a faint, gasping voice:

'Mrs. Mercer?'

'Yes. You were helping her at Solway Lodge, weren't you? Did she tell you she had a toothache the day Mr. Everton was shot?'

'Oh no, miss, she didn't.'

It was obvious that the question was a relief, and the answer an easy one.

'Did you know that she'd been having toothache?'

'Oh no, miss, I didn't.'

'You didn't know she'd had trouble with her teeth?'

'Oh no, Miss.'

'But I suppose she used to talk to you a good bit?'

'Sometimes she would and sometimes she wouldn't,' said Mrs. Ashley — 'not if Mr. Mercer was anywhere about. But if we were by ourselves in the bedrooms as it might be, she'd tell me how she'd lived down by the sea when she was a girl the first time she was in service. She thought a lot about that place Mrs. Mercer did. There was a lady and a little boy, and the gentleman a lot away from home. There was a baby too, but it was the little boy she thought the world of.' Mrs. Ashley paused for

74

breath. The topic seemed to have reassured her, and she had stopped looking like something in a trap.

Hilary brought her firmly back from Mrs. Mercer's reminiscences to Mrs. Mercer herself.

'Then you didn't know she had a toothache?'

'Oh no, miss.'

Hilary let the toothache go.

'What time did you leave — on the 16th, I mean?'

The frightened look came back into Mrs. Ashley's face. She showed the whites of her eyes like a nervous horse as she said:

'I had my tea and went same as usual.'

Now what was the matter with her?

'And what time was that?' said Hilary.

Mrs. Ashley's mouth opened and shut. She looked dreadfully like a fish on a hook.

'Six o'clock,' she said on an almost inaudible gasp.

'And you didn't see anything out of the way?'

Mrs. Ashley shook her head.

'Or hear anything?'

Mrs. Ashley turned the colour of a tallow candle and her eyes bolted, but she shook her head again.

Hilary, exasperated, took a step towards her and said with all the severity of her twenty-two years:

'Mrs. Ashley, you *did* hear something. It's no good your saying you didn't, because I can see that you did, and if you won't tell me what it is, I shall just have to think about going to the police.'

It wasn't possible to look more frightened, but it was possible to shiver. Mrs. Ashley shivered, and clutched at the table for support.

'I went away at six o'clock — gospel truth I did.'

Hilary came darting at her with, 'But did you come back again, Mrs. Ashley — did you come back?' And then and there the woman collapsed, going down on her knees by the table, sobbing and weeping, her hands

75

pressed over her eyes and her tongue stumbling and failing under a landslide of words.

'I told her I wouldn't tell, *and* I never. I promised her sure and certain I wouldn't tell. I told the police I went away at six like I always done and no reason why I shouldn't and take my gospel oath on it for true's true and I went away like I said and no one never arst me nothing more except that pore lady and I promised her faithful I wouldn't tell *and* I never.'

Hilary felt a little cold and bewildered. The sound of Mrs. Ashley's sobs filled the room. She had let go of the table and was crouched in a sort of heap against one of the rickety legs, rocking herself to and fro and crying.

'Mrs. Ashley — listen to me! What are you talking about? Who made you promise not to tell?'

'I never!' said Mrs. Ashley with a rending sniff. 'The police come, and I don't know how I kep' myself, but I *never*.'

'Who did you promise? You must tell me who you promised.'

Mrs. Ashley's sobs redoubled.

'She come here, *and* I told her. And she sat in that chair and she arst me to promise. Not three months off her time she was. And I promised, and I kep' my promise.' She pushed the hair from her face with a trembling, dabbing hand and stared at Hilary in a sort of weak pride. 'I didn't tell the police — I didn't tell no one — only *her* — only Mrs. Grey.'

Hilary knelt down on the shabby floor so that she could face her eye to eye.

'What did you hear?' she said in a young, small voice.

Mrs. Ashley rocked and sobbed. Hilary's voice went down into a whisper.

'Tell me — Mrs. Ashley, tell me — I've got to know. It won't hurt anyone now — Geoff's in prison — the case is closed. I'm Marion's cousin — you can tell me. You see, I know that you came back. I've got to know what happened — I've got to know what you heard.' She put out a hand and took the woman by the wrist. 'Mrs. Ashley, why did you go back?'

'I dropped my letter.'

'What letter?'

'I've got a boy that went for a sailor. He's seventeen — and it's his first trip — and he wrote to me from India — and I took the letter for to show Mrs. Mercer — she and me used to talk about my boy, and about the one she set such store by in her first place — and when I got home I hadn't got my letter, so I come back — '

'Yes?' said Hilary.

Mrs. Ashley pushed back her damp hair.

'Mr. Mercer he'd have burnt it or tore it up, Mr. Mercer would. No feelings for a mother, Mr. Mercer hasn't — many's the time me and Mrs. Mercer have said it when he wasn't by. So I dursn't leave it over till next day and I come back. I knew where I must have left it for certain, because it was when Mr. Everton was out and I was doing the study, and Mrs. Mercer come in and I read her the letter. And I put it back in my pocket in a hurry because we heard Mr. Mercer, and it must have slipped out and seeing I was tight up against the curtains I'd good hope no one 'ad seen it. So I waited till I thought Mr. Everton 'ud be at dinner and I come along.'

'Yes!' said Hilary — 'yes?'

Mrs. Ashley had stopped crying. She sniffed and gulped, but she was fairly launched.

'I come back and I thought no need to let anyone know. And I thought a fine evening like this the study window'll be open right down to the ground, and no more than to put my hand inside and take my letter if it was there, and if not I must just leave it and take my chance of a word with Mrs. Mercer.' She paused and rocked herself, and stared at Hilary with frightened eyes. 'I made sure Mr. Everton 'ud be at dinner, but I come along tight up to the wall and I hadn't got to no more than a yard or two from the study window than I heard Mr. Everton call out and there come the sound of a shot, and I turned around and I ran.' She choked on a sob. 'I didn't see no one, and no one didn't see me. I don't know how I got home — I don't indeed.'

Hilary felt exactly as if someone had dashed cold water in her face. She was braced, eager, and steady. Something in her mind kept saying, 'The time — the time that she heard the shot — that's what matters — the time — the time of the shot.' She said it aloud in a clear, firm voice.

'What time was it? What time did you hear the shot?'

Mrs. Ashley stopped rocking. Her mouth fell open. She seemed to be thinking.

'There was a clock struck when I come along Oakley Road —'

'Yes — yes?'

'Eight o'clock it struck.'

Hilary drew a long joyful breath. It was only five minutes walk from Oakley Road to Solway Lodge. That is to say, Geoff had made five minutes of it. A woman would probably take seven or eight minutes, and a dreep like Mrs. Ashley might take ten. But if Mrs. Ashley had heard that shot fired at ten minutes past eight, it couldn't have been fired by Geoffrey Grey. Geoff couldn't possibly have reached Solway Lodge before a quarter past eight, and even then you had got to allow time for him to meet his uncle and quarrel with him if you were going to believe the Mercers' evidence. She said in an eager, trembling voice:

'Then it couldn't have been later than ten past eight when you heard that shot?'

Mrs. Ashley sat back on her heels and stared. Her

78

hands had fallen palm upwards in her lap. She said in a flat voice:

'No, miss — it would be later than that — a good bit.'

Hilary's heart gave a jump.

'It couldn't be! You couldn't take more than ten minutes from Oakley Road — nobody could.'

'Oh no, miss.'

'Then it couldn't have been more than ten minutes past eight.'

Mrs. Ashley opened and shut her mouth exactly like a fish. Then she said, 'It was a good bit later than that,' in her meek, flat voice.

'How *could* it be?'

She moistened her lips again.

'A good ten minutes out that clock have been ever since I been going to the house.'

'Which way out?'

Mrs. Ashley blinked.

'It must have been getting on for the half hour.'

'You mean the clock was slow?'

'A good ten minutes out.'

Hilary's heart sank. The joy went out of her. No wonder Marion had asked this woman to hold her tongue. If she had really heard the shot at twenty past eight, her evidence would just about have finished Geoff. She winced sharply away from the picture of Marion — fine, proud Marion — going down on her knees to this woman to ask her to hold her tongue and give Geoff a chance, a bare chance, of escaping the hangman. She stood for a moment pressing her hands together. Then she said:

'Mrs. Ashley — you're quite sure about that clock being ten minutes slow?'

'A good ten minutes, miss. I used to pass the remark to Mrs. Mercer many and many a time. "Nothing to go by that church clock of yours," I used to say. "And all very well for you that's got a watch, but many's the time it's given me a turn, and all for nothing." They've put it right since, someone was telling me, but I don't go that way now so I couldn't say for sure.'

'Did you hear anything besides the shot?' Hilary was dreadfully afraid of this question, but she had to ask it or be a coward. And immediately she knew why she had been afraid. Panic looked at her out of Mrs. Ashley's eyes and a trembling hand went up and covered her mouth. Hilary shook too. 'What did you hear? You *did* hear something — I know you did. Did you hear voices?'

Mrs. Ashley moved her head. Hilary thought the wavering movement said 'Yes.'

'You heard voices? What voices?'

'Mr. Everton's.' The words were stifled against the woman's palm, but Hilary caught them.

'You heard Mr. Everton's voice? You're sure?'

This time the movement of the head was almost a jerk. As far as Mrs. Ashley could be sure of anything she was sure that she had heard James Everton's voice.

'Did you hear any other voice?'

Again the wavering movement said 'Yes.'

'Whose voice?'

'I don't know, miss — not if it was my last word I don't, and so I told Mrs. Grey when she came and arst me, pore thing. It was only just so I could say there was someone there quarrelling with Mr. Everton.'

Quarrelling . . . Hilary's very heart was sick. Damning evidence against Geoff — damning corroboration of Mrs. Mercer's evidence. And not bought, not cooked up, because this woman had nothing to gain. And she had held her tongue. She had been sorry for Marion, and she had held her tongue.

Hilary drew in her breath and forced herself on.

'You didn't hear anything the other person said?'

'Oh no, miss.'

'But you recognised Mr. Everton's voice?'

'Oh yes, miss.'

'And you heard what he said?' Hilary was pressing her hard.

'Oh *yes*, miss.' And at that her voice broke in choking sobs and her eyes rained down tears.

One bit of Hilary wondered furiously how anyone could produce such a continuous water flow, whilst another bit of her was cold and afraid on the edge of knowing what James Everton had said. She heard herself whisper:

'What did he say? You must tell me what he said.'

And then Mrs. Ashley, with her face in her hands, choking out:

'He said — oh, miss, he said, "My own nephew!" Oh, miss, that's what I heard him say — "My own nephew!" And then the shot, and I ran for my life, and that's all. And I promised pore Mrs. Grey — I promised her faithful that I wouldn't tell.'

Hilary felt perfectly cold and stiff.

'It doesn't matter now,' she said. 'The case is closed.'

CHAPTER TEN

Hilary walked along Pinman's Lane with heavy feet and a much, much heavier heart. Poor Marion — poor, poor Marion, coming here with a flickering hope as Hilary had come, and hearing this damning evidence as Hilary had heard it. Only much, much worse for Marion — unbelievably, dreadfully worse. She mustn't ever know that Hilary knew. She must be able to believe that she had shut Mrs. Ashley's mouth on the evidence which would certainly have hanged Geoffrey Grey.

She turned the corner of Pinman's Lane and walked back blindly along the way by which she had come. Was it well to save a man for years, monotonous years, of deadening prison life? Wouldn't the sharp wrench have been better — better for Geoff, and better for Marion too? But even in retrospect she shrank back from the thought. There are things beyond enduring. She shuddered away from this one, and came back with a start to the outside world.

She must have taken a wrong turning, for she was in a street she did not know at all. Of course she didn't know any of the streets really, but this one she was sure she had never seen before — little raw houses, barely finished yet already occupied, semi-detached, with one half of a house painted bice green and the other half mustard yellow, red curtains in one family's windows, and royal blue next door, and roofs tiled in every imaginable shade. The effect was very new and clean, and the houses like bright Christmas toys just unpacked and set out all in a row.

It was when she was thinking they looked like toys that she heard a footstep behind her, and in the moment of hearing it she became conscious that the sound was not a new one. It had been going on for quite a long time, probably ever since she had turned out of Pinman's Lane. It had been there, but she hadn't been listening to it. She listened now, walking a little faster. The footsteps quickened too. She looked over her shoulder and saw a man in a Burberry and a brown felt hat. He had a fawn muffler pulled well up round his throat, and between hat brim and muffler she had a glimpse of regular features, a clean-shaven upper lip, and light eyes. She looked away at once, but it was too late. He lifted his hat and came up with her.

'Excuse me, Miss Carew — '

The sound of her name startled her so much that she forgot all the rules. If people speak to you in the street, you don't say anything, you just walk on as if they hadn't ever been born. If you can manage to look as if you had been brought up in a refrigerator, so much the better, and you simply mustn't blush or look frightened. Hilary forgot all these things. A bright annoyed colour sprang to her cheeks, and she said:

'What do you want? I don't know you.'

'No, miss, but if you'll excuse me I should like a word with you. I was on the train with you the other day, and I recognised you at once, but of course you wouldn't know me unless you happened to notice me in the train.' His manner was that of an upper servant, civil and respectful. The 'miss' was reassuring.

Hilary said, 'In the train? Do you mean yesterday?'

'Yes, miss. We were in the carriage with you, me and my wife, yesterday on the Ledlington train. I don't suppose you noticed me, because I was out of the carriage a good part of the time, but perhaps you noticed my wife.'

'Why?' said Hilary, looking at him rather disconcertingly. Her bright no-coloured eyes had the frank stare of a child.

The man looked past her. He said:

'Well, miss, I thought you two being alone in the carriage as it were — well, I thought perhaps you might have got into conversation.'

Hilary's heart gave a little jump. Mercer — it was Mercer. And he thought perhaps she had talked to Mrs. Mercer in the train, and that Mrs. Mercer had talked to her. She didn't believe for a moment that he had recognised her yesterday. Of course he *might* have. Mrs. Mercer had recognised her, and Mrs. Thompson had, but all the time Mercer was in the carriage she had sat looking out of the window, and when he came back she herself had gone out into the corridor and stayed there until the Ledlington stop. He had stood aside to let her pass, and of course he might have recognised her then, but she didn't think so, because if he had, and if there was anything he wanted to say, he could have followed her down the corridor and said it there. No, he had got it out of his poor draggly wife afterwards and now he wanted to find out just what the poor thing had said. How he had found her, she just couldn't imagine, but when she thought about it afterwards she wondered whether he had been at Solway Lodge on some business of his own or of Bertie Everton's and had seen her looking in through the gate, or whether he had followed her all the way from the flat. Both these thoughts gave her a nasty creepy feeling down the back of her neck. She said with no perceptible pause:

'Oh yes, we talked a little.'

'Begging your pardon, miss, I hope my wife didn't make herself troublesome to you in any way. She's quiet enough as a rule or I wouldn't have left her with a stranger, but as soon as I came back into the carriage I could see she'd been working herself up, and when I saw you turning the corner of the road just now I thought I would take the liberty of catching up with you and saying I hope she didn't saying anything she shouldn't or give any offence. She's quiet enough as a rule, poor thing, but I could see she was all worked up, and I shouldn't like to think she'd offended a young lady that was connected with a family where we'd been in service.'

Hilary turned that bright look on him again. A very superior, well-spoken man, but she didn't like his eyes. They were the blankest eyes she had ever seen — light, hard eyes without a trace of expression in them. She thought of Mrs. Mercer weeping in the train, and she thought a man with eyes like that might break a woman down. She said:

84

'You were in service with Mr. Everton at Solway Lodge?'

'Yes. A very sad affair, miss.'

They were walking along between the bright toy houses. Hilary thought, 'I'd rather live in one of these than under those dripping trees at Solway Lodge.' Everything clean, everything new. Nobody else's sins, and follies, and crimes, and loves, and hates hanging around. Little gay bandbox rooms. A little gay garden where she and Henry would prodigiously admire own marigolds, own Canterbury bells, own Black-eyed Susans.

But she wasn't ever going to have a house with Henry now. Mercer's words echoed faintly in her mind — 'A very sad affair.' She blinked sharply twice and said,

'Yes, it was.'

'Very sad indeed. And my wife not being very strong in her head, she can't properly get over it, miss, and I should be very sorry if she'd annoyed you in any way.'

'No,' said Hilary — 'no, she didn't annoy me.' Her voice had an abstracted sound, because she was trying to remember just what Mrs. Mercer *had* said . . . *'Oh, miss, if you only knew.'* That was one of the things. If she only knew what? What was there for her to know? . . .

She didn't see Mercer look sharply at her and then look away, but his voice came through her thoughts.

'She's in very poor health, miss, I'm sorry to say, and it doesn't do to let her talk about the case, because she gets all worked up and doesn't hardly know what she's saying.'

Hilary said, 'I'm sorry.' She was trying to think what else Mrs. Mercer had said . . . *'I tried to see her.'* Her — that was Marion — poor Marion, with the trial going on. *'Miss, if I never spoke another word, it's true as I tried to see her. I give him the slip and I got out.'*

Mercer's voice came through again.

'Then she didn't say anything she oughtn't to, miss?'

'Oh no,' said Hilary a little vaguely. She wasn't really

thinking about what she said. She was thinking about Mrs. Mercer giving her husband the slip, with Geoff being tried for murder and the Mercers the chief witnesses against him. And Mrs. Mercer had tried to see Marion, tried desperately. *'Miss, if I never spoke another word, it's true as I tried to see her.'* The woman's very tone of horror sounded in her mind, and the way her light wild eyes had been fixed as she whispered, *'If she'd ha' seen me,'* and then, *'She didn't see me. Resting — that's what they told me. And then he came and I never got another chance. He saw to that.'* It had meant nothing to her at the time. It began to mean something to her now. What had Mrs. Mercer been going to say, and what chance had been missed because poor worn-out Marion had been persuaded to take a brief uneasy rest? . . .

Mercer was saying something, she didn't know what. She wrenched away from that train journey and turned on him with a sudden energy.

'You were a witness at Mr. Grey's trial — you were both witnesses?'

He kept his eyes down as he answered her.

'Yes, miss. It was very painful to me and Mrs. Mercer. Mrs. Mercer's never got over it yet.'

'Do you believe that Mr. Grey did it?' The words came to Hilary's lips without thought or purpose.

Mercer looked at the pavement. His tone had a note of respectful reproof.

'That was for the jury to say, miss. Mrs. Mercer and me we had to do our duty.'

Something boiled up in Hilary so suddenly that she nearly lost her self-control. She felt a strong uncivilised urge to slap Mercer's smooth, well-featured face and give him the lie. Fortunately it was *nearly*, and not quite. Civilised young women do not slap butlers' faces in the street — it simply isn't done. She turned hot and cold all over at her narrow escape and walked a little faster. The new road had run into an old one, and she could hear the roar of a thoroughfare not too far away. She wished passionately to catch a bus and leave Putney and Mercer to their own devices.

He still kept up with her and went on talking about his wife.

'It's no use raking things up that's bound to be painful to all concerned, and so I've told Mrs. Mercer many a time, but being weak in the head — it's her nerves the doctor says — she kinds of harps on the case and blames herself because she had to give evidence. But as I said to her, "You're bound to say what you know, and no blame to you if it goes against anyone." "You can't tell lies," I said — "not on your Bible oath in a court of law, you can't. You've got to tell what you've seen or heard, and it's the judge and the jury that does the rest, not you." But there, she goes on harping on it, and I can't stop her. But as long as she didn't annoy you, miss — I'm sure you'd be one that would make allowances for her not being what you might call quite right in the head.'

'Oh yes,' said Hilary.

The thoroughfare was most helpfully near. She walked faster and faster. That was at least six times Mercer had told her that Mrs. Mercer wasn't right in the head. He must be very anxious for it to soak right in. She wondered why. And then she thought she knew. And then she thought that if he said it again, she would probably scream.

They emerged upon the High Street, and her heart jumped with joyful relief.

'Good morning,' she said — 'I'm catching a bus.' And caught one.

CHAPTER ELEVEN

Hilary sat in the bus and thought. She thought about the Mercers. She thought a great deal about the Mercers. Mrs. Mercer might be off her head, or she mightn't. Mercer was uncommonly anxious to make it clear that she *was* off her head — he kept on saying it every five minutes. There was something in Shakespeare — how did it go — 'Methinks the lady doth protest too much.' Mercer was rather like that about Mrs. Mercer — he protested so much that you couldn't help having the feeling that perhaps he was overdoing it. 'What I tell you three times is true.' That was Lewis Carroll in *The Hunting of the Snark*. That seemed to fit Alfred Mercer very well. If he went on saying that Mrs. Mercer was mad often enough it would be believed, and to all intents and purposes mad she would be, *and nobody would take any notice of what she said*.

An idiotic rhyme cavorted suddenly amongst these serious deliberations:

> 'If I had a husband like Mr. Mercer,
> I should want him to be a sea-going purser
> And go long voyages over the main
> And hardly ever come home again.'

Quite definitely and unreasonably, she didn't like Mercer. But that didn't necessarily mean that he was telling lies. You may dislike a person very much, and yet they may be telling the truth. Hilary reflected on this curious fact, and decided that she must not allow herself to be biased. Mercer might be speaking the truth and Mrs. Mercer might be off her head, but contrariwise he might be telling lies and Mrs. Mercer might be what she had appeared to Hilary to be — just a poor thing, a dreep — a frightened poor thing with something on her mind. If there were even once chance in a thousand that this was true, something ought to be done about it.

Hilary began to consider what she could do. The Mercers had left the train at Ledlington. She could, of course, go down to Ledlington and try to find Mrs. Mercer, but just how you began to look for a stranger in a strange place like Ledlington she really had no idea. What she wanted was someone to talk the whole thing over with. How could you think a thing like that out all by yourself? What you wanted was someone to say 'Nonsense' in a loud commanding voice and having said it, to take up his stand on the hearth rug and lay down the law with that passionate indifference to argument or contradiction which was one of Henry's most marked characteristics. But she probably wasn't ever going to see Henry again. She blinked hard and stared out of the window of the bus. There really did seem to be an unnecessary amount of misery in the world. She would never have believed that she could have thought with yearning of Henry laying down the law. What was the good of thinking about Henry when she wasn't going ever to see him again and couldn't possibly ask his advice?

Hilary gave herself a shake and sat up. What was there to prevent her from asking Henry's advice? They had been friends. They had thought they would like to be married, and had become engaged. And then they had found out that they didn't want to be married and had become disengaged. Considered rationally, the next step should be a reversion to friendship. It was completely irrational to be dead cuts with a man just because you weren't going to marry him.

With a slightly quickened pulse, and in what she told

herself was a calmly deliberative frame of mind, Hilary decided that she would go and see Henry and ask his advice. She must talk to someone, and she couldn't talk to Marion. She would be calm and perfectly friendly. At their last interview she had been scarlet in the face with rage. She had stamped, she had come very near to screaming at Henry. But that was because he simply wouldn't stop talking or let her get in a word edgeways. It would be pleasant to show him that she could behave with poise and dignity, polite but aloof, courteous, and unruffled.

She left the bus, and walked on air. She was going to see Henry, and only half an hour ago she had never expected to see him again. She looked at her watch and found it was half past twelve. Suppose Henry had gone out to lunch. Well, suppose he had — 'I can see him some other time, can't I?' Something that felt as heavy as a lorry-load of bricks crashed down on Hilary's spirits. Easier to bear the thought of never seeing Henry again than to feel that he might be out now, at this very minute, when she had counted on seeing him. 'Please, please, *please* don't let him be out!'

She turned the corner, and there across the roaring flood of the Fulham Road was Henry's shop, or rather the shop which Henry's godfather had bequeathed to him, and which Henry was in two minds whether to accept or not. Hilary's heart gave a foolish jump when she saw it, because she and Henry had been going to live in the flat over the shop when they got married. The Fulham Road may not be everyone's idea of the Garden of Eden, but so inveterately romantic is the human heart that when Henry kissed Hilary and asked her if she could be happy in a flat over a shop, and Hilary kissed Henry and said she could, it is a fact that to them the noisy crowded thoroughfare became a mere boundary of their own particular paradise.

Hilary reminded herself that she was now perfectly calm, perfectly detached. She crossed the road, read the legend, 'Henry Eustatius, Antiques,' and stood looking in at the window. She did this because something odd seemed to have happened to her knees. They didn't seem to be aware that she was being calm. They wobbled. Impossible to confront Henry with any poise while your knees were wobbling. She gazed earnestly in at the window and noticed that the Feraghan rug which they had been going to have in their dining-room was no longer to be seen. It used to hang on the left-hand wall, and they had had a joke about it, because Henry said that if anyone came in and asked the price, he would say a thousand pounds, and *she* had said he wouldn't have the nerve. Something tugged at her heart. It was gone. It was their very own dining-room carpet, and it was gone. Henry had sold it away into slavery to be someone else's carpet, and she felt most desolate, robbed, and homeless. It was her own dining-room carpet, and Henry had stolen it.

For the first time she really believed that everything was over between them. It seemed quite impossible to walk into the shop and see Henry, and be cool and dignified. It seemed equally impossible to cross the Fulham Road again. And then as she stood looking in through the window past the inlaid table with the red and white chessmen, and the Queen Anne bureau, and the set of high-backed Spanish chairs, she saw a movement in the dark corner where a screen of stamped and gilded leather hid the door, and round the edge of it came Henry and a man.

Hilary wanted to run away, but her feet wouldn't move. She didn't dare look at Henry, so she looked at the other man. He seemed short beside Henry, but he wasn't really short. He was just a very ordinary height, slim, pale, irregular-featured, with greenish hazel eyes, and red hair worn negligently long. He had on a soft collar and a tie not quite like other people's ties, a sort of floppy bow. There seemed to be something rather odd about the cut of his suit too. It reminded Hilary of a Cruikshank caricature. It was of a slaty blue colour, and the tie was mauve. Hilary didn't think she had ever seen a man wearing a mauve tie before. Frightful with that red hair — and he had matched his handkerchief to the tie, and his socks to the handkerchief. She had begun by looking at him because she didn't want to look at Henry, but after the first glance her interest was riveted, because this was Bertie Everton. She had only seen him once before, at Geoff's trial, but he was the once-seen-never-forgotten sort. No one else in the world had hair like that.

Henry was talking as they came into the shop. He pointed at a tall blue-and-white jar, and both men turned to look at it. Hilary let her eye slide rapidly over them. It slipped off Bertie Everton and rested upon Henry. He was talking in quite an animated manner — laying down the law, Hilary decided, but he looked pale, paler than when she had seen him last, if you didn't count that hurried glimpse at the station yesterday. Of course when she had seen him last — *really* seen him — they had been quarrelling, and colour and temper are apt to rise together. He looked pale, and he appeared to be laying down the law to Bertie Everton with a good deal of gloomy emphasis. She reflected that if he was talking about the jar, Bertie probably knew a lot more about it than he did. She wondered if he remembered that Bertie was a collector. At first she hoped he didn't, because it would serve him right if he tripped over his own feet and took a toss. And then with a rush of angry compunction she knew just how dreadfully she would mind if Henry gave himself away. Her feet came unstuck from the pavement, and almost before she knew what she was going to do she had pushed open the glass door of the shop and walked in.

Henry had his back to her. He did not turn round. He was saying a beautiful piece which he had memorized with great care from one of his godfather's books on ceramics. It was calculated to impress anyone except a real collector, who would probably recognise the passage and suspect that it had been learnt by heart.

When he had finished the paragraph, Bertie Everton said, 'Oh, quite,' and took a step towards the door, whereupon Henry turned round and saw Hilary. After which he sped the departing Bertie with an almost indecent haste. The door closed. The red-haired young man covered his red hair with a soft black hat, looked over his shoulder once at the girl who appeared to be admiring that remarkably fine set of ivory chessmen, and passed out of sight.

With a long striding step Henry arrived at the other side of the inlaid table which supported the chessmen. He said 'Hilary!' in a loud shaken voice, and Hilary dropped the white queen and backed into a grandfather clock, which rocked dangerously. There was a pause.

Emotion affects people in different ways. It induced in Henry a stare of frowning intensity, and in Hilary an inability to meet that stare. If she did she would either laugh or cry, and she didn't want to do either. She wanted to be cool, calm, detached, and coldly polite. She wanted to display tact, poise, and *savoir faire*. And here she was, dropping chessmen and backing into grandfather clocks. And both she and Henry were in full view of everyone who happened to be walking down that part of the Fulham Road. Her cheeks were burning like fire, and if Henry was going to go on standing there and saying nothing for another five seconds, she would simply have to do something, she wasn't sure what.

Henry broke the silence by saying in a tone of gloomy politeness,

'Is there anything I can do for you?'

Rubbish for Henry to talk like that. She looked up with a bright sparkle in her eyes and said,

'Don't be silly, Henry — of course there is!'

Henry's eyebrows rose. A most annoying trick.

'Well?'

'I want to talk to you. We can't talk here. Let's go through to the Den.'

Hilary was feeling better. Her knees were still wobbling, and she wasn't being properly aloof and cold, but she had at least got herself and Henry away from the window, where they must have been presenting a convincing tableau of The Shoplifter Detected.

Without further speech they passed round the screen and along a bit of dark passage to the Den, which had been the office of old Mr. Henry Eustatius. It was of course Captain Henry Cunningham's office now, and it was a good deal tidier than it had been in his godfather's day. Henry Eustatius had corresponded voluminously with collectors in every part of the world. Their letters to him lay about all over the table, all over the chairs, and all over the floor, and his replies, written in a minute spidery hand, were often very much delayed because they were apt to get engulfed in the general muddle. They probably arrived in the end, because the woman who did for Henry Eustatius was quite clever at recognising his writing. She never interfered with any of the other papers, but whenever she saw one covered with that spidery handwriting she would pick it up and put it right in front of the table where it could not help being seen. Henry Cunningham's correspondence was not so large. He kept unanswered letters in one basket and answered letters in another, and when he wrote a letter he took it to the post at once.

CHAPTER TWELVE

Hilary sat down on the arm of a large leather-covered chair. She was glad to sit down, but it put her at a disadvantage, because Henry remained standing. He leaned against the mantelpiece and gazed silently over the top of her head. *Enraging.* Because if you wanted to stop Henry talking you couldn't — he merely raised his voice and continued to air his views. And now, when you wanted him to talk, he went all strong and silent and looked over the top of your head. She said, in rather a breathless voice,

'Don't do that!'

Henry looked at her, and immediately looked away again. 'As if I was a black beetle!' said Hilary to herself.

He said, 'I beg your pardon?' and Hilary forgot about her knees wobbling and jumped up.

'Henry, I really won't be spoken to like that! I wanted to talk to you, but if you're going to be a perfectly polite stranger, I'm off!'

Henry continued to avert his gaze. She understood him to say in a muffled tone that he wasn't being a polite stranger, and inside herself Hilary grinned and heard a little jigging rhyme which said,

> 'Henry is never very polite,
>   But when he is he's a perfect fright.'

She emerged, to hear him enquire what he could do for her, and all at once her eyes stung, and she heard herself say,

'Nothing. I'm going.'

Henry got to the door first. He put his back against it and said,

'You can't go.'

'I don't want to go — I want to talk. But I can't unless you'll be rational.'

'I'm perfectly rational,' said Henry.

'Then come and sit down. I really do want to talk, and I can't whilst you go on being about eleven feet high.'

He subsided into a second leather chair. They were so close that if she had been sitting in the chair instead of on the arm, their knees would have touched. She had now a slight advantage, as from this position it was she who looked down on him whilst he looked up to her. She thought it an entirely suitable arrangement, but had serious doubts as to its ever becoming permanent. Even now Henry wasn't looking at her. Suppose he wasn't just putting it on — suppose he really didn't want to look at her any more . . . It was a most unnerving thought.

Quite suddenly she began to wish that she hadn't come. And just at that moment Henry said rather gruffly,

'Is anything the matter?'

A new, warm feeling rushed over Hilary. Henry only spoke like that when he really minded, and if he really minded, it was going to be all right. She nodded and said,

'That's what I want to talk to you about. Things have been happening, and I can't talk to Marion because it upsets her, and I feel as if I must talk to someone, because of course it's very, very, *very* important, so I thought we — we — well, we *were* friends — and I thought if I talked to you, you'd tell me what I ought to do next.'

There! Henry ought to adore that — he liked them meek and feminine. At least he did in theory, but in practice he might get bored.

'Henry would like his wife to be meek
If he had a new one once a week.'

Henry brightened a little.

'You'd better tell me all about it. What have you been doing?'

'Nothing.' Hilary shook a mournful head. 'At least I only got into a wrong train by mistake — and that wasn't my fault. I — I just saw someone who — who frightened me, so I got into a Ledlington train by mistake and didn't find it out for ages.'

'Someone frightened you? How?'

'By glaring. It's very unnerving for a sensitive young girl to be glared at on a public platform.'

Henry looked at her with suspicion.

'What are you getting at?'

'You,' said Hilary, and only just stopped herself saying 'Darling.' 'You've no idea how you glared — at least I hope you haven't, because it's much worse if you meant it. But I was completely shattered, and by the time I'd picked up the bits, there I was in a lonely carriage in a Ledlington train with Mrs. Mercer having suppressed hysterics in the other corner and beginning to clutch hold of my dress and confide in me, only I didn't know it was Mrs. Mercer or I'd have encouraged her a lot more.'

'*Mrs. Mercer?*' said Henry in a very odd tone indeed.

Hilary nodded.

'Alfred Mercer and Mrs. Mercer. You won't remember, because you'd gone back to Egypt before the trial came off — Geoff's trial — the Everton Case. The Mercers were James Everton's married couple, and they were the spot witnesses for the prosecution — Mrs. Mercer's evidence very nearly hanged Geoff. And when I was in the train with her she recognised me, and then she began to cry and to say the oddest things.'

'What sort of things, Hilary?' Henry had stopped being superior and offended. His voice was eager and the words hurried out.

'Well, it was all about Marion and the trial, and a lot of

97

gasping and sobbing and staring, and a funny sort of story about how she'd tried to see Marion when the trial was going on. She said she went round to the house where she was staying and tried to see her. She said, "Miss, if I never spoke another word, it's true I tried to see her." And she said she'd given her husband the slip. And then she said in quite a frightful sort of whisper things like "If she had seen me." But she didn't see her, because she was resting. Poor Marion, she was nearly dead by then — they wouldn't have let her see anyone — but Mrs. Mercer seemed most dreadfully upset about it. And then she said her husband came and she never got another chance. She said *he* saw to that.'

Henry was looking straight at her for the first time.

'It really was Mrs. Mercer?'

'Oh yes. Marion showed me a photograph and I recognised it at once. It was Mrs. Mercer all right.'

'What did she look like?'

'Do you want me to describe her?'

'No — no. I want to know how she seemed. You said she was having hysterics. Did she know what she was saying?'

'Oh yes, I should think so — oh yes, I'm sure she did. When I said hysterics, I didn't mean she was screaming the place down. She was just awfully upset, you know — crying, and gasping, and trembling all over, and every now and then she'd pull herself together, and then she'd break down again.'

'Something on her mind — ' said Henry slowly. Then, with a good deal of emphasis, 'You didn't think of her being *out* of her mind, did you?'

'No — no, I didn't — not after the first minute or two. I did at first because of the way she stared, and because of her bursting out that she knew me, and things like "Thank God *he* didn't," and, "He'd never have gone if he had." '

'He?'

'Mercer. He went along the corridor. I — I'd been looking out of the window, and when I turned round I just
saw a man getting up and going along. I'd been picking
up the bits, you know — the ones you shattered by
scowling across the platform at me — so I hadn't been
noticing who was in the carriage, and when I'd got
myself put together again, and turned round, there was
the man going out into the corridor and the woman staring at me, and I did think she was mad for about a
minute and a half.'

'Why?'

'Why did I think she was mad at first — or why didn't I
think so afterwards?'

'Both.'

'Well, I thought she was mad at first because of her
staring and saying "Thank God" at me — anyone would.
But when I found out that she really did know me because of seeing me with Marion at the trial, and that the
reason she was all worked up and emoted was because she
was frightfully sorry for Marion and couldn't get her off
her mind, I didn't think she was mad any more. That
sort of person gets gulpy at once if they're fond of someone who's in trouble, so I just thought it was that, but
when I found out who she was, all the rather odd things
she'd been saying came up in my mind, and I wondered.'

'You wondered whether she was mad?'

'No — I wondered what she'd got on her mind.'

Henry leaned forward with his elbow on his knee and
his chin in his hand. 'Well, you said yourself that her
evidence nearly hanged Geoffrey Grey.'

'Yes, it did. She'd been up to turn down Mr. Everton's
bed, you know, and she swore that when she came down
again she heard voices in the study and she thought
there was a quarrel going on, and she was frightened and
went to the door to listen, and she swore that she recog-

99

nised Geoffrey's voice. So then she said she thought it was all right, and she was coming away, when she heard a shot, and she screamed, and Mercer came running out of his pantry where he was cleaning the silver. The study door was locked, and when they banged on it Geoff opened it from inside with the pistol in his hand. It's frightful evidence, Henry.'

'And Grey's story was?'

'His uncle rang him up at eight and asked him to come along at once. He was very much upset. Geoff went along, and he would have got there at between a quarter and twenty past eight. He went into the study through the open French window, and he said his uncle was lying across the writing-table and the pistol was on the floor in front of the window. He said he picked it up, and then he heard a scream in the hall and the Mercers came banging at the door, and when he found it was locked he unlocked it and let them in. And there were only his finger-prints on the handle and on the pistol.'

Henry said, 'I remember.' And then he said what he had forborne to say during the six months of their engagement — 'That's pretty conclusive evidence. What makes you think he didn't do it?'

Hilary's colour flared. She beat her hands together and said in a voice of passionate sincerity,

'He didn't — he didn't really! He *couldn't*! You see, I know Geoff.'

Something in Henry responded to that sure loyalty. It was like trumpets blowing. It was like the drum-beat in a march. It stirred the blood and carried you along. But Hilary might whistle for the comfort of knowing that she had stirred him. He frowned a little and said,

'Is Marion as sure as you are?'

Hilary's colour failed as suddenly as it had flamed. She wasn't sure, poor Marion — she wasn't sure. She was too worn out with pain to be sure. A cold terror peered at her from her own thoughts and betrayed her from within.

Hilary looked away and said in a voice of sober courage,

'Geoff didn't do it.'

'Then who did?'

'Mrs. Mercer knows,' said Hilary. Her own words startled her so much that she felt herself shaking. She had not known that she was going to say that. She hadn't even known that she was thinking it.

'Why do you say that?' said Henry quickly.

'I don't know.'

'You *must*. You can't say a thing like that without knowing why you said it.'

Henry was riding the high horse. Its trampling had a reviving effect upon Hilary. She might marry Henry, or she might not marry Henry, but she simply wasn't going to be trampled on. She stuck her chin in the air and said,

'I can. I don't know why I said it, because it just popped out. I didn't first think, "Mrs. Mercer knows," and then say it — I just said it, and then I felt perfectly certain that she did know. That's the way my mind works — things I've never thought about at all come banging out, and then when I do start thinking about them they are *true*.'

Henry came down off the high horse with a bump. She was so comic when she talked like that with her colour glowing again, and her eyes as bright as a bird's, and the little brown curls all shining under her perky hat. She wanted shaking and she wanted kissing, and meanwhile he burst out laughing at her.

'It's all very well to laugh!' But in her inside mind she laughed too and sang a little shouting song of joy, because once you begin to laugh together, how can you go on quarrelling? You simply can't. And she was tired right through to the very marrow of her bones of quarrelling with Henry.

'Prize fool!' said Henry, no longer strangely polite.

Hilary shook her head and caught the inside corner of her lip between her teeth, because she wasn't going to laugh for Henry to see — not yet.

'That's only because you can't do it yourself. And you've got a nasty jealous disposition — I've told you about it before — and if you ever marry anyone, Henry, you'll have to watch it because she'll either walk out on you or else turn into a dreep because you've broken her spirit by giving her an ingrowing inferiority complex.'

Henry's gaze rested on her with something disturbing in it. This was the Henry who could laugh at you with his eyes, and make your heart beat suddenly and hard.

'I haven't noticed any signs of it,' he said.

'Oh, I'm the sort that walks out,' said Hilary, and met his eyes with a hardy sparkle in her own.

Henry said nothing. He didn't intend to be drawn. He continued to look at her, and in a panic Hilary returned to Mrs. Mercer.

'Don't you see, Henry, if you don't believe Mrs. Mercer's evidence — and I *don't* — well then, she must know who did it. She wouldn't just go telling all those lies to amuse herself — because she wasn't amused, she was frightfully, frightfully miserable — or to spite Geoff, be-cause she was frightfully, frightfully miserable about Geoff and about Marion. So if she was telling lies — and I'm sure she was — it was because she wanted to screen somebody else. And we've got to find out who it is — we've simply got to.'

CHAPTER THIRTEEN

Henry stopped laughing at Hilary with his eyes and frowned instead, not at her, but past her at the Mercers, and the Everton Case, and the problem of finding about a quarter of a needle in several hypothetical bundles of hay. It was all very well for Hilary to propose a game of Spot the Murderer, but the trouble was that so far as he himself was concerned he had a conviction amounting to certainty that the murderer had already been spotted, and was now expiating his exasperated shot at the uncle who had cut him out of his will. It was, and had been all along, his opinion that Geoffrey Grey had got off light and was uncommonly lucky not to have been hanged.

Henry's regiment was in Egypt, and after a leave spent very pleasantly in the Tyrol he had gone back to Cairo. James Everton was shot a couple of days before his leave was up. He had, at the time, been a good deal preoccupied with trying to make Hilary see the question of an engagement in the same light as he did. In the end they more or less split the difference, Henry asserting that they were engaged, whilst Hilary maintained that being engaged was stuffy. Snippets about the Case filtered through to Egypt. Hilary wrote voluminously about it from a passionately personal and partisan point of view, but he had never really read the evidence. He accepted the verdict, was sorry for Marion Grey, and counted the days till he could get home and make Hilary marry him. And here she was, without any intention of marrying him at all and every intention of trying to drag him into a wild goose attempt at re-opening the Everton Case. He reacted in the most obstinate and natural manner, focused the frown on Hilary, and said in his most dogmatic voice,

'You'd better let it alone — the case is closed.'

Hilary beat her hands together again.

'It isn't — it can't be! It won't ever be closed until the real murderer is found and Geoff is free — and the more I think of it, the more I feel quite, quite sure that Mrs. Mercer knows who it is. Henry, it's a hunch!'

Henry frowned upon the hunch.

'What's the good of talking like that? You say yourself that your first impression of the woman was that she was mad. I don't mean to say she's a raving lunatic, but she is obviously a morbid, hysterical person. If she was fond of the Greys she would naturally feel having to give evidence against Geoffrey. I can't see anything in what you told me except that having given the evidence she apparently tried to crash in on Marion and make a scene about it.'

'No,' said Hilary — 'no. No, it wasn't that. She'd got something eating into her — I'm sure she had. Why did she say, "If I'd only seen her?" '

'Why does a hysterical person say anything?'

'And why did she say things like "I didn't get another chance — *he* took care of that," and the bit about thanking God Mercer didn't recognise me, because he wouldn't ever have left us alone together. Why did she say that?'

Henry shrugged his shoulders.

'If you've got a mad wife, you do your best to stop her annoying people — I don't see anything in that. As a matter of fact I believe she really is unhinged.'

'I should *hate* to be married to Mercer,' said Hilary.

Henry burst out laughing.

'Hilary, you really *are*!'

Hilary looked at him in a melting manner which it had taken her a good deal of time and trouble to acquire. She had copied it from a leading film star, and she wanted to see what effect it would have on Henry. It didn't seem to have any effect at all, and as she began to feel that it was going to bring on a squint, she permitted a natural sparkle of anger to take its place.

> 'When you make eyes at Henry, he
> Behaves as if he didn't see,'

said Hilary's imp in a sort of piercing mosquito whisper. The angry sparkle became a shade brighter. Henry was a beast — he really was. The man in the film had gone down like a ninepin. It really wasn't the slightest use making eyes at Henry, and if he was the last man left in London she wouldn't marry him. She would almost rather be married to Mercer. *No, she wouldn't.* A shiver went all down the back of her neck, and she said in a hurry,

'You know what I *mean.* It would be enough to *drive* anyone into a lunatic asylum, I should think.'

'Then you agree that she's mad.'

'No, I don't. And the more Mercer follows me round and tells me she is about twice in every sentence, the less I'm going to believe it.'

Henry got up.

'What are you talking about?'

'Mercer. Henry, his name's Alfred. Isn't it awful?'

'Hilary — has he been following you?'

She nodded.

'Yes, darling — I told you he had — most persistent. I should think he probably followed me all the way from Solway Lodge to Pinman's Lane to where I got on to my bus, because he was talking to me most of the way and telling me about Mrs. Mercer being out of her mind, and when he'd said it more than six times I began to wonder why he was saying it.'

Henry sat down on the arm of the chair beside her. There was just room and no more.

'Perhaps because it was true,' he said.

'Or perhaps because it wasn't.'

Their shoulders were touching. She looked round at him with a defiant gleam in her eye and prepared to do battle. But Henry had dropped his point. He put his arm round her in a sort of matter-of-course way as if they were still engaged and said,

'That's odd.'

'What is?'

'Mercer's following you round like that.'

Hilary nodded. Henry's arm made a good back — something nice to lean against. She said,

'He'd found out that it was me in the train. I expect he bullied it out of her, poor thing. And he wasn't quite sure what she'd said to me, but he was going to make sure that whatever it was, I wasn't going to believe it. Now if he could make me believe that she was mad — Henry, don't you *see*?'

Henry's arm tightened a little.

'I don't know — she might really be mad,' he said. 'But it's funny — was it today he followed you?'

'Just now — just before I came here. Why, Henry?'

'Well, it's funny that he should have been saying it to you just about the same time that Bertie Everton was saying it to me.'

Hilary whisked round so suddenly that she would have fallen off if Henry hadn't clutched her.

'Here — hold up!'

'*Bertie Everton!*' said Hilary, taking no notice of being clutched.

'That's what I said. He went out as you came in. Didn't you see him?'

'Of course I did — he's not the sort of person you can miss. Did he tell you Mrs. Mercer was out of her mind?'

'Several times — same as Mercer did to you.'

'Henry, you're not making it up to pull my leg or anything of that sort? Because if you are —'

'What?' said Henry with interest.

Hilary wrinkled the top of her nose at him.

'I don't know, but it'll probably begin with never speaking to you again.'

'That would give you lots of time to think out what you were going to do next! All right, I'm not for it this time. And I'm not pulling your leg.'

'Bertie Everton came here on purpose to tell you Mrs. Mercer was out of her mind?'

'Not ostensibly — nothing so crude as that. He knew old Henry Eustatius — said he'd bought a set of Chippendale chairs from him and was doing needlework covers for the seats — *petit point* or something of that sort. And I was afraid he'd find out that I had only a very hazy idea of what *petit point* was, so I tried to switch him off on to china — I've been burning a lot of midnight oil over china lately — and he said, "Oh, yes," and "Quite." And then he mentioned you, and said were you a friend of mine, and I said "Yes" — which was a bit of a lie, of course.' Here Henry paused, the obvious intention being that Hilary should (a) burst into tears, (b) contradict him, or (c) fall into his arms.

Hilary didn't do any of these things. Her colour rose brightly and her tongue flicked out at him and back again.

Henry frowned and went on as if he had never stopped.

'And then, I think, he got me to mention Marion, and after that it was all plain sailing — something on the lines of what an unpleasant thing it was for the whole family, and a bit about Geoffrey's temper, and then to Mrs. Mercer by way of everyone liking him, and — "My uncle's housekeeper has never got over having to give evidence against him. She's gone clean off her head, I believe." And then he went off at a tangent about that big blue jar in the shop, but after a bit Mrs. Mercer cropped up again, and he said what a queer thing it was that she should have got so worked up over the Everton Case. "She can't think or talk about anything else," he said — "pretty bad luck on her husband, and all that". And then a piece about what a decent soul Mercer was, and then a bit more about the blue jar. And then you come in and he went out. And there we are.'

'Um —' said Hilary.

She began to rock gently to and fro. She was trying to get Henry to rock, too, but Henry wouldn't. His arm had about as much resilience as a crowbar, but it was fortunately not quite so hard to lean against. She stopped trying to rock, and became mournful and earnest on the subject of Bertie Everton.

'He would have done so beautifully for the murderer if it hadn't been for his alibi. Darling, don't you simply hate alibis? I do.'

'What are you talking about?'

'Bertie Everton, of course.'

'Has he got an alibi?'

'Dozens,' said Hilary. 'He's simply stuck all over with them. And, mind you, Henry, he wanted them, because poor old James had just made a will in his favour after not being on speaking terms with him for years, or practically not, so Bertie had a pretty strong motive. But with all the motives in the world, you can't shoot anyone if they're in Putney and you're in Edinburgh.'

'And Bertie was in Edinburgh?'

Hilary gave a dejected nod.

'Sworn to by rows of people in the Caledonian Hotel. James was shot at eight o'clock in the evening on July 16th. Bertie dined with him on the evening of the 15th — just about twenty-four hours too soon to have been the murderer. He then caught a train at King's

Cross and fetched up at the Caledonian Hotel in time for a late breakfast on the morning of the 16th. From then till a quarter past four half the people in the hotel seem to have seen him. He made a fuss about the bell in his room, and the chambermaid saw him writing letters there, and soon after four he was in the office asking about a telephone call. And then he went out and had too much to drink. And the chambermaid saw him again at about half-past eight, because he rang for biscuits, and then she saw him again next morning at nine o'clock when she brought his tea. And if you can think of any way he could possibly have shot poor old James, I wish you'd tell me. I sat up the best part of last night reading the inquest and the trial all over again, and I can't see how anyone could have done it except Geoff. And today I ferreted out the daily help who used to work at Solway Lodge, and she told me something that makes it all look worse than ever. And yet I don't believe it was Geoff. Henry, I don't, I don't, I *don't*!'

'What did she tell you?' said Henry quickly.

'I can't tell you — I can't tell, and I *made* her, so I can't tell anyone.'

'Hilary,' said Henry with a good deal of vehemence, 'you've got to drop it! You're only stirring up mud, and Marion won't thank you for that. What do you think you're doing?'

She pulled away from him and stood up.

'I want to find out what Mrs. Mercer knows.'

'Drop it!' said Henry, getting up too. 'Let the mud settle. You won't help Geoff, you won't help Marion. Let it alone!'

'I can't,' said Hilary.

CHAPTER FOURTEEN

Hilary came away from Henry Eustatius, Antiques, with a flaming colour and a determination not to be downed by Henry Cunningham. If she once let Henry down her, her spirit would be broken and she would rapidly become a dreep. Like Mrs. Mercer. Like Mrs. Ashley. Horrible and repellent prospect. They had both probably started quite young and pretty — the Ashley daily help certainly had — and some man had downed them and trampled on them until they had just given up and gone quietly down the drain. She could imagine Mercer breaking any woman's spirit if she was fool enough to let him, and the other poor creature had probably had a husband who trampled on her, too. That was what was the matter with Henry — he was a trampler born, and bred, and burnt right in. But she wasn't going to be the person he trampled on. If he wanted a door-mat he could go and marry a door-mat, and it wasn't going to be Hilary Carew.

She had walked nearly a quarter of a mile before her cheeks cooled. She stopped being angry, and thought what a pity it was that they couldn't have had lunch before they quarrelled. Henry was a hearty breakfast eater. He had probably had eggs, and sausages and bacon, and things like that no longer ago than nine o'clock, but Hilary had had toast and tea at eight, and it seemed so long ago that she had forgotten all about them. Prowling round Putney, and interviewing housekeepers and daily helps, and quarrelling with Henry were all things that made you very hungry, especially quarrelling with Henry. If Henry hadn't been determined to quarrel he would have taken her out to lunch first, and now she would have to go and have a glass of milk and a bun in a creamery with a lot of other women who were having buns and milk, or bovril, or milk with a dash of coffee, or a nice cup of tea. It was a most frightfully depressing thought, because one bun was going to make very little impression on her hunger, and she certainly couldn't afford any more. Extraordinarily stupid of Henry not to have given her lunch first. They could have quarrelled comfortably over their coffee if he was absolutely set on quarrelling, instead of uncomfortably in the Den with nothing inside you and no prospect of anything except a bun. It was a bad, bleak, bitter, and unbearable business. And it was all Henry's fault.

Hilary found her creamery and ate her bun — a peculiarly arid specimen. There were little black things in it which might once have been currants but were now quite definitely fossils. Not a good bun. Hilary's imp chanted mournfully:

> 'How bitter when your only bun
> Is not at all a recent one.'

When she had finished it she got out her purse and counted up her money. There was just about enough to buy a third-class return to Ledlington. She looked at the coins and wondered whether it was the slightest use for her to go there. There was no reason to suppose that it would be any use at all. She tossed her head. There are always such a lot of reasons why you shouldn't do a thing that if it were not that something pushed you along in spite of yourself, you would never do anything at all. She was unaware that Dr. Johnson had moralised upon this theme to Boswell, or that he had called the something which impels you the pressure of necessity. There are many necessities, to each his own — a driving force which will not be denied. Hilary's necessity was to find out what Mrs. Mercer knew. She didn't reason about it. If she had, common sense would have urged that Ledlington is a considerable place, and that she hadn't the slightest idea of how to find the Mercers — she hadn't even the slightest idea of how to begin to look for them. To all this she opposed a firm and unreasoning purpose. She was going to buy a third-class ticket, go down to Ledlington, and look for Mrs. Mercer.

Henry had a much better lunch than Hilary. He felt a kind of gloomy satisfaction in having held his own. Once let Hilary think that she could take her way without reference to him and in disregard of his opinion and of his advice, and their married life would become quite impossible. The trouble about Hilary was that she always wanted her own way, and just because it was her own way it had to be the right one. She didn't listen to reason, and she wouldn't listen to him. She just took the bit in her teeth and bolted. It was a pity, because — here Henry faltered a little — she was — well, she was Hilary, and at her silliest and most obstinate he loved her better than he had ever loved anyone in all his life. Even when she was being supremely aggravating there was something about her which put her on a different footing to everyone else. That was why he was simply bound to keep his end up. If he didn't, she'd be trying to run him, twisting him round her little finger, making a fool of him. It was when he felt all this most acutely that Henry's voice took its hardest tone and his eye its most dominant stare. And behind all this protective armour there was a Henry who shrank appalled from the picture of a world without Hilary, a life without Hilary. How could she leave him when she was his, and knew, as she must know, that he was hers? They belonged to each other and could not be divided.

Henry frowned at his chop and considered what he was going to do next. Hilary would come back. He could let her run foot-loose now, because she was bound to come back in the end. Meanwhile there was this damned Everton Case. It had been closed a year ago, and here it came, cropping up again and making trouble, and if Hilary insisted on going grubbing into it, there was going to be more trouble. His frown deepened. Infernal cheek of that man Mercer to go following her in the street. Something fishy about it too — something fishy about the Mercers — though he'd see Hilary at Jericho before he encouraged her in this insensate nonsense by admitting it.

He went on frowning and finishing the chop whilst he considered the possibility of turning some expert eye upon the Mercers and their doings. One might find out where they were, and what they had been doing since James Everton's death. One might direct the expert attention to the question of their financial position. Was there anything to suggest that it had been improved by James Everton's death? He seemed to remember that there had been some small legacy which would be neither here nor there, but if there was any solid financial improvement, it would bear looking into. The expert might also be instructed to delve into the Mercers' past. He supposed that this would have been done at the time of the inquest, but with Geoffrey Grey so compromisingly in the limelight as the guilty person, it was possible that these enquiries had not gone very far. He thought there was undoubtedly work for an expert here.

He went back to the shop and rang up Charles Moray, who was some sort of seventeenth cousin and a very good friend.

'That you, Charles? . . . Henry speaking.'

'Which of them?' said Charles with a slight agreeable tinge of laughter in his voice. A very good telephone voice. It sounded exactly as if he was in the room.

'Cunningham,' said Henry.

'Hullo — 'ullo — 'ullo! How's the antique business?'

Henry frowned impatiently.

'That's not what I rang you up about. I wanted to know — that is, didn't you say the other day — '

'Get it off the chest!' said Charles.

'Well, you were talking about a detective the other day — '

Charles gave an appreciative whistle.

'Somebody been pinching the stock?'

'No, it's not for myself — that is, it's for someone I'm interested in. I want to have some enquiries made, and I want to be sure that the person who makes them is all right. I mean, I don't want someone who'll go round opening his mouth.'

'Our Miss Silver will do you a treat,' said Charles Moray.

'A woman? I don't know — '

'Wait till you've seen her — or rather wait till she's delivered the goods. She does, you know. She pulled me out of the tightest corner* I ever was in in my life — and that wasn't in the wilds of South America, but here in London. If your business is confidential, you can trust her all the way. Her address — hang on a minute and be ready with a pencil . . . Yes, here you are — 16, Montague Mansions, West Leaham Street, S.W. . . . And her telephone number? . . . No, I haven't got it — this is an old one. You'll find it in the book — Maud Silver. Have you got that?'

'Yes, thanks very much.'

'Come round and see us,' said Charles affably. 'Margaret says what about dinner? Monday or Wednesday next week.'

Henry accepted for Monday and rang off. Then he went out to the British Museum, where he spent an intensive two hours over the Everton Case. He read the inquest and he read the trial. He came away with the

* See *Grey Mask*.

conviction that Geoffrey Grey must have been born very lucky indeed to have escaped being hanged. As he read it, there had never been a clearer case. It was as plain as a pikestaff. James Everton had three nephews. He loved Geoffrey Grey. He didn't love Bertie Everton. And Frank Everton was neither here nor there — a mere remittance man. Everything was for Geoffrey — the place in his uncle's firm, the place in his uncle's home, the place in his uncle's will. And then, quite obviously, Bertie comes along and tells a tale out of school. He dines with his uncle, and in the most almighty hurry James Everton cuts out Geoffrey and puts in Bertie in his place. Incidentally, he cuts out poor old Frank too, but probably that hasn't got anything to do with it. The cutting out of Geoffrey is the peg on which everything hangs. Geoffrey must have gone off the rails somewhere, and Bertie had tumbled over himself to give him away. Result, Uncle James changes his will, sends for Geoffrey to tell him what he has done, and Geoffrey shoots him in a sudden murderous fit of rage. No knowing just how serious Geoffrey's misdemeanour may have been. It may have been so serious that he couldn't afford to have it come out. His uncle may have threatened him with exposure. Geoffrey wouldn't necessarily know that Bertie Everton had split on him — he mightn't ever know that Bertie knew. He loses his head and shoots, and Bertie comes in for everything.

Henry wondered idly whether Bertie was continuing Frank's allowance. There didn't seem to be any other doubt about the case. There didn't seem to be any reason at all for calling in Miss Maud Silver. After which Henry went to the telephone and called her up.

CHAPTER FIFTEEN

He came into her waiting-room, and after a very short pause found himself being ushered into a most curiously old-fashioned office. There was a good deal more furniture than there had been in Charles Moray's day, and the chairs were not modern chairs. They looked to Henry like the ones he had sat in as a schoolboy when he visited his grandmother and his grandmother's friends. The mantelpiece was crowded with photographs in gimcrack frames.

Miss Silver herself sat at a good solid writing-table of the mid-Victorian period. She was a little person with a great deal of mousey grey hair which was done up in a bun at the back and arranged in a curled fringe in front. Having worn her hair in this way through a period of practically universal shingling varied only by the bob and the Eton crop, she had become aware with complete indifference that she now approximated to the current fashion.

Yet however she had done her hair, it would have appeared, as she herself appeared, to be out of date. She was very neatly dressed in an unbecoming shade of drab. Her indeterminate features gave no indication of talent or character. Her smooth sallow skin was innocent of powder. She was knitting a small white woolly sock, and at the moment of Henry's entrance she was engaged in counting her stitches. After a minute she looked up, inclined her head, and said in a quiet toneless voice,

'Pray be seated.'

Henry wished with all his heart that he hadn't come. He couldn't imagine why he had asked for this woman's address, or rung her up, or come to see her. The whole thing seemed to him to be absolutely pointless. If he had the nerve he would get up and walk out. He hadn't the nerve. He saw Miss Silver put down her knitting on a clean sheet of white blotting-paper and take a bright blue copybook out of the top left-hand drawer of her writing-table. She opened the book, wrote down his name, asked him for his address, and then sat, pen in hand, looking mildly at him.

'Yes, Captain Cunningham?'

Henry felt that he was making the most complete fool of himself. He also felt that this was Hilary's fault. He said in an embarrassed voice,

'I don't think I really ought to have troubled you.'

'You will feel better when you have told me about it. I don't know if you read Tennyson. He seems to me to express it so very beautifully:

> 'Break, break, break,
>   On thy cold grey stones, oh sea.
>   And I would that my heart could utter
>   The thoughts that arise in me.'

It is always difficult to make a beginning, but you will find it easier as you go on.'

'It's about the Everton Case,' said Henry abruptly.

'The Everton Case? Quite so. But it is closed, Captain Cunningham.'

Henry frowned. An obstinate feeling that having made a fool of himself, he might as well see it through stiffened his courage.

'Do you remember anything about the case?'

Miss Silver had picked up her sock and was knitting rapidly in the German manner. She said, 'Everything,' and continued to knit with unbelievable rapidity.

'I've been going through it again,' said Henry. 'I've read the inquest and I've read the trial, and — '

'Why?' said Miss Silver.

'I missed a good deal of it at the time — I was abroad — and I must say — '

'I'd rather you didn't,' said Miss Silver. Her needles clicked. She gazed mildly at him. 'You see, Captain Cunningham, I always prefer to draw my own conclusions. If you will tell me in what way I can help you, I will do my best.'

'It's about the Mercers. They were the chief witnesses against Geoffrey Grey. I don't know if you remember.'

'Mr. Everton's cook and butler. Yes?'

'I would like some information about those two.'

'What sort of information?'

'Anything you can lay hands on. Their antecedents, present circumstances — in fact, anything you can get. It has — well, Miss Silver, it has been suggested that these people committed perjury at the trial. I can't see any reason why they should, but if they did commit perjury, they must have had a reason. I want to know if they're any better off than they were. In fact, I want to know anything you can find out about them. I don't expect you to find out anything damaging, but — well, the fact is I want to convince — someone — that there's nothing to be gained by trying to re-open the case. Do you see?'

Miss Silver dropped her knitting in her lap and folded her hands upon it.

'Let us understand one another, Captain Cunningham,' she said in her quiet voice. 'If you employ me, you will be employing me to discover facts. If I discover anything about these people, you will have the benefit of my discovery. It may be what you are expecting, or it may not. People are not always pleased to know the truth.' Miss Silver nodded her head in a gentle deprecating manner. 'You've no idea how often that happens. Very few people want to know the truth. They wish to be confirmed in their own opinions, which is a very different thing — very different indeed. I cannot promise that what I discover will confirm you in your present opinion.' She gave a slight hesitating cough and began to knit again. 'I have always had my own views about the Everton case.'

Henry found himself curiously impressed, he couldn't think why. There was nothing impressive about mouse-coloured hair, indeterminate features, and a toneless voice. Yet Miss Silver impressed him. He said quickly,

'And what was your opinion?'

'At present I should prefer not to say.' She put down her knitting and took up her pen again. 'You wish me to get any information I can about the Mercers. Can you give me their Christian names?'

'Yes — I've just been going through the case. He is Alfred, and she is Louisa Kezia Mercer.'

'I suppose you don't know her maiden name?'

He shook his head.

'I'm afraid I don't. I don't know anything about either of them except what came out in the evidence. I don't know where they are living or what they are doing — and I want to know.'

Miss Silver wrote in the bright blue exercise-book. Then she looked up at Henry.

'I could help you more if you would trust me, Captain Cunningham. Nearly every client is the same — they hold something back, and the thing they hold back is the thing which would help me most. It always comes out in the end, but frankness in the first instance would save me a good deal of trouble.' She coughed again. 'For instance, it would assist me greatly to know when and where your friend encountered the Mercers, and what happened when she encountered them. Quite obviously it was something which encouraged her to think that the case might be re-opened. You did not agree, and you are employing me because you hope that I shall enable you to support your opinion with evidence which your friend will accept.'

The colour rose in Henry's face. He hadn't mentioned Hilary. The last thing he wanted was to mention Hilary. He was prepared to swear that he had got no nearer mentioning her than to say that there was someone whom he wanted to convince. This infernal little maiden aunt of a woman had nosed Hilary out and guessed at an encounter with the Mercers. He felt secretly afraid of her, and looked up with a frown to find that she was smiling at him. Miss Silver had a smile which seemed to belong to quite a different person. It changed her face to that of a friend. Quite suddenly Henry was telling her about Hilary getting into the wrong train and finding herself in the same compartment as the Mercers.

Miss Silver listened. Her needles clicked. She said 'Dear, dear!' at one point, and 'Poor thing' at another. The 'Poor thing' referred to Marion Grey. Mrs. Mercer's stumbling, agitated sentences repeated by Henry in a completely unemotional voice drew forth a fit of coughing and an 'Oh, dear me!'

'And they got out at Ledlington, Captain Cunningham?'

'She says they did, but I don't suppose she really knows. She got out there herself because it wasn't her train and she had to get back to town.'

'And she hasn't seen either of them since?'

'Well, yes, she has.'

Heny found himself telling her about Alfred Mercer following Hilary through the byways of Putney for the purpose, apparently, of informing her that his wife was out of her mind. And then, before he knew where he was, he had thrown in Bertie Everton's visit to himself upon what seemed to be a similar errand.

Miss Silver looked up from time to time and then looked down again. She was knitting so rapidly that the woolly sock appeared to rotate.

'And you see, Miss Silver, if there is something fishy going on, I don't want Miss Carew to get mixed up in it.'

'Naturally.'

'But at the same time I can't say I think that there's any doubt at all about the murder. Grey did it all right. I just want —'

Miss Silver drew out a needle and stabbed it into the wool again.

'You just want to have your own opinion confirmed. I have told you that I can only undertake to provide you with facts — I cannot guarantee that they will be to your liking. Do you still wish to employ me?'

Henry had the strangest feeling. It was just as if a shutter in his mind had jerked open. Light and air rushed in upon a dark place — bright light, strong air. And then the shutter banged to again and everything was dark.

He said, 'Yes, please,' and was astonished at the firmness of his own voice.

CHAPTER SIXTEEN

Hilary caught the two o'clock train to Ledlington. She got into a carriage with a pair of lovers, a pretty girl, and a woman with nine parcels. At least there ought to have been nine parcels, but it presently appeared that there were only eight. As the train had now started, it wasn't possible to do anything about it except rummage along the seats and under the seats in a vague, unhappy manner, apologising profusely the while. Hilary helped in the search, the pretty girl read a sixpenny novelette, and the lovers held hands.

The owner of the lost parcel was a fat, worried woman with a flow of quite extraordinarily disconnected talk.

'I don't know where I could have left it *I'm* sure, unless it was Perry's. Johnny's socks it'll be — two good pairs. Oh, dear me — gone down the drain as you may say! And what Mr. Brown'll say I reelly don't know. I never knew a child so hard on his heels as what Johnny is, though I don't say Ella isn't a caution, too. Excuse *me*, miss, but you don't happen to be sitting on a little parcel of mine, I suppose? It's a soft stuff, so you mightn't notice it. I didn't ask you before, did I? I'm sure I'm ever so sorry if I did, but if you didn't mind — well, I'll just count them again ... I can't make them more than eight, try how I will. And it might be Mabel's scarf, and if it is, she won't half go on, and I don't know whatever Mr. Brown is going to say.'

Hilary heard a good deal more about Mr. Brown, who was the fat woman's husband, and Johnny and Mabel, who were her almost grown-up son and daughter, and Ella who was an after-thought and a great deal younger than the other two. She heard all about what Mr. Brown did in the war, and how Johnny had three relapses when he had scarlet fever, and how troublesome Mabel had been when she had to wear a band on her front teeth — 'Stuck right out like a rabbit's, they did, but they've come in lovely, and no thanks to her — fret, fret, fret, and whine, whine, whine, and "Must I wear this horrid thing, Mum?" if you'll believe me! You'd never credit the trouble I had with her, and now it's over, she doesn't say thank you — but that's what girls are like. Why, when Ella had the whooping-cough — '

Hilary heard all about Ella's whooping-cough, and Johnny's mumps, and the time Mr. Brown went off his food and couldn't fancy anything but a lightly-boiled egg, thus leading up to the day when the egg was bad and what Mr. Brown said after he had spat it out.

Owing to these reminiscences, the journey was so much lost time as far as working out a plan of campaign was concerned. Hilary had meant to sit with her eyes shut and think hard all the way to Ledlington, instead of which she was fully occupied in following Mrs. Brown's acrobatic leaps from one family illness to another and in murmuring at suitable intervals, 'How inconvenient!' and 'How dreadful!' She therefore walked out of Ledlington station without any idea of what she was going to do next. She gazed around her, and felt her heart sink like a stone. Ledlington was quite a place. Ledlington would in fact have been very much offended if it had struck a stranger as anything but a full-sized town. How did you find a woman whose address you didn't know in a full-sized town? The post-office wouldn't give you an address, it would only forward a letter. And it would be no good writing to Mrs. Mercer, because Mercer would certainly read the letter. No, what she wanted was what she had had and had thrown away — ten minutes alone with the woman whose evidence had sent Geoff to penal servitude for life. There is one drawback to breaking a woman's spirit — and Mercer might live to become aware of it. A broken spring no longer holds the lock — it has lost its resistance, and any resolute hand may jar it open. Hilary felt a good deal of confidence in her own ability to make Mrs. Mercer speak, but she hadn't the faintest idea of how to find her.

She stood still in the station yard just clear of the traffic and thought. The post-office wasn't any good, but there were food shops — butchers, bakers, grocers, dairies. The Mercers would have to eat, and unless they went out and shopped everything themselves, and paid for it on the nail and carried it home, one or other of these food shops would have their address. The thing you are least likely to go out and shop for yourself is milk. Nearly everyone lets the milkman call. Hilary thought she would begin with the dairies. She made enquiries and was given the names of four.

As she walked in the direction of Market Square, it seemed to her that she had made a beautiful plan, and one that was practically sure of success unless:

(a) The Mercers were passing under another name,

(b) they were living in a boarding-house or an hotel, in which case they wouldn't be doing their own catering.

She didn't think they would have changed their name. It would be a definitely fishy thing to do, and Mercer couldn't afford to be fishy. He'd got to be the brave, honest butler with a wife who was out of her mind. And she didn't think they would be in an hotel, or a boarding-house, because of the danger of Mrs. Mercer wailing and breaking down. Landladies and fellow-boarders have gaping ears and galloping tongues. No, Mercer would never risk it.

She came round the corner into Market Street, and saw the first dairy straight in front of her. They had no customer of the name of Mercer, but the woman behind the counter tried to sell Hilary a *special* cream-cheese, and some *very* special honey. She was such a good sales-woman that if Hilary had had anything in her purse except her return ticket and sevenpence-halfpenny, she would almost certainly have succumbed. As it was, she emerged a little breathless, and hoped that everyone in Ledlington wasn't going to be quite so brisk and efficient.

There was neither briskness nor efficiency in the second dairy. A mournful elderly man said he had no Mercers on his books, and then coughed and called her back from the door to enquire if she had said Perkins.

It was the girl in the next dairy who introduced the first real ray of sunshine. It was a good, strong, hopeful ray, but it petered out in a very disappointing manner. The girl, a plump, rosy creature, reacted immediately to the name of Mercer.

'Two of them, Mr. and Mrs. — a pint a day. Would that be them?'

Hilary's heart gave a jump of pure joy. She hadn't realised just what a hopeless, needle-in-the-hay kind of business she had embarked upon until she heard those stirring words. Her imp chanted:

'A pint of milk a day
Keeps despair away.'

She said eagerly, 'Yes, they might be. What were they like?'

The girl giggled a little.

'She didn't look as if she could call her soul her own. I wouldn't let a man get the upper hand of me like that. Silly, I call it.'

'Can you give me the address?' said Hilary.

'They were staying with Mrs. Green round in Albert Crescent — rooms, you know.'

'What is the number?' said Hilary quickly.

The girl yawned, covering her mouth with a plump white hand.

'Oh, they're not there any longer. Just a matter of one night, that was all.'

The disappointment was quite dreadful.

'They're not here any longer?'

The girl shook her head.

'Friends of yours?' she enquired with a sort of easy curiosity.

'Oh, no. I just want to find them — on a matter of business.'

'You've got to be careful,' said the girl. She put her plump elbows on the counter and leaned towards Hilary. 'I wouldn't have liked to say anything if they were friends of yours, but Mrs. Green wasn't half pleased to get rid of them. She liked him well enough but Mrs. just about gave her the creeps. Like a ghost about the house, she said, and a bit queer by all accounts. But what put her out more than anything else was her waking everyone up screaming in the night. Never heard anything like it, Mrs. Green said. And him trying to calm her down, and apologising all round. Quite the gentleman she said he was. And it was then he let out about her not being right in the head, and "Mr. Mercer," says Mrs. Green — I know all about it, because she's a friend of Aunt's and come round and told her — "Mr. Mercer," she says, "I'm sorry for you, and if your wife's afflicted, I'm sorry for her, but this isn't a home for the afflicted and I'll trouble you to go elsewhere." And Aunt said she done perfectly right, because you've got to think about your own house, and screams in the night are just what might get a house a bad name. And Mr. Mercer said he was very sorry, and it shouldn't occur again, and they were leaving, anyway.'

'They've gone?' said Hilary in the woeful voice of a child.

The girl nodded.

'First thing. Closed their account and all.'

'You don't know where they've gone?'

The girl shook her head.

'Not to say *know*. There was a cottage to let out Ledstow way. Mrs Green passed a remark about it.'

A cottage — that was just what she had thought of — a place where there wouldn't be anyone for Mrs. Mercer to talk to — a lonely cottage where a woman might scream without being heard. A shiver ran all the way down her spine as she said,

'Can you tell me how to get to this cottage?'

The girl shook her head again.

'Sorry — I can't.'

'Mrs. Green might know.'

Another shake of the head.

'Not her! Why, she told Aunt someone had told her about the cottage, but she didn't know who it was. And

Aunt said one of the agents would know, but Mrs. Green would have it that it was being let private and nothing to do with the agents. And then all of a sudden it came over her who it was told her about the cottage.'

'Yes?' said Hilary — 'yes?'

The girl giggled and lolled on the counter.

'It was Mr. Mercer himself. Funny — wasn't it? It came back to her as clear as anything. He'd heard about the cottage from a friend, and he thought maybe he'd go and have a look at it. So that's what he must have done. She didn't take any notice at the time, but it came to her afterwards.'

The ray had faded out completely.

'How far is Ledstow?' said Hilary in a discouraged voice.

'A matter of seven miles,' said the girl.

Seven miles. If Hilary's heart could have sunk any lower, it would have done so. It was a nasty dull, grey, foggy afternoon. It would be early dark, and still earlier dusk. The cottage might be as far away as the last of the seven miles between Ledlington and Ledstow. There was a horrible sagging inexactness about that 'out on the Ledstow road'. She couldn't just walk into the fog with the prospect of perhaps having to do fourteen miles and returning in the dark. Somewhere at the back of her mind she was remembering that Mercer had followed her this morning, and all of a sudden she was occupying herself with how he had come to be in Putney, and why he had followed her. The Mercers had gone down to Ledlington yesterday afternoon, presumably on their way to look at the cottage on the Ledstow road. They had slept at Mrs. Green's — or, rather, they hadn't slept, because Mrs. Mercer had screamed and raised the house. And Mrs. Green had given them notice and they had gone away 'first thing'. Well, that left time for Mercer to get up to Putney and go to Solway Lodge. But what had he done with Mrs. Mercer? And why had he gone to Putney? And why did Mrs. Mercer scream in the night? Yes, why did Mrs. Mercer scream in the night?

CHAPTER SEVENTEEN

Hilary gave it up. She felt as small and mean as one of the little scuttling things that you turn up under a stone in the garden, but she gave it up. The urge to follow Mrs. Mercer and find out whether she was out of her mind or not failed and faded away before the prospect of a fourteen-mile walk in the dark along a country road which she did not know in search of a cottage which might not even exist and a woman who might be anywhere else in England. She had lunched on milk and a bun and she wanted her tea. You can't buy much tea with sevenpence halfpenny, of which twopence has to be reserved for a bus fare at the other end, but she did her best with it.

Sitting in the train which was taking her back to London, she found that her opinion of herself was rising. Perhaps it was the tea, perhaps it was merely the revival of common sense which made her feel that she had done the right thing. Silly to lose herself in dark lanes, and impossible to frighten Marion by not getting home till all hours. Tonight of all nights Marion would want someone to come home to. It always took her days to get over one of those tormenting visits to Geoff. No, she was doing perfectly right to come back. Where she had been a stupid ass was in starting to go down to Ledlington in the afternoon. The thing to do was to get down there bright and early, say not later than ten o'clock, and so have plenty of time to look for the cottage and Mrs. Mercer by daylight. Horrid beyond words to think of being benighted, and hearing perhaps a footstep following her in the dark as Mercer had followed her this morning. She hadn't liked it very much then, but what had been just vaguely unpleasant in a Putney street by daylight took on a nightmarish quality when she thought of it happening in the black dark without a house in call.

These arguments placated her conscience easily. The cottage wouldn't run away. If Mrs. Mercer was there, she wouldn't run away either. Tomorrow she would pawn Aunt Arabella's ring and go down to Ledlington on the proceeds. It was the most hideous ring Hilary had ever seen in her life — a very large, badly-cut ruby practically buried in enormous heavy masses of gold. It weighed like lead and was quite unwearable, but it could always be trusted to produce a fiver at a pinch. Hilary decided that this was definitely a pinch. She planned to hire a bicycle and so escape an interminable search on foot. And that being off her mind, she went to sleep and slept peacefully all the way to town. She had a dream about Henry — a very encouraging dream — in which he told her that he had been in the wrong, and that his only wish was to be forgiven. This agreeably improbable picture was extremely solacing, but even in a dream this contrite and humble Henry seemed a little too good to be true. She awoke with a start, and dreamed no more.

Marion Grey came home that night in a state which made Hilary feel thankful that she was there and not in Ledlington. Marion was cold, strained, and exhausted beyond belief. She fainted twice before Hilary could get her to bed, and when there just lay and stared at the ceiling in wordless misery. There was no question of going down to Ledlington next day, or for the rest of the week. Marion was ill and had to be nursed, coaxed into taking food, petted and cajoled out of the thoughts which were consuming her. She must rest, but she mustn't be left alone. She must be talked to, read to, interested, and fed. Aunt Emmeline sent a cheque, but Hilary had to do the work — keep the flat, buy and cook the food, and look after Marion. For the time at least, Ledlington was off the map and the Mercer's didn't exist.

It was during this time that Henry Cunningham paid a second visit to Miss Silver. He was rung up and invited to call. The gentle, precise tones of her telephone voice gave him no clue as to whether she had any news for him, or whether she had merely sent for him in order to tell him that there was no news to be had.

She received him with the same slight inclination of the head as before, and she appeared to be knitting the same white woolly sock. When she was seated she took out a tape-measure and did some minute measuring with it. Then, as she rolled up the yard measure again, she said in a pleased, brisk voice,

'Well, Captain Cunningham, I have some news for you.'

Henry, not so pleased, was a good deal taken aback, and showed it. What was going to be raked up now? News on a detective's lips was unlikely to be anything pleasant. He felt a very active impatience with the Everton case, and a very decided reluctant to hear what Miss Silver's news might be. Those indeterminate eyes of hers rested upon him mildly. She said in her ladylike voice,

'Something rather surprising has come to light, Captain Cunningham. I felt that you should know about it at once.'

With a good deal of apprehension Henry said, 'Yes?' He could not for the life of him think of anything else to say — and felt a fool, and feeling a fool, felt cross.

Miss Silver's needles clicked.

'Decidedly surprising, I thought. But you will judge

for yourself. After you had left me the other day I put on my hat and went to Somerset House. You were not able to supply me with Mrs. Mercer's maiden name, but I thought I would see if I could trace her marriage. In a case of this sort previous history is all important. Her Christian names, one unusual in itself, and the two certainly unusual in juxtaposition, encouraged me to hope for success. It was unlikely that there would be more than one Louisa Kezia who had married an Alfred Mercer.'

'Yes?' said Henry again.

Miss Silver paused for a moment to count her stitches.

'Ten — twelve — fourteen,' she murmured. 'Knit one, slip one, knit two together — '

The sock rotated, and a fresh needle stabbed into the wool.

'Well, Captain Cunningham, fortune — or I should prefer to say providence — favoured me. I was able to trace the marriage. Mrs. Mercer's maiden name appears to have been Anketell — Louisa Kezia Anketell. The uncommon surname ought to make it easy to trace her antecedents. But there is more than that. There is a circumstance connected with the marriage itself — a circumstance connected with the date of the marriage.'

'Well?' said Henry Cunningham. He was not cross any longer, he was excited. He did not know what he expected to hear, but he was impatient to hear it.

Miss Silver stopped knitting for a moment.

'The date gives food for thought, Captain Cunningham. Alfred Mercer and Louisa Kezia Anketell were married on the seventeenth of July, Nineteen-thirty-five.'

'*What?*' said Henry.

'The seventeenth of July,' said Miss Silver — 'the day after Mr. Everton's death.'

'*What?*' said Henry again.

Miss Silver resumed her knitting.

'Think it over, Captain Cunningham. I told you it provided food for thought.'

'The day after James Everton's death? But they had been with him for over a year as a married couple.'

Miss Silver primmed her lips.

'Immorality is not confined to the upper classes,' she said.

Henry got up from his chair and stood there looking down at her across the table.

'The day after James Everton's death — ' he repeated. 'What does that mean?'

'What does it seem to you to mean, Captain Cunningham?'

Henry was no longer frowning. This was too serious an occasion. He looked most seriously perturbed as he said,

'A wife can't be made to give evidence against her husband — '

Miss Silver nodded.

'Quite correct. That is one of the occasions on which the law regards husband and wife as one, and a man cannot be forced to incriminate himself, though he may make a confession, and a wife may give evidence if she wishes to. The law, if I may say so, is extremely inequitable in its treatment of married people. It regards them as one in such a case as this, and they pay income tax as one person, thus bringing both incomes on to a higher rate of taxation, yet when it comes to death duties the spouses are regarded as two, and the survivor is mulcted.'

Henry was not listening to all this. His mind was completely occupied with the Mercers. He said,

'She couldn't be made to give evidence against him — he was in a blazing hurry to shut her mouth — '

Miss Silver nodded again.

'It certainly has that appearance. I should be glad if you would resume your seat, Captain Cunningham — it is difficult to talk to someone who is, so to speak, towering.'

'I beg your pardon,' said Henry, and sat down.

'I have a nephew who is six-foot-one,' said Miss Silver, knitting busily. 'Very much your own height, I should say — and I have constantly to remind him that it is very tiring to converse with someone who, so to speak, towers. But we must return to the Mercers. There might, of course, be other explanations of this sudden marriage, but at first sight it certainly does suggest a desire on Alfred Mercer's part to make sure that his associate could not be compelled to give evidence against him. But if you accept this suggestion, you will find yourself forced to a most sinister conclusion.' She laid down her knitting and looked directly at Henry. 'Consider the date of the marriage.'

'The day after the murder.'

'Yes. But consider, Captain Cunningham. You cannot just walk into a register office and get married — notice has to be given.'

'I know that, but I don't know how much notice.'

'One clear week-day must elapse between the giving of the notice and the actual marriage. The Mercers were married on Wednesday the seventeenth of July. They must have given notice to the registrar not later than Monday the fifteenth, and Mr. Everton was not murdered until eight o'clock on the evening of Tuesday the sixteenth. If the marriage was designed in some way to shelter the criminal, then the crime must have been coldly planned at least thirty-six hours ahead — it was no affair of a sudden quarrel, a sudden violent impulse of anger or resentment. The words "malice aforethought" will occur to you, as they did to me.' She coughed a little. 'You see, Captain Cunningham?'

Henry saw. He put his head in his hands, and saw a number of things which did not come into Miss Silver's view. He saw the Everton case being re-opened and a flood of unpleasantness let loose. He saw Hilary plunging into the flood and getting splashed, and mired, and stained all over. He saw her openly triumphant because she had been right and he had been wrong all along. He found himself quite unable to believe that Geoffrey Grey was innocent. He didn't see how he could possibly be innocent. If the Mercers were in it, too, if Alfred Mercer had married his wife to stop her mouth, it merely made matters worse for Geoffrey Grey, since it proved that the murder was premeditated and not, as he had believed after reading the case, the outcome of Geoffrey's ungovernable fury on learning that he had been disinherited. That was what he had believed, what the jury had believed, and what practically everybody who read the case had believed. But if the murder had been planned ... He recoiled in horror from the thought of the added suffering and discredit which might be brought upon Marion and Hilary should this be established.

Miss Silver watched him without speaking for a time. At last she said,

'Well, Captain Cunningham? Do you wish me to go on? It is for you to say.'

Henry lifted his head and looked at her. He never knew quite how he came to a decision, or what impelled this decision. He said,

'I want you to go on.'

CHAPTER EIGHTEEN

Marion Grey went back to work after five days of Hilary's nursing. It was about this time that Jacques Dupré wrote to his sister in Provence:

> *I saw Marion in the street today. It breaks one's heart — she looks like a shadow carved in stone . . .*

But then Jacques was a poet, and he had loved her vainly for years — one of those endless, hopeless loves.

Hilary urged a longer rest, but was silent when Marion said,

'Don't stop me, Hilary. If I stop I shall die. And if I die, Geoff won't have anyone.'

It was this speech more than anything else which took Hilary down to Ledlington again just a week after her last fruitless visit. She wasn't going to be caught in the dark this time, so she took the 9.30, and found her way out of the station yard and into Market Street with a good fat slice of the morning still before her, to say nothing of the afternoon — only she hoped she would have found Mrs. Mercer long before it came to that. She had duly pawned Aunt Arabella's ring, and was comfortably conscious of being a capitalist with four pounds ten and sixpence in her purse. She had brought it all with her, because you never know, and bicycle shops have a way of asking for a deposit before they will hire a machine to a stranger. Even a deposit does not always incline them to what they regard as a chancy transaction.

Hilary tried three bicycle shops before she encountered a very pleasant and impressionable young man who not only produced a bicycle but gave her floods of information about all the cottages between Ledlington and Ledstow. He had a most surprising crop of fair hair which stood up a sheer four inches from his freckled forehead, and he was one of the most friendly creatures Hilary had ever met. He hadn't heard of any strangers taking any cottages — 'But then you never know, miss — I'll just pump that back tyre up a bit. It might be Mr. Greenhow's cottage, best part of a mile and a half along the Ledstow road and turn to the left down the the the lane — there isn't more than one thereabouts. I did hear he'd gone to stay with his married daughter in London, but Fred Barker told me he'd come back again. Or it might be the new house Mr. Carter was building for his daughter, only she never got married at all and it was up to be let. I don't know that you'd hardly call it a cottage, but you might try there. And there's the Miss Soameses. They always let in the summer, but you wouldn't hardly call it summer now, and they're a good half-mile off the main road.'

'I shouldn't think that would be it.'

The young man stopped pumping and stood up.

'There's Humpy Dick's place,' he said doubtfully. 'Nasty old tumble-down shack though. I shouldn't think anyone 'ud take it, though you never can tell — can you?'

It didn't sound attractive, but Hilary wasn't looking for attractions. A broken-down woman might very well be hidden away in a broken-down shack.

She said, 'How do I get to it?' and was rewarded with another flood of information.

'Third bridge you come to there's a lane going off to the right — well, 'tisn't hardly a lane, but you might call it one. Well, you don't take any notice of that, you go straight on, and then there's a bit of a wood, and then there's a pond, but you don't go as far as the pond. There's a footpath all along by the side of the wood, and you keep right on till you come to Humpy Dick's. Only I don't suppose there'll be anyone there, because it's stood empty ever since Humpy fell over the quarry in the dark last January and his brother fetched him away. I did hear a London gentleman had bought it — some kind of an artist — but he wouldn't hardly move in this time of year, I shouldn't think. Anyhow, it was empty a fortnight ago, because I was up that way myself and seen it.' He went on telling her about cottages, until she received a comforting impression that the Ledstow road had fallen a prey to ribbon building, and that cottages fairly jostled one another over the whole seven miles.

She thanked the young man, left a deposit of two pounds, and tore herself away. She would much rather have continued to listen to his friendly discourse than go the round of the house-agents and then start looking for Mrs. Mercer.

The house-agents were a complete wash-out. They were neither chatty nor helpful. The name of Mercer evoked no response. They knew nothing of any cottage being taken. The Miss Soames never left in winter. Mr. Greenhow's cottage had not been in their hands. Mr. Carter was going to live in his new house himself. The late Mr. Humphrey Richard's cottage had been sold about a month ago. They were not at liberty to give any information about the purchaser. Thus three agents with admirable discretion. But at the fourth a very young clerk told Hilary that the place had been bought for a song by a Mr. Williams, a gentleman from London, who wanted it for a weekend cottage in summer.

By this time Hilary was hungry, and today she wasn't lunching on a bun and a glass of milk. You didn't pawn Aunt Arabella's ruby ring every day of the week, and when you did you didn't lunch on buns — you splashed, and had a two-course lunch, and cream in your coffee.

It was about half past one when she rode out of Led-lington past rows of little new houses, some finished and lived in, some only half-grown, and some just marked out, mere sketches on the ground. Hilary rode past them on the hired bicycle, bumping a little where the road had been cut up, and thinking that the shock-headed young man had been too zealous with his pumping. However, hired bicycles had a tendency to leak, so perhaps it was all for the best.

Once clear of the houses, she had an expanse of per-fectly flat green fields on either side under the lowering grey arch of the sky. The morning had been fine, and the weather forecast one of those which thoughtfully pro-vides for every contingency. Hilary, having picked out the pleasant words 'bright intervals', hadn't really bothered about the rest of it, but as she looked at that low grey sky, lost fragments emerged uneasily from the corners of her mind. There was something about 'colder', and it was certainly turning colder. That didn't matter, but there was also a piece about 'rapid deterioration later', and she had a gloomy feeling that the word fog came into it somewhere. She ought to have read it more carefully, but the honest truth was that she hadn't wanted to. She had wanted to get on with this business and get it over, and really, in November, if you allowed yourself to be put off by what the weather forecast said, you might just as well throw in your hand and hibernate. All the same she did hope there wasn't going to be a fog.

The fog came on at about four o'clock. Hilary had been to fifteen cottages and six small houses. They all said that they didn't let, though some of them varied the answer by admitting that they wouldn't mind taking in a quiet lady or gentleman in the summer. One of them went so far as to say that she was used to actresses and didn't mind their ways. They all seemed to regard Hilary as desirous of forcing herself upon them at an unsuitable

time of year when people expected to be left to themselves after the labours of the holiday season. She must
have overshot the footpath to Humpy Dick's cottage, because though there were several patches of woodland she
never identified the young man's pond. This was not very
surprising, as he had quite forgotten to tell her that it
had dried out in the drought of 1933 and had never had
any water in it since. She arrived at Ledstow feeling that
she never wanted to hear of a cottage again.

At Ledstow she had tea. She had it in a sort of parlour
in the village pub. It was very cold, and stuffy with the
stuffiness of a room whose windows have not been
opened for months. Everything that could be cleaned
was very clean, and everything that could be polished
was very highly polished. The red and green linoleum
shone like a mirror, and a smell of soap, varnish, tur-
pentine, bacon, onions, and old stuffed furniture thick-
ened the air. There was a sofa and three padded chairs
upholstered in an archaic tapestry whose original colour
or colours had merged into an even drab. There were
paper shavings in the fire-place and, on the mantelshelf
above, a bright blue vase with a bunch of pansies painted
on it, a copper lustre sugar-bowl with a wreath of lumpy
pink and blue fruits below the rim, a horrid little orna-
ment displaying the arms of Colchester (why Colchester?), a brass bedroom candlestick, shining like gold,
and a pet of a zebra, all stripy, feeding out of a little girl's
hand. The little girl had a sprigged dress with a yellow
petticoat, and the zebra carried a pair of panniers,
one heaped up with fruit and the other with flowers.
Hilary loved him passionately at sight, and by dint of
dwelling fondly upon his stripes contrived to forget that
the tea was bitter and the butter rancid, and that she
was no nearer finding the Mercers than when she had
set out.

It was perhaps as well that the room afforded neither

warmth nor comfort, because even its cold stuffiness was hard to leave. If there had been a fire and a comfortable chair, Hilary might have found it almost impossible to wrench herself away and go out into the dark. It wasn't quite dark yet, but it was going to be, long before the lights of Ledlington came into view. And there was certainly going to be a fog. No, there was a fog already, and it looked like getting worse. Well, it was no good staying here, she had better be going. She would just have to give up any idea of finding the Mercers today. She opened the parlour door, and saw Alfred Mercer coming down the passage.

CHAPTER NINETEEN

Hilary's mind went perfectly cold and stiff, but her hand shut the door. She stood on the other side of it and waited without thought or movement. She did not know how long she waited.

She began to think again. Was he coming in here? No, he wasn't. The footsteps went past. She lost them. What was Alfred Mercer doing here? She didn't know. She wanted to know, but there wasn't any way of finding out. Had he followed her? She *must* find out. She went to the fire-place and rang the bell.

It seemed a long time before anyone answered it. Then the girl who had brought the tea came in and said there was eighteenpence to pay. Hilary took out two shillings and a sixpence, put one shilling and a sixpenny bit into the girl's hand, and held the other shilling between finger and thumb.

'I wonder if you could tell me the name of the man who came in just now?'

The girl was plump and good-tempered — a heavily built young thing with a high colour. She looked at the shilling and said,

'Oh, no, miss, I couldn't.'

'You don't know his name?'

'Oh, no, miss, I don't.'

'You've seen him before — he's been here before?'

'Oh, no, miss, he hasn't.'

'You mean he's a stranger?'

'Oh, no, miss.'

Hilary could have stamped with rage. Did the girl know anything, or didn't she? She seemed impenetrably stupid, but you never could tell. And she couldn't afford to stay here and perhaps be caught asking awkward questions. Whether the girl knew Alfred Mercer or not, it was very certain that Alfred Mercer would know Hilary Carew, and that blighted girl had left the door open when she came in. Hilary Carew had got to make herself scarce, and she'd got to look slippy about it.

She looked slippy, but she didn't look slippy enough, for just as she got to the end of the passage and had her hand on the outer door, Alfred Mercer came walking briskly back by the way he had gone. Hilary looked sideways and saw him, and with the same movement she pulled the door towards her and slipped out.

There was a recessed porch and some steps. Her bicycle was leaning against the steps, but someone had knocked it down and she had to pick it up. She was very, very quick about it. One moment she was groping for the bicycle, and the next she was wobbling out on to the road and leaning forward to reach the electric lamp and switch it on. Nothing seemed to happen when she did this. It wasn't as dark as it was going to be later on, but it was quite dark enough, and there was quite a lot of fog. It was her own fault for stopping to have tea, but there comes a point when you care more about having your tea than about doing what you ought to do, and Hilary had reached that point. She now used some bitter expressions about the shock-headed young man who had sent her out on a foggy afternoon with a lamp which had probably died last winter.

When she had gone a few hundred yards and had nearly run into a ditch because the road turned off sharp to the right and the bicycle kept straight on, she got off and had a look at the lamp. Not a glimmer. She shook it, poked it, opened it, and closed it again with an exasperated bang. A beautiful bright beam of light instantly disclosed the fact that she had somehow got into a field. She got back on to the road, mounted, and began to ride as fast as the fog would let her in the direction of Ledlington, hoping passionately that Alfred Mercer hadn't got a bicycle, too. She felt tolerably sure that he wouldn't have a car, but he might have a bicycle. And then the voice of common sense, speaking in a very faint and unconvincing manner, enquired why on earth Alfred Mercer should want to follow her. He had already told her about two hundred times that his wife was out of her mind. Common sense was of the opinion that this should suffice him. Something that wasn't common sense kept urging in a low and horrid whisper, 'Ride, Hilary — ride for your life! He's coming after you — he's coming now!'

As a matter of fact Mr. Mercer was drinking beer in the bar. He had recognised Hilary when she turned her head, and he had seen her through the half open door, but he had followed her no farther than the bottom step. The bicycle which he had stumbled into and knocked over was gone. That meant that Miss Carew had taken it. He wasn't running down any dashed road after any dashed bicycle; not much he wasn't. He went into the bar, ordered a pint of beer, laced it — deplorably — with gin, and awaited the arrival of his principal, who was late on account of the fog. His principal would arrive by car. If Miss Carew was to be followed, they could follow her comfortably in the car. He expended some profanity on the weather, and addressed a good deal more to Miss Hilary Carew.

About ten minutes later a car drew up in front of the inn, and after no more than five minutes went on again with a passenger. It took the Ledlington road.

The fog was deepening steadily. When she struck a bad patch Hilary had to get off and walk. It was better to walk than to run into a ditch or a tree. The prospect of getting hurt and lying out on a clammy road all night was too repellent. There began to be more and more bad patches, and she began to wish more and more fervently that she had never come on this wild goose chase. Her imp produced an appropriate rhyme:

> 'If you want to chase a goose
> That's flying loose,
> You really should take care
> The goose is there.'

She rode a little way, and then had to get off again. It was funny how much safer she felt when she was riding the bicycle. As a matter of actual fact she was probably safer on her feet, but every time she dismounted the feeling that she was stepping down into danger came over her. It was exactly as if there was another mist upon the Ledlington road, a steadily rising mist of fear. When she was on the bicycle she was a little above it, but each time she got off, it was deeper and colder about her.

She found herself listening, straining her ears for any sound that would break the silence which the fog had brought. If she stood still she could hear her own breathing, but nothing else — not a bird's wing, not a twitter, not a breaking twig or a leaf brushed aside by any moving wild thing. Nothing was abroad, nothing moved except Hilary Carew, who wouldn't be here if she wasn't an obstinate little fool who thought she knew better than anyone else. Anyone else meant Henry. She had actually come to the point where she felt that Henry had been right when he told her to leave the Everton case alone — in case of something worse happening. To whom? To Hilary Carew, on a dark foggy road where nobody passed, and where no one would *know* — for a long, long time.

'Idiot!' said Hilary to herself. 'What's the good of thinking of that sort of thing now? Stop it, do you hear — stop it at once! And you're not to think about Henry either! It's undermining. He isn't here, and if he was he'd probably be hating you like poison.'

'But he wouldn't let me be murdered in the dark.'

This was another Hilary who was so afraid that she had no proper pride and would have flung herself with passionate relief into the arms of Henry Cunningham even if he was hating her.

It was at this point that she heard the car.

She felt so much relief that for the moment she was quite herself again. It was the silence that had been so horrid. The familiar, comfortable sound of traffic on the King's highway broke into this paralysing silence, and with it Hilary's fear. Even the fog didn't seem to be quite so dense, and she had the bright thought that the car would probably be running slow, and that she might be able to follow its tail-light into Ledlington as a guide.

She pedalled along carefully, making up her mind that she had better jump off when the car was near so as to be sure of getting well out of the way. There would be plenty of time, because, as she could hear, the car wasn't going at all fast. It couldn't, of course. About ten miles an hour would be anyone's limit, unless they wanted to run off the road at the first bend.

Afterwards Hilary could remember everything quite clearly down to this point. She particularly remembered thinking that she would be able to keep up with the car if it wasn't doing more than ten miles an hour, but after that there was a confusion. There was light — and a noise. The car must have had its fog-light on or its headlights dipped. The noise was the car roaring down upon her, rushing into sudden speed — a big car. And she had jumped. If she hadn't had the plan ready in her mind she wouldn't have had time to jump clear, but because she had planned to jump off on to the grass as the car came near she did jump, and saved herself. Heat, and a grinding sound, and her head coming crash against something hard. Stars in the darkness — catherine wheels and golden rain — and then nothing at all. She had fallen heavily and knocked her head hard enough to be stunned for about a minute and a half. If it had been longer, there would have been no more Hilary Carew.

She came back to a pain in her head — to being lifted — to a voice that said, 'Only stunned. Quick now, and we'll make a job of it!' She didn't know the voice at all, and what it said had no meaning for her. Her mind was open, empty, and without power to grasp anything. The things that passed through it meant nothing to her at all. She knew that she had a pain in her head, nothing more. That was the whole world.

Something else came into this world. Grit — cold, wet grit against her mouth. Horrid. She moved, and touched something sharp, something that cut her hand. She wasn't being lifted any more. She was lying on her face with grit in her mouth, her cheek on something wet, and hard, and cold. The road — she was lying in the road. She was lying on her face in the road. And she had cut her hand. It hurt. She had cut it on something sharp. She remembered the bicycle, and thought it was all smashed up, and how was she going to get into Ledlington now?

All these thoughts really took no time at all. Consciousness came back and they were there, waiting for the light to touch them. She became aware of two things simultaneously, and then a third. The car with its engine running, and its lights shining on her — those two things first. And then the slam of a door. Someone had slammed the door of the car.

The man at the wheel put the car into bottom gear and jammed his foot down hard on the accelerator.

Hilary heard the sudden roar of the engine. It came to her as sound, as danger, as terror itself. The two men who had carried her from the grass verge had laid her on her face in the track of the car with the broken bicycle beside her. If you fall from a bicycle, you are more likely to fall on your face than on your back. The men had considered this, and they had laid Hilary on her face in the road. She would be found broken and dead in the morning, a casualty of the fog. If they had cared less for probabilities and had laid her on her back, the plan would have gone off without a hitch, but they had laid her on her face. A half stunned girl on a wet and slippery road has just about twice as much chance of scrambling to her feet from this position.

At that roaring sound Hilary raised herself upon her hands, stared at the orange foglight of the car, and saw it rush towards her. But as it rushed, she threw herself sideways — scrambling, slithering, thrusting herself up from the road. She got somehow to her feet and went blundering and stumbling across the grass verge until she was brought up short by a hedge. Blind terror has an instinct of its own. There were thorns which she did not feel, blackberry trails which came across her face, across her mouth, as she went down on her knees burrowing and groping to find a gap which would let her through. Her hair caught, her coat ripped, an interlacing tangle of twigs and branches held her back, but she pushed and

146

struggled until she was through, and there on the other side of the hedge she crouched with her head on her knees and the stuff of her skirt clutched hard against her face to muffle the sound of her panting breaths. She was almost fainting, but not quite. Thought swung between oblivion and nightmare. Then steadied. They would come back. They would look for her. They mustn't find her.

She got up and ran as fast as she could away across the field.

CHAPTER TWENTY

Down the road the car came to a standstill with a grinding of brakes. One of the men got out and ran back. There was a difference of opinion between him and the driver as to what had happened. The fog had made it impossible to see. The wheels had bumped over something. With any luck Miss Hilary Carew was a corpse.

He reached the spot. There was no corpse on the road. There was a good deal of smashed bicycle, scattered, fragmentary, and excessively dangerous. He trod on the rim of a wheel, and half a dozen broken spokes came flicking up at him, tearing his trouser leg and stabbing into the palm which he thrust out to fend them off. He swore, shouted, barked his shin on a pedal, and getting clear, ran back to the car.

All this took a minute or two. By the time explanations and recriminations had been bandied, and an electric lamp extracted from a crowded cubby-hole, Hilary had blundered into a second hedge. If she had not been so giddy she would have run straight down the deep field, and she would probably have been overtaken there, for the men soon found the place where she had forced her way through the first hedge. With the fog to help her she might have escaped, but there were two of them, able-bodied and active, and they had a torch. They had also a great deal at stake. But then so had she, and if she was weak and shaken, her very weakness helped her and she had run anything but straight. Her head was swimming, and without knowing it she bore hard to the right. This took her across a corner of the field and brought her up short against a hedge which ran in from the road. She scrambled through it, being lucky enough to strike a gap, and then, finding her feet on a downhill slope, she followed them. They took her into a deep hollow place set about with bushes. When she got there she stopped, crouched down and trembling all over. The bushes closed her in and hid her, and the fog hid the bushes. Here, in this dreadful dark lonely place, like a hunted wild thing she had a sanctuary. The earth supported her shaking limbs. The darkness was a shelter. The stripped wintry bushes stood sentinel. If a foot moved against her, or a hand stretched out to do her harm, there would be an alarum of snapping twig and creaking branch.

Gradually she relaxed. Her heart quieted. Her head cleared. She listened, and could hear no sound of pursuit.

After what seemed like a very long time a faint sound came to her, a sound of voices. Just that — just voices, just an indistinguishable murmur of sound a long way off. She strained in an agony, waiting for it to come nearer, to break upon her. Instead there was silence. Then, suddenly sharp and clear, the slam of a door, and upon that again an engine throbbing.

Hilary's hands came together and held one another tight. They had got into the car, banged the door, and started the engine. They had given up looking for her, and they were going away. Oh, joyful, joyful, joyful, joyful, joyful!

A cold drop trickled suddenly between her shoulder-blades. Suppose it was a trick. Suppose they were only pretending to go away. Suppose she climbed back into the road and found them waiting for her there. A hand at her throat — suddenly — in the dark. A voice behind the curtain of fog, whispering under its breath, 'Quick, and we'll make a job of it!' They wouldn't miss her a second time. The car would smash her as it had smashed the bicycle. *She wouldn't ever see Henry any more.* That hurt so sharply that it did her good. She felt a fierce determination to see Henry again. She was going to. She didn't care what they did, she was going to.

She became suddenly quiet and balanced. She was conscious of a new courage. It was not the young courage which says with a light heart, 'Dreadful things happen — in the newspapers — to other people — but of course they couldn't happen to me or to the people I love.' They had happened to her, they had happened to Marion, they had happened to Geoffrey Grey. If she found courage now, it was the older, colder courage which says, 'This thing has got to be faced, and it's up to me to face it.'

She sat up, pushed back her hair from her face, winced as she touched a long deep scratch, and heard the car go down the road and away. It was heading for Ledlington. The sound of it faded out upon the foggy air. It didn't stop suddenly, as it would have done if they had run on for a bit and then pulled up. It lessened gradually and died away in the distance.

And yet it might be a trick. There had been two men. One of them might have stayed behind to catch her when she came out upon the road again. They would surely count on her having to find her way back to the road. She thought of a still black figure, a featureless wickedness, standing there under the hedgerow, waiting. Her thought was quite steady and calm. It wouldn't do to go out on the road. Neither could she risk trying to stop a passing car. It would probably be impossible in a fog like this anyhow.

She began to try and think what she had better do.

Fields belong to somebody. There might be a path somewhere near, or a cottage — some place which she could reach without going out upon the road again. She tried to remember the way she had come, and to make out where she was now. She thought about half way to Ledlington, but she couldn't remember any place like this hollow among the bushes, and she didn't know how far off the road she was. Not far by the noise of the car, which had sounded startlingly close.

She was, had she only known it, at the bottom of the pond which had been offered to her as a landmark by the shock-headed boy when he was telling her how to find Humpy Dick's cottage. He had omitted to tell her that it had gone dry in the drought, and she had omitted to notice it as she rode past. A glint of water was what she had been looking for, and, missing that, she missed the footpath, too.

She found it now. Climbing up out of the bottom and pushing through the bushes, she came upon it almost at once, a rutted path deeply scored by the passing of laden carts. Carts meant people, and people meant a house. She began to follow the ruts away from the road.

It wasn't easy. Without that deep scoring of the ground she would have been lost, but the furrows kept her to the path. If she ceased to stumble and turn her ankles, she knew at once that she was bearing away from the track, and so felt her way back to it and stumbled on again. It was very weary work. Suppose there wasn't any house. Suppose this wasn't a real place at all. Suppose she had got into a nightmare where an endless path went on, and on, and on through an everlasting fog. That was a very stupid thought. If you had one single grain of sense you didn't let yourself think that sort of thought when you were trying to find your way in a fog. Here Hilary's imp cocked a snook at her and said rudely: 'If you had a grain of sense you wouldn't have come.' He made a sort of jingle of it, and it went echoing round and round inside her head:

'You'd have stayed at home, you wouldn't have come.
You wouldn't have come, you'd have stayed at home.'

She went on feeling for the ruts with her feet, walking with one hand stretched out in front of her in case of a wall or another hedge.

It was a gate she touched. Her hand went over it, and it brought her up short with a bar at her waist and another across her knees. She felt for the latch, lifted it, and walked through. It wasn't big enough to be a field gate, and there were no ruts inside it, just a hard path which might at some time have been laid down in gravel. It was quite hard to walk on — hard, and narrow. She bore too far to the right, and went in up to her ankle in the soft earth of a garden bed. And then, before she came to it, she was aware of the house. It was much too dark to see anything, and her outstretched hand touched only the empty air, yet some sense told her that the house was near. Two more cautious steps, and there it was — a wall covered with creepers — the wood of a window frame, cold glass. She was off the path and must get back to it again. Groping, she came to a step, and a wooden door with a heavy metal knocker. The enchanting vision of a lighted room — a fire, hot tea — rose gloriously upon the fog. Open, Sesame! She had only to knock on the door and someone would open, and the enchantment would come true. She had the knocker in her hand, and nothing so easy as to let it fall — nothing so easy, and nothing so hard.

She stood there, and with every passing second it was harder to move at all. Her hand cramped on the heavy metal ring. If someone had followed her in from the road, the sound of the falling knocker would give her away. Perhaps there was no one in the house. There was no light in any window, and no sound at all. She laid the knocker gently back against the wood and began to feel her way round the house.

It was only a cottage really, for almost at once she was at the corner and groping along a side wall. Another corner, and the back of the house. If there was anyone at home, this was where they would be. Life in a cottage centres round the kitchen, and the kitchen is always at the back of the house.

As she turned the corner, she saw a shining in the fog, a silver shining which disclosed its secret currents. The light came from a window on the ground floor, and the fog moved in it with a slow upward movement like the rising of some sluggish tide. To Hilary that dim shining was like the first created light — very good. It broke the yoke of the darkness from her mind, and the nightmare slipped away. She went up to the window and looked in.

There was no curtain, at least none that was drawn. There was a sink below the sill, and taps. There was no light in the room, which seemed to be a scullery and very small, but a door stood open into the kitchen, and a lamp on the kitchen table shone upon the window and upon the fog. It shone in Hilary's eyes and dazzled her, so that at first she could see nothing except the lamp and the blue and white checked tablecloth which was spread between it and the table. In spite of being dazzled she kept her eyes wide and looked through the open door. Then she saw something else. She saw Mrs. Mercer turn round from the range with a teapot in her hand. The range was beyond the table and the lamp, a big old-fashioned range with a glowing fire. Mrs. Mercer turned round from it with the teapot. She set it down upon a tray beside the lamp — an old-fashioned tin tray with a gold pattern on it. Then she straightened herself up as if she had been carrying something heavy.

Hilary knocked on the window.

For a moment nothing happened. Then Mrs. Mercer came round the table and through the scullery door. She unlatched the window above the sink, and pushed it open, and said in a weak, dragging voice,

'Is that the milk? I didn't expect you in all this fog.'

Hilary leaned well in over the sill. She wasn't going to have any windows shut in her face. If it was humanly possible to have some of the tea in that fat brown teapot, she meant to have it. She hoped earnestly that the milk-jug she now saw on the tray was not empty, and it revived her a good deal to notice that there was only one cup. Alfred was evidently not expected home to tea. She let the light fall on her face, and she said,

'Good evening, Mrs. Mercer.'

Mrs. Mercer caught at the edge of the sink and swayed. The lamp was behind her, and her face just a blur. After a minute she said weakly,

'It's Miss Carew?'

Hilary nodded.

'Won't you let me in? I'd like a cup of tea — you don't *know* how much I'd like a cup of tea. I've just had a fall off my bicycle. I expect I look as if I'd been dragged through a hedge. May I come in and tidy up?'

Mrs. Mercer still held on to the sink with one hand. The other was at her side. She said,

'Oh, miss — you frightened me!'

'I'm so sorry if I did.'

She stared at Hilary.

'Perhaps you've got to catch a train,' she said.

'I can't think how I'm going to get to the station — my bicycle's all smashed up. Won't you let me in and give me some tea?'

'My husband don't like visitors. I'm expecting him.'

'There's only one cup on the tray.'

Mrs. Mercer began to shake.

'Can't I say who I want in my house and who I don't? I didn't ask you to come here, did I? If you'd got any sense in you you'd stay away. Haven't you got anything to do at home that you must needs come trapesing and trailing after those what don't want you? You be off quick! And the quicker the better, because if Mercer comes home — if Mercer comes home — '

Up to that first mention of the man's name she had used an angry whisper, but now it failed. Her eyes were fixed with terror, not upon Hilary, but upon some picture called up by her own words, some picture of Alfred Mercer coming home and finding them here — together.

'Mrs. Mercer — ' Hilary's voice was urgent — 'I want to ask you something. I don't want to stay — I've got to get back to town.'

Mrs. Mercer's pale tongue came out and moistened her lips.

'Go!' she said. 'Go — go — go — while you can — '

Hilary nodded.

'I want to go every bit as much as you want me to. I'll go the very minute you've told me what I want to know. And if you don't want Mercer to find me here we'd better get on with it. But I do wish you'd let me in.'

The pale tongue touched the pale lips again.

'I darsn't. He'd — cut my heart out.'

Hilary's spine crept, not so much at the words as at the sick look of terror which went with them. It was no good going on like this. She leaned in as far as she could and dropped her hand on Mrs. Mercer's wrist. It was icy cold, and the fingers clenched on the stone edge of the sink.

'Look here,' she said, 'I want to know what you meant when you said you tried to see Mrs. Grey while the trial was on.'

Mrs. Mercer strained away from the sink and from Hilary.

'I did go — I did try — nobody can't say I didn't try. I thought he'd have killed me then.'

'You tried to see her, and she was resting. Why did you try? What did you want to say to her?'

She felt the crazy leap of the pulse that was under her hand. Her grasp tightened. Her head swam with all the unhappiness that had been since then. It wasn't battle, murder, and sudden death that were the most dreadful things — it was having to go on after they had scorched your life to the bone. She thought of Marion as she had been, Marion as she was now. She said in a breaking voice,

'You asked me about Marion. She's so changed. If you could see her you wouldn't be able to bear it — you wouldn't *really*. Won't you tell me why you went to see her, and what you were going to say? You said *if* she had seen you — you said it in the train. *If* she had seen you — what were you going to tell her if she had seen you?'

Mrs. Mercer stopped pulling away. The hand at her side dropped limply. She said in a faint, exhausted tone,

'It's too late.'

'Tell me,' said Hilary.

Mrs. Mercer shook her head, not with any energy, but as if, being weak, she could not keep it from shaking.

'Let me go!' she said.

Hilary held the cold wrist.

'What were you going to tell her?'

Mrs. Mercer began to cry. Her nose twitched and the tears ran down beside it into her mouth.

'It's no use,' she said with a gasping sob. 'I was brought

up religious, and I know what I done. I darsn't read my Bible, and I darsn't say my prayers, and I darsn't go back on what I promised Mercer. If I had told her then, maybe it wouldn't have been so bad, but what's said now won't mend what's gone, nor it won't save me from what I done. Only if Mercer was to know he'd kill me, and then I'd be in hell.' She had stopped gasping. The words came out with hardly any breath behind them, her voice failing but never quite gone.

Hilary shook the wrist she was holding.

'Hell's now,' she said — 'when you're doing something wicked. No wonder you're unhappy. Tell me what you were going to say to Marion. *Please* tell me. I won't go till you do. Do you want Mercer to come back and find me here? I don't. But I can't go till you've told me.'

Mrs. Mercer leaned towards her across the sink.

'He'll kill you,' she said in a whispering voice — 'with the bread-knife or something — and say I did it as like as not — and say I'm mad. He tells everyone I'm mad, and when he's killed you that's what he'll say — "My wife done it." And they'll take me away and lock me up — because he'll say I'm mad.'

Hilary's heart banged against her side. Was it true? Was it? *Was* it? She said, very slow, and afraid, and like a child,

'Are you mad, Mrs. Mercer?'

The woman broke into a flood of tears.

'I'm not, I'm not! Not without he sends me mad with all his wickedness! Oh, miss, I wish I was dead — I wish I was dead!'

Hilary stopped feeling afraid. She managed to pat the heaving shoulder, and felt it pitifully sharp and thin.

'Mrs. Mercer, do stop crying. If you said what wasn't true at the trial — and I think you did, because I know Geoff never killed anyone, I really know it — if you did a wicked thing like that, don't you see your only chance is to tell the truth now and put it right? I don't wonder you feel like that about hell, with Geoff in prison and Marion so unhappy. But just think how awful it would have been for you if he'd been hanged and there wasn't anything you could do that would bring him back and put things right again. Doesn't that make you feel a bit better? Because you can put it right now. You don't want to go on being miserable like this — do you?'

Mrs. Mercer wrenched sharply away.

'I don't know what you're talking about!' she said. 'You get along out of here, or something'll happen!'

The tears stung Hilary's eyes. She had thought — she had been sure — the wildest hopes had dazzled her — and then suddenly everything was gone.

Mrs. Mercer had retreated into the doorway. She stood there leaning against the jamb. There was a wretched triumph in her voice.

'You go back on to the road and turn to the left, and you'll get to Ledlington! Where's your bicycle?'

Hilary straightened herself. She was stiff from leaning over the sill.

'Smashed.' And then, 'They tried to kill me.'

Mrs. Mercer put up a hand, touched her lips, and let it fall again. The lips parted and said,

'Who?'

'Don't you know?' said Hilary with a little scorn in her voice.

Mrs. Mercer backed away from her into the kitchen. When she was clear of the door she thrust at it with her hands and with her knee. The door fell to with a clap. Hilary was alone in the foggy dark.

She felt her way back round the house and out at the gate. Then she followed the ruts again.

CHAPTER TWENTY-ONE

Marion Grey was showing a dress called Moonlight. There was very little of it, but what there was was quite well named. The time was five o'clock in the afternoon. Harriet St. Just's showroom was full of women, some of whom had come there to amuse themselves and not to buy. Most of them called her Harry, or darling. She charged incredible prices for her clothes, and had contrived a quite astonishing success in the three years of her venture. She and Marion had been at school together, but she recognised no friendships during business hours. From ten to six Marion was simply Vania, and one of the best mannequins in London.

A dark, stooping woman, lined and haggard, called across half a dozen people.

'Harry, that's divine! I'll have it just as it is. Ask her to turn round and let me see the back again.'

Marion turned slowly, gracefully, looked over a shadowy shoulder, and held the pose. Her dark hair was knotted on her neck. She was made up to a smooth, even pallor. The shadows under her eyes made them look unnaturally large, unnaturally dark. She did not look as if she were really there at all. The dress followed the lovely lines of her figure, softening them like a mist.

Harriet St. Just said, 'That will do. You can show the black velvet next.'

Marion went out trailing her blue-grey moonlight. A girl called Celia who had been showing a bright green sports suit giggled as the showroom door closed behind them.

'Old Katie's got a nerve! "I'll have that"!' She mimicked the dark woman's voice. 'Gosh — what a hag she'll look in it! I call it a shame — a lovely dress like that!'

Marion said nothing. With the skill of long practice she was slipping the dress off over her head. She managed it without ruffling a single hair. Then she took down a black velvet dress with a matching cloak and began to put it on.

A short, fair woman with thick fluffy eyebrows put her head round the door.

'Someone wants you on the 'phone, Vania.'

Celia giggled again.

'Well, I wouldn't be you if old Harry gets to know about it! In the middle of a dress show! I say, Flora, have I really got to show that ghastly pink rag? It's not my style a bit. I wouldn't be seen dead in it in the Tottenham Court Road — and I can't say fairer than that.'

'You just hurry!' said Flora and shut the door on her.

Marion lifted the receiver from the office telephone. Flora ought to have said she was engaged. She couldn't imagine who could possibly be ringing her up here. They had no business to do it. Flora was much too good-natured — a sort of cousin of Harriet's who did about six people's work and was never out of temper, but she couldn't say no. She put the receiver to her ear, and heard a man's voice say rather faintly,

'Mrs. Grey?'

'Yes.'

The black velvet was slipping from her shoulder. She shifted her hand and pulled it up.

'Marion, is that you?' And all at once she knew who was speaking. Her face changed. She said in a low, hard voice,

'Who are you? Who is speaking?' But she knew very well.

'Bertie Everton,' said the voice. 'Look here, don't ring off — it's important.'

'I've nothing to say to you.'

'I know, I know — you feel like that. It's my misfortune. I wouldn't trouble you, but it's something about Geoffrey I thought you ought to know. Just a chance, but there it is. I thought I'd tell you.'

She leaned with her free hand on Harriet's writing-table, leaned hard, and said,

'I can't see you. If you've anything — to say — you can see my solicitor.' Her lips were so stiff that they shaped the words with difficulty. After a confused moment she wondered whether they had shaped them at all, because he was saying,

'Then I'll call for you at six.'

That broke the stiffness anyway. She said with a rush of anger,

'You can't come here — you must know that.'

'Then I'll be at your flat at half past six. You'll be home by then?'

'I can't see you. There's a dress show. I shall be late.'

'I'll wait,' said Bertie Everton, and with a click the line was dead.

Marion went back to show the black velvet gown, which was called Lucrezia Borgia. It had a stiff full skirt and a tight bodice embroidered with pearls after the Renaissance fashion. The heavy sleeves were slashed from shoulder to wrist over deep-toned ivory satin. She saw herself in a mirror as she opened the showroom door, but it was not the dress she saw reflected there, it was the anger in her eyes.

The dress had a great success. It was bought by a wispy fair-haired woman who sniffed and dabbed continually the tip of her nose with a small square of magenta chiffon. She was somebody's friend from the country, and if she fancied herself as Lucrezia Borgia, it was nobody's business but her own.

CHAPTER TWENTY-TWO

Hilary reached the outskirts of Ledlington at a little after half past six. The first street-lamp almost brought tears into her eyes, she was so glad to see it. When you have been wandering in one of those dark places of the earth which are full of cruelty, and when you have only just escaped being murdered there, omnibuses, and trams, and gas-lamps, and crowds of people really do seem almost too good to be true.

The crowds of people looked oddly at Hilary. It didn't occur to her at first that they were looking oddly, because she was so rapturously pleased to see them, but after she had got over the first of that the oddness began to soak in, and she woke up with a start to realise that she had been slithering about on wet roads and scrambling through hedges, and that she was probably looking like a last year's scarecrow. She gazed about her, and beheld on the other side of the road the sign of The Magpie and Parrot. The sign was a very pleasant one. The magpie and the parrot sat side by side upon a golden perch. The magpie was very black and very white, and the parrot was very green. They advertise one of Ledlington's most respected hotels, but nobody knows how it got its name.

Hilary crossed the road, mounted half a dozen steps, and entered such a dark passage that she was instantly filled with confidence. It might appear gloomy later on when she had washed her face, but at the moment it was very comfortable. She told the pleasant elderly woman at the desk that she had had a bicycle accident, and immediately everyone in the hotel began to be kind and helpful. It was very nice of them, because really when Hilary saw herself in the glass she looked the most disreputable object it is possible to imagine. All one side of her face was plastered with mud. She remembered the grit of the road under her cheek. She had lost her hat — she didn't remember anything about that — and the mud had got into her hair. There was a long scratch running back across her temple, and another fairly deep one on her chin. They had bled a good deal, and the blood had run into the mud. Her coat was torn, and her skirt was torn, and her hands were torn.

'Golly — what a mess!' she said, and proceeded to get it off.

There was lovely hot water, and lots of soap, and a large rough towel, and a little soft one produced by a very kind chambermaid — 'because it'll be soft on those scratches, miss.' With these and a large bathroom to splash round in she made a good job of getting the mud off, whilst the chambermaid put in some first aid on the ripped-up coat. They brought her tea which was quite terribly good (the Magpie and Parrot pays six shillings a pound for its tea), and a time-table which was not so good, because the minute she began to look up trains it came over her that there wasn't anything in the world that would get her into one of those trains with the prospect of travelling up to London by herself tonight. It wasn't any use arguing or calling herself a coward. Her courage had run out and she simply couldn't do it. Any carriage she got into would either be empty to start with, or it would go empty on her at the very first stop. And then one of *them* would get in, and there would be an accident on the line, and an end of Hilary Carew. Because if they had wanted to kill her an hour ago on the Ledlington road, nothing had happened since to make them change their minds. Contrariwise, as Humpty Dumpty says. And if they wanted to kill her, they would certainly watch the station, because they would expect her to catch a train, and it would occur to them as it did to her that very few people would be taking the London train on a night like this. Nobody would if they weren't obliged to. And that was the trouble — Hilary was obliged to. There was Marion for one thing, and there was the money question for another. Aunt Arabella's ring had produced a fiver. Out of that, getting here and back would account for about twelve bob. She had left two pounds on deposit for the bicycle, and she would have to go and tell the shock-headed boy that it was all smashed up and pay whatever they valued it at. She couldn't possibly risk an hotel bill on the top of that. What she could do, and what she immediately made up her mind to do, was to ring up Henry.

There was a sort of shiny office stool in the telephone-box. It was very slippery and uncomfortable, but it was better than nothing. As Hilary sat on it and waited for her call, it came over her that it wasn't any good quarrelling with Henry — it didn't really seem to make any difference. They had a sensational Row and broke off their engagement, and the first minute Mrs. Mercer wept at her and Mercer followed her in the street she could no more help making a bee line for Henry than she could help breathing. Well, then they had a second row, and Henry forbade her to go hunting the Mercers, and she had done it, and they hadn't spoken for a week. Yet the minute people tried to murder her and she was frightened, here she was, ringing him up and quite sure that he would come and fetch her. He would probably say 'I told you so', and they were practically certain to quarrel again. They would probably quarrel all the way back to town. The prospect was a *most* comforting one. How nice, how safe, how exhilarating to have Henry to quarrel with in that railway carriage instead of being murdered by a person or persons unknown.

The bell went ping, and as she snatched up the receiver, Henry said 'Hullo!'

'Hullo!' said Hilary brightly.

'Who is it?'

'Don't be ridiculous!'

'Oh, it's you?'

'Idiot!' said Hilary in a soft insinuating voice.

Henry set himself to disguise his reactions. He supposed Hilary wanted something or she wouldn't be ringing him up. There was satisfaction in the thought that she couldn't get on without him, but he wasn't giving anything away. He had a dark suspicion that she used that voice because she knew it did things to his feelings. Like poking up the tiger with a sugar-stick.

He said, 'What do you want?' in the tone of one who has been rung up by a boring aunt.

'You,' said Hilary, nearly forty miles away. She said it so softly that it only just reached him, and he wasn't sure whether the little wobble in the middle was a laughing wobble or a crying one.

If she was really — but suppose she wasn't —

He said, 'Hilary —' and she blinked back some tears which she hadn't expected, and said in a breathless kind of way,

'Henry — will you come and fetch me — *please?*'

'Hilary — what's the matter? Is anything the matter? I wish you'd speak up. I can't hear a word you say. You're not crying, are you? Where *are* you?'

'L-l-ledlington.'

'You sound as if you were crying. Are you crying?'

'I th-think so.'

'You must know.'

A bright female voice said, 'Thrrree minutes," to which Henry, regardless of the fact that it wasn't his call, replied with a firm demand for another three. After which he said,

'Hullo!' and, 'Are you there?' And then, 'Tell me what's the matter with you at once!'

Hilary steadied her voice. She had only meant to let it thrill a little at Henry, but it had let her down and she was really crying now, she couldn't think why.

'Henry, please come. I want you — badly. I can't tell you on the telephone. I'm at the Magpie and Parrot at Ledlington. I've smashed a bicycle, and I don't think I've got enough money to pay for it.'

'Are you hurt?'

He said that much too quickly. Why should she be hurt? But she was crying. She wouldn't cry because she was hurt. He was horribly frightened, and angry with Hilary because she was frightening him. Little fool! Little damned darling fool!

He heard her say, 'No — only scratched,' and then, 'You can't drive — it's too foggy. Will you ring Marion up and tell her you're fetching me? You needn't say where I am.'

The girl at the exchange said 'Six minutes.' Hilary said, 'Golly!' And Henry said, 'Another six,' and Hilary giggled, and Captain Henry Cunningham blushed because now he really had given himself away.

'There's a train at seven-forty,' said Hilary sweetly. 'We don't want any more minutes — it's much too expensive. You hurry up and catch that train, darling.'

The telephone bell tinkled and the line went dead.

CHAPTER TWENTY-THREE

There was no one but Hilary in the lounge of the Magpie and Parrot when Henry walked in about an hour and a half later. He picked her up and kissed her as if they had never broken off their engagement, and Hilary kissed him back as she had never done while they were still engaged. It was still only a very little while since the sharpest edge of her despair had been, 'I shall never see Henry again.'

Henry completely forgot all the things he had been going to say. He kissed her, and went on kissing her, and at intervals he asked her if she was sure she wasn't hurt.

'If I was — would you mind?'

'Don't say things like that!'

She burrowed her nose into his neck.

'Why should you, darling? I mean we're not engaged any more. You wouldn't have had to wear a black tie if I'd been murdered.'

Henry's arms went all stiff and hard. It was most uncomfortable.

'You're not to say things like that!'

'Why, darling?'

'I don't like it.' He held her tight and kissed her hard.

Nice to have Henry's arms round her. Nice to be kissed.

All of a sudden he wasn't kissing her any more. He was making a plan.

'Look here, we've got to catch the nine-fifty. Have you had any food?'

'No — I waited for you. I thought it would be nice if you paid for it.'

'Then we must eat, and you can tell me what you've been doing. You're sure you're not hurt?'

'Mortally wounded, but I'm being brave about it.'

Henry frowned at the scratches.

'I can't think what you've been doing to yourself,' he said, and got a mournful glance.

'My fatal beauty is wrecked! What a good thing we're disengaged, because I should simply have to be noble and break it off if we weren't.'

'No fishing!' said Henry, and marched her off to the dining-room, where the head waiter informed them that the nine-fifty had been nine-forty-five since the first of October, and though of course it might be late on account of the fog, he wouldn't advise them to chance it. He recommended soup and a cold veal and ham pie, and he thought they had better have a taxi from Mr. Whittington's garage, and if they wished him to do so, he would get the hall porter to ring up about it.

It didn't seem to be the moment for explanations. The soup was good, the veal and ham pie was very good, and the coffee was delicious. The head waiter hovered like a ministering angel. Hilary thought how nice it would be if she and Henry were here on their honeymoon instead of escaping from murderers. And then something made her blush, and she looked up and met Henry's eye and blushed more brightly still.

They caught their train, and had a carriage to themselves — an empty train and an empty carriage, but not frightening any more, because Henry was there too. As the engine started and their carriage banged clanking into the buffers of the one in front of it, Henry said,

'Now, Hilary — what have you been up to? You'd better get it off your chest.'

Hilary got it off her chest. They were facing one another in two corner seats. She could see exactly how

Henry was taking it, and he could see the scratch on her chin, and the scratch on her forehead, and just how little colour there was in her cheeks.

'You see, darling, I simply *had* to find Mrs. Mercer, so it's no good going over that part of it, because we're sure to quarrel, and if we once start quarrelling, I shan't ever get on with telling you about the people who tried to murder me.'

'Hilary — stop! What are you saying?'

She gave a little grave nod.

'It's true. I want to tell you about it.' Then, suddenly off at a tangent, 'I say, I do hope the young man I hired the bicycle from doesn't think I've embezzled it, because he's rather a lamb, and I shouldn't like him to think I was an embezzler.'

'He won't. The hotel is going to tell him to send in his bill. You get on with telling me what happened.'

Hilary shivered.

'It was perfectly beastly,' she said — 'like the stickiest kind of nightmare. I kept on hoping I'd wake up, but I didn't. You see, I found out that the Mercers had been in Ledlington and their landlady hoofed them out because Mrs. Mercer screamed in the night. And the girl in the milk-shop said she thought they'd moved into a cottage on the Ledstow road, so first I went to the house-agents to find out about cottages, and then I did a gloomy trek right out to Ledstow, forcing my way into cottages as I went. And everyone was very nice, only none of them was Mrs. Mercer. By the time I got to Ledstow I felt as if I had been hunting needles in bundles of hay for years, and it was tea-time. So I had tea at the village pub, and when I opened the door to get my bill, there was Mercer walking down the passage like a grimly ghost.'

'Hilary!' Henry's tone was very unbelieving.

'Word of honour, darling. Well, of course, I shot back into the room, and rang, and paid my bill and fled. But just as I was opening the outside door, there he was coming back again — *and I think he saw me.*'

'Why?' said Henry.

'Because of what happened afterwards.'

'What did happen?'

'Well, it was practically pitch-dark, and there were wallops of fog lying about loose all over the place, and whenever I came to one I had to get off and walk, so I wasn't getting on very fast. And every time I had to get off I got a most horrid nightmare kind of feeling that *something* was coming after me, and that it was going to catch me up.'

There was a pause.

Henry said, 'Nonsense!' in a rough, reassuring way, and Hilary said in rather a wavering voice,

'Henry — would you mind — if I held your hand — because — '

Henry pulled her across the carriage on to his knees, put both arms round her, and rocked her as if she was a baby.

'First — class — prize — silly — little — fool!'

'Um — ' said Hilary, a good deal comforted.

'Now you can go on,' said Henry.

She went on with her head against his shoulder.

'Wasn't nice. Was horrid. Like being lost dog in a bad dream. And just when it got to its worst a car came blinding out of the fog and I jumped for the side of the road. Henry, I only just jumped in time. They weren't coming so fast at first, and I thought I'd try and follow them into Ledlington, and then I think they saw me, and they tried to run me down.'

'Nonsense!' said Henry with his arms round her.

'No,' said Hilary, in a soft, sighing voice.

'They couldn't!'

'They did. And I jumped, and hit my head, and I must have passed out, because the next thing I knew they were carrying me. And one of them said I was only stunned. And then he said, "Quick now, and we'll make a job of it!" And then, Henry — then — they put me down in the road and got back into the car and got ready to drive it over me.'

Henry stopped rocking. His arms tightened about her. Behind the jab she had just given to his nerves his mind said, 'You know this can't possibly be true. She got run down in the fog and hit her head. The rest of it isn't anything at all — she dreamt it.'

She turned her head on his shoulder. By craning backwards she could see his profile with the ceiling light behind it. It was one of those strong, silent profiles. She gave a little gentle sigh and said,

'You're not believing me.'

It was really very difficult for Henry. The last thing on earth he wanted was to start another quarrel, but he had by nature the gift which Thomas the Rhymer so indignantly refused at the hands of the Queen of Elfland — the tongue that can never lie.

' "My tongue is mine ain," True Thomas said,
    A gudely gift ye wad gie to me!
I neither dout to buy nor sell,
    At fair or tryst where I may be.

' "I dout neither speak to prince or peer,
    Nor ask of grace from fair ladye." '

In fact, a most uncomfortable and embarrassing gift. It wasn't Henry's fault — he hadn't asked for it. He often found it extremely inconvenient, especially in his dealings with women. In reply to Hilary's sigh and 'You're not believing me,' he could do no better with his tongue than to make it keep silence.

Hilary sighed again. Then she put her head back on his shoulder.

'That means you're not. I don't know why you want to marry me if you don't believe a word I say.'

Henry kissed her, which was quite easy and committed him to nothing. When she could speak again she said, 'I shouldn't kiss someone I thought was a liar, but I suppose men are different. I'm too tired to quarrel about it.'

'I don't think you're a liar.'

'Well, what do you think?'

'I think you had concussion. You say you knocked your head. I think the rest of it was a sort of dream. You have them when you're concussed.'

'I don't! Henry, you've got a very stubborn disposition. I think I'm behaving exactly like Patient Griselda not to quarrel. I'm admiring myself a lot for it, so I hope you are too. I suppose it's no good going on telling you what happened — if you're not going to believe it, I mean.'

Henry shook her a little. He also said, 'Go on.'

She went on in a small meek voice with her lips quite close to his ear.

'Of course if you say it was only a dream, it must have been one — Henry the Never Wrong and all that sort of thing. Well, in this perfectly horrid dream they did put me down in the road and got ready to run me over. I was all muzzy, and I'd have let them do it, only when they banged the door of the car something went click like when you put the electric light on, and I got my head up and saw the car coming for me, and I did a sort of slither and got off on to the grass and through the scratchiest hedge in England. And after that there was a sort of hollow with bushes, and I hid there. And when they couldn't find me they got into the car again and went away. And I was afraid to go back on to the road because of not knowing it was a dream and being afraid of them waiting there to grab me, so I walked brightly up a lot of ruts till I came to a gate. And then I walked round a cottage till I came to a scullery window, and there was Mrs. Mercer making tea.'

Henry held her away so that he could look at her.

'Hilary — are you making this up?'

He got a mournful shake of the head.

'I'm not nearly clever enough. And, oh, Henry, it was the most crashing disappointment, because first she was angry and then she began to say things like she did in the train.'

'What sort of things?'

'Well, she said, "Go! Go, while you can!" and that she didn't dare let me in. She said *he*'d cut her heart out — and of course she meant Mercer. And the way she looked when she said it made me feel perfectly sick. I shouldn't feel frightfully safe myself in a lonely cottage with Mercer if he thought I was giving the show away, and that's what she was on the edge of doing. You know she told me in the train that she tried to see Marion when the trial was going on. Well, I pressed her about that, and she looked as if she was going to flop, and said, "It's too late." I grabbed hold of her wrist — we were talking across the scullery sink — and she began to cry, and said she couldn't say her prayers, and why hadn't she told Marion, only if she had Mercer would have killed her, and then she'd have gone to hell. So I swore I wouldn't go until she told me, and I asked her if she wanted Mercer to find me there when he got back. And then she went all flesh-creeping and said he'd kill me — with the bread-knife — and say she'd done it, and then they'd take her away and lock her up, because he'd make them believe she was mad.'

'She must be mad. What's the good of believing what a mad woman says?'

Hilary gave a faint, shaky laugh.

'Is she mad in my dream, or mad really? I'm ónly telling you a dream, you know — at least you said it was only a dream. And the way I dreamt it she wasn't mad, she was just horribly frightened — and if it's my own dream,

I ought to know, oughtn't I? Any how, I asked her bang out.'

'You asked her *what*?'

'I asked her if she was mad — just like that. I said, "Are you mad, Mrs. Mercer?" And she said, "Not without he sends me mad with his wickedness." And then she cried buckets, and wished she was dead. And just when she'd got to the point when I thought she was going to tell me what she'd got on her mind, she shut right up like a clam and pulled her hand away from me and ran into the kitchen and banged the door. And I don't know how many miles I walked into Ledlington after that, but when I saw the first lamp-post I felt as if I could have kissed its boots.'

Henry said nothing. He was wondering how much of Hilary's story was concussion, and how much was true. The way he straightened it out in his own mind she had taken a toss off her bicycle and had wandered away across the fields. If she had really seen Mrs. Mercer, the woman had said some very odd things. But had she seen her, or had she dreamed the whole thing? He had begun by being sure that she had, but his conviction had begun to weaken. Hilary did not appear to be at all concussed. She didn't look muzzy, or excited or dazed, she just looked tired. And the very fact that she didn't flare up and go into a rage in defence of her story did more to shake him than anything else could have done. Hilary went into rages rather easily, but when it came to this story of hers she had just stuck to it with a rather convincing calm.

She said suddenly, close to his ear, 'Do you still think I'm telling lies?'

There wasn't a spark of resentment in her voice. It was engagingly soft. Henry liked soft-voiced women. He was a good deal shaken and melted. He said,

'Hilary —'

'Yes, darling?'

'What I mean to say is — well, it isn't easy to put it the way I want to, but — look here, are you really sure that all this happened?'

'Cross my heart!'

'You're sure you didn't dream it?'

'Quite, quite, quite sure. Henry, I didn't really — it all *happened*.'

'Well then, suppose it happened — I don't say whether it did or it didn't, but suppose it did.'

'What do you want to suppose?'

'I want to go back to the smash. You say there were two men in the car that knocked you over?'

'There were two men in the car that ran me down,' said Hilary firmly.

'Did you see them?'

'No, I didn't.'

'Then how do you know there were two men?'

Hilary put out the tip of her tongue and drew it back again.

'Because they carried me. One of them had me by the shoulders, and the other one by the knees. Besides — one of them spoke — I told you. He said, "Be quick — we'll make a job of it!" And he wasn't talking to *me*.'

'Did you know his voice?'

Hilary said 'No' with heartfelt regret. It would have been so nice and easy if it had been Mercer's voice and she could have sworn to it. But it wasn't, and she couldn't, so she had to say so. As a matter of fact this did her good with Henry, because if she had dreamed the whole thing she would probably have tacked the voice on to Mercer.

He frowned and said, 'You only heard one man speak?'

'That's all. But there were two of them carrying me, and they dumped me face downwards in the road and got into the car again to run me over.'

Henry stiffened perceptibly. A beastly dream if it was a dream. And if it wasn't . . . He felt as if he was walking in the dark upon a road which might at any moment collapse. A preliminary tremor stirred the very ground upon which his foot rested, and at the next step he might become aware of an opening gulf. If Hilary's life had really been attempted, there must be some strong motive behind the attempt. If the attempt had failed, the motive remained. If it was strong enough to impel murder once, would it not be strong enough again? He wished with all his heart he could be sure that it was all a dream.

He looked down at the stains on the front of Hilary's dress and coat. She said that they had put her down on her face in the road. Her jumper was stained right up to the throat. He knew what he wanted to believe, but there is no help in believing what isn't true. He said,

'Who do you think the two men were? Have you any idea?'

'Yes, of course I have. I think one of them was Mercer.'

'But not the one you heard speak?'

'No, not that one.'

'Mercer wouldn't have a car.'

He was arguing as if the thing was true instead of being fantastic.

'Oh no — the car belonged to the other man. It was a big car.' She gave a little shudder as she remembered it rushing down upon her. Then she said in a defiant voice, 'It was Bertie Everton's car. I'm sure it was.'

'What makes you say that? What have you got to go on?'

'Nothing — I'm just sure. And he did come round to the shop on purpose to tell you Mrs. Mercer was mad after she'd talked to me in the train.'

Henry felt a most overwhelming relief. He had very nearly swung over to believing in Hilary's villains, but thank goodness he had been pulled up in time. The whole thing was fantastic. On this point at least he could bring proof.

'Look here, Hilary, you mustn't go saying things like that — you'll be getting yourself into trouble. And you're wrong — it couldn't have been Bertie Everton because he was in London.'

'Oh — did you see him?'

'No, but Marion did.'

'*What?*'

'Marion saw him. You know you told me to ring her up and say I was bringing you home. Well, he'd just left her then. She was in a white rage about it. He rang her up at her shop. She only just managed to choke him off coming there, I gather, and when she got back to the flat he was waiting for her. So you see — you mayn't like Bertie Everton, but he didn't try and run you down. He's got a perfectly good alibi.'

Hilary lifted her head with a jerk.

'I think Bertie Everton has too many alibis,' she said.

CHAPTER TWENTY-FOUR

Marion was still in a cold rage when they arrived at the flat. A hot anger would have been so much easier to meet. When you love someone and they look at you as if they had never seen you before and never want to see you again, it does rather take the edge off coming home.

Hilary subsided on to the floor in front of the fire. There was a chair to lean against. She folded her arms on the seat and pillowed her head upon them. Henry, in the open doorway, was very well aware that he hadn't been asked to come in, and that he was not expected to stay.

Marion had walked to the window. As she turned, Henry came in and shut the door. With a lift of her eyebrows, she said,

'I think Hilary ought to go to bed.'

Hilary said nothing. Henry said,

'I think you'd better hear what she's got to say first. It concerns you — quite a lot.'

'Not tonight. I've had one visitor already, and I've run out of polite conversation.'

'So I gather.'

'Then will you please go, Henry.'

'Not just now.'

Without lifting her head Hilary spoke in a muffled voice.

'Please, Marion.'

Marion Grey took no notice.

'I really want you to go,' she said.

Henry leaned against the door. He had his hat in his hand.

'Just a minute, Marion. And I think you'd better listen, because — well, I think you had better. Hilary's had a very narrow escape.'

She took him up there and echoed the word.

'*Escape*. From what?'

'Being murdered,' said Hilary in a mournful, muffled tone.

Marion turned her head sharply.

'What are you talking about?'

'Being murdered. I nearly was. Henry can tell you — I'm too tired.'

Marion looked from one to the other. She saw Henry's brows drawn together, frowning. She saw the look in his eyes as they rested on Hilary's untidy curls. Something melted in her. She let herself down into a chair and said,

'All right, Henry, say your piece.'

Henry said it. The odd thing was that repeating Hilary's story gave him the feeling that it was true. He continued to assert that he was not convinced, but as he told her tale he found himself endeavouring to convince Marion, and in the end he didn't know whether he had convinced her or not. He simply didn't know. She was leaning her head on her hand. Her eyes were screened. Her gaze was turned inward upon her own guarded thoughts.

'The heart knoweth its own bitterness, and a stranger intermeddleth not with its grief.' She was not angry now, but she was still cold. There was no warmth in her. When he had finished she sat silent, and when the silence had gone on too long Henry broke it bluntly.

'You've had Bertie Everton here. Hilary thinks he was one of the men who tried to do her in. It's quite unreasonable, but she does think so — there you are. I think you've got to tell her what time he rang you up, and when he rolled up here, and how long he stayed. Hilary seems to think it's rather compromising to have an alibi, but the fellow can't have been in two places at once.'

'I didn't say he could,' said Hilary in a buried voice. Then she lifted her head about an inch. 'An alibi isn't being in two places at once — it's doing a crime in one place and pretending you were somewhere else.'

Henry burst out laughing.

'When did you make that up?'

'Just now,' said Hilary, and dropped her head again.

Marion said, without looking at either of them,

'He rang me up about five o'clock. I was showing some models which had just come in. We sold three of them. It was just after five — I heard the clock strike as I came out of the showroom.'

'Did he say where he was calling you from?'

'No. He must have been in town though, because he

178

suggested coming round to Harriet's, and when I said he couldn't possibly, he said he'd go to the flat and wait for me. He was here when I got back.'

'And what time would that be?'

'Some time after seven. I told him I should be late — I thought it might put him off.'

'What did he want?' said Hilary to the chair.

Marion stiffened. Her hand dropped. Her eyes blazed.

'I don't know how he dared to come here and talk about Geoff!'

'What did he say?' said Hilary quickly.

'Nothing. I don't know why he came. He had some rambling story about having met someone who had seen Geoff get off the bus the evening James was shot, but he didn't seem to know who the man was, and it didn't seem to add anything to the evidence. Anyhow, it couldn't do any good now. I don't know why he came.'

'I do.' Hilary sat up and pushed back her hair. 'He did it to have an alibi. If he could get you to believe that he was in London all the afternoon, well then he couldn't be murdering me on the Ledstow road — could he?' Her hair stood up in little fluffy curls. Her no-coloured eyes were as bright as a tomtit's.

'But, my blessed darling child!' said Henry. He laughed. 'You're a bit groggy about alibis tonight. Have you any idea what time you had your smash?'

She considered.

'Well, I hadn't got a watch, and it wouldn't have been any good if I had because of the fog and being dark, but I had tea at the pub in Ledstow because it was tea-time, and it wasn't dark then — only foggy and Novemberish. And I suppose I was there about half an hour, so should think it was about five when I saw Mercer and bolted. And after that I don't know how long I was. It seemed ages, because I had to keep getting off my bicycle — the fog was simply lying about in lumps. It's very difficult to say, but I should think the smash was somewhere getting on for half past five.'

'Well, then, with the worst will in the world, it couldn't have been Bertie Everton who ran you down if he was in London telephoning to Marion at five o'clock.'

Hilary wrinkled her nose.

'*If*,' she said.

'Well, Marion says it was five o'clock.'

Marion nodded.

'I heard the clock strike.'

'I'm sure he telephoned at five o'clock,' said Hilary. 'He meant to — it was part of his alibi. He knew very well that Marion wouldn't let him come round to Harriet's, and he could telephone from Ledstow or from an A.A. box and she'd never think for a minute that he wasn't ringing up from his rooms in town. That's how you do alibis if you're a criminal. I should have been very good at it.'

'And suppose she had said, "All right, come along"?'

'She wouldn't. Marion never lets anyone go anywhere near Harriet's. She'd get the sack if she did. He could bank on that.'

Marion looked hard at her.

'Well, then what happened? This is your story. What happened next?'

'Well, he must have picked up Mercer at the pub. And after they'd tried to kill me and I'd got away, I think he just stamped on the gas like mad, because he was bound to get back to London and finish up his alibi. I expect he shed Mercer in Ledlington, and then he either just got a train by the skin of his teeth, or else drove on like fury up the London road. I looked up trains while I was waiting for Henry, and there's a five-forty from Ledlington that gets in at seven. It's a non-stop theatre train. He could have caught that, and it would account for their not going on looking for me any longer than they did. You see, he'd simply got to have that alibi if I escaped. But I don't really think he went by train, because he wouldn't want to leave his car in a Ledlington garage and have someone remembering about it afterwards.'

'An hour and a half from Ledlington would be pretty good going in a fog,' said Henry. 'I don't believe it can be done.'

Hilary tossed back her hair.

'You wait till you've tried to murder someone and you've *got* to have an alibi to save you, and then you just see if you can't break a record or two. Even people who aren't making alibis go blinding along in a fog — you know they do.'

Marion spoke again.

'It must have been quite ten past seven before I got back. Mrs. Lestrange and Lady Dolling didn't go away until twenty past six, and then we'd all the models to put away, and Harriet wanted to tell me about her brother's engagement, and there was the fog. It never takes me less than half an hour to get back.' She looked at Henry. 'What time was it when you rang me up?'

'Oh, it was after half past seven. I was ringing up from the station just before my train went.'

'There!' said Hilary, 'he'd have had plenty of time. I told you so. And I think' — she sat bolt upright and clasped her knees — 'I think we ought to get a detective on to that other alibi of his, because I'm quite sure he made that up too, and if he did, a really clever detective would be able to find him out. Marion —'

'No,' said Marion.

Hilary scrambled up, ran across, and caught her by the hand.

'Don't say no, darling — don't don't, *don't*! It couldn't do any harm. It couldn't hurt Geoff. Marion, don't say no! I know you can't bear to have it all raked up — I know exactly how you feel — but won't you let Henry have the file and go through it with someone? Geoff didn't do it. There's some devil at the back of this who has made it look as if he did, but he didn't — I *know* he didn't.'

Marion pushed her away and got up. Without a look or an answer she went to the door, opened it, and went out. It closed behind her. They heard her bedroom door close too.

Hilary ran to the chest, flung up the lid and came running back with the file in her outstretched hands.

'Here it is! Take it and fly! Quick — before she comes back and says you're not to!'

CHAPTER TWENTY-FIVE

Hilary woke up in the dark. One minute she was very fast asleep, plunged in the drowning depths where no dreams come, and the next minute she was clear awake and a little frightened, with the night air coming in smoky and cold through the open window. The curtain was pulled right back, but the room was dark. There was a middle-of-the-night sort of feeling. But if it was still the middle of the night, she could only have been asleep for a very little time, because it was well after midnight when she got into bed.

Something had waked her, she didn't know what. Something had frightened her awake. She had come up with a rush out of the deep places of her sleep, and she had waked afraid. But she didn't know what she was afraid of.

She got out of bed, went softly to the door, and opened

it. The sitting-room door was open too. The light shone through it into the hall, and in the lighted room Marion was talking to someone in a low, desperate voice. Hilary heard her say,

'Why don't you tell me you did it? I'd rather know.'

And with that she went back and sat on the edge of her bed, and didn't know what to do next. Marion — at this hour! Who was she talking to? Who could she possibly be talking to? It just didn't fit in — it wasn't true — Marion wouldn't. It wasn't any good your eyes and ears telling you the sort of things you simply couldn't believe.

Well, if you didn't believe this, what did you do next?

Hilary got up, put on her dressing-gown, and crossed the hall. The sitting-room door stood open about half-way. Without touching it or pushing it she stood by the left-hand jamb and looked into the room.

There was no one there but Marion Grey. She was in her nightgown. Its pale green colour made her look even paler than she was. Her hair hung loose — fine, waving, black hair that touched her shoulders and then turned up in something which was not quite a curl. In this soft frame her face had a young, tormented look. Its mask of indifference and pride was down. Her eyes brimmed with tears. Her lips were soft. They trembled. She was kneeling on the hearth, her hands spread out to the fire that had died an hour ago.

Hilary felt as if her heart would break with pity and relief.

She said, 'Darling — ' just under her breath, and Marion said in a low voice of pain,

'You don't tell me. I could bear it if I knew — if I knew why. There must have been a reason — you wouldn't have done it without a reason. Geoff, you wouldn't! Geoff — Geoff'

Hilary caught her breath. Marion wasn't talking to

her, she was talking to Geoff. And Geoff was in Dartmoor.

She began to plead with Geoffrey Grey whose body was in Dartmoor but whose visible image moved and spoke in her dream. She put up a hand as if to hold him.

'Geoff — Geoff — why don't you tell me? You see, I know. She told me — that daily woman. You didn't know about her. But she came back. She had dropped something in the study and she came back for it, and she heard you talking — quarrelling. And she heard what James said. She heard him say, "My own nephew!" and she heard the shot. So you see, I know. It won't make any difference if you tell me now — they won't hang you now. She won't tell — she promised she wouldn't tell. Geoff, don't you see that I've got to know? It's killing me!' She got up from her knees and began to walk in the room, to and fro, bare foot and silent, with the tears running down her face. She did not speak again, but once in a while she sighed.

Hilary did not know how to bear it. She didn't know what to do. That sighing breath was more piteous than any sob. She was afraid too of waking Marion, and she was afraid to let her go on dreaming this sorrowful dream.

And then Marion turned from walking up and down and came towards the door. Hilary had only just time to get out of the way. She would not have had time if Marion's hand, stretched out before her, had not gone to the switch. With a click the light went out. The bulb glowed for a moment and faded into darkness. Marion's fingers touched Hilary on the cheek — a cold, cold, icy touch which left her shivering.

Hilary stood quite still, and heard no sound at all. It was very frightening to be touched like that in the dark and hear no sound. It needed an effort to go back to her own room and put on the light. She could see then that Marion's door was ajar, but the crack showed no light there. She took a candle, pushed the door softly, and looked in. Marion was in bed with the clothes pulled round her and only her dark head showing against the pillow.

Hilary shut the door and went back to bed shaking with cold. As soon as she got warm she went to sleep, and as soon as she was asleep she began to dream. She dreamt that she was talking to Mrs. Mercer in a railway carriage, only instead of being an ordinary railway carriage it had a counter down one side of it. Mrs. Mercer stood behind the counter measuring something on one of those fixed yard measures which they have in draper's shops. Hilary stood on the other side of the counter and wondered what she was doing. She could see everything else in the dream quite plainly, but the stuff in Mrs. Mercer's hands kept slipping, and changing, and dazzling so that she couldn't see what it was, so she asked — and her own voice frightened her because it boomed like a bell — 'What are you measuring?' And Mrs. Mercer said, with the stuff slipping, and sliding, and shimmering between her hands, 'That's just my evidence, Miss Hilary Carew.'

In her dream Hilary said, 'Do you sell evidence? I didn't know it was allowed.' And Mrs. Mercer answered and said, 'I sold mine.' Then Hilary said, 'What did you sell it for?' And Mrs. Mercer said, 'For something I'd have given my soul to get.' And then she began to sob and cry, and to say, 'It wasn't worth it — it wasn't worth it, Miss Hilary Carew.' And all at once Alfred Mercer came along dressed like a ticket-collector, only somehow he was the shop-walker as well. And he took a breadknife out of his trouser pocket and said in a loud fierce voice, 'Goods once paid for cannot be returned.' And Hilary was so frightened about the bread-knife that she ran the whole way down the train and all up the Fulham Road. And just as she got to Henry's shop a car ran over her and she woke up.

CHAPTER TWENTY-SIX

Henry rang up at a quarter past nine, a time nicely calculated to ensure that Marion would have left the flat. Hilary stopped in the middle of making her bed, put the receiver to her ear, and stuck out her tongue at the mouthpiece.

'Hilary —' said Henry at the other end of the line.

'Thank goodness it's you!' said Hilary.

'Why shouldn't it be me? Who did you expect it to be?' Hilary giggled.

'Darling, you don't know how nice it was to hear your voice — I mean a man's voice. The telephone has been too, too exclusively female and completely incessant this morning.'

'What about?'

'First of all Aunt Emmeline's Eliza rang up to say she was in bed with a chill — Aunt Emmeline, not Eliza, she doesn't hold with chills — and she was selling at a stall for the Infant Bib Society, or something of that sort this afternoon — still Aunt Emmeline — Eliza doesn't hold with infants, or bibs, or bazaars —'

'Hilary, what are you talking about?'

'Darling, it was grim! Aunt Emmeline wanted me — *me*, Henry — to take her place — to go and help at a bazaar for Infant Bibs! I said to Eliza, "As woman to woman, would you do it?" And she coughed and said she

186

didn't hold with bazaars and well Miss Carew knew it, so I said "Nothing doing," and rang off. And about half a minute later the secretary of the Bib Society rang up and said Miss Carew had told her I was kindly taking her place, and about two minutes after that a girl with an earnest voice said that as we were going to work together at the basket stall — '

'Hilary, dry up! I want to talk to you.'

'I told them all there was nothing doing, but they didn't seem to take it in. People with the bazaar habit are like that, and once they get hold of you you never get out alive. I'd love to talk to you, darling. What did you particularly want to say?'

'I want you to come round at once to 15, Montague Mansions, West Leaham Street.'

'If it's a bazaar, I'll never speak to you again.'

'It's not. Don't be an ass! I'll meet you there. And you'd better take a taxi — I'll pay for it.'

Hilary was very pleasantly intrigued. It didn't very often run to taxis, and she liked them. She liked the way they whisked in and out of traffic and cut corners as if they didn't exist. She looked out of the window and found it a pleasant day — just enough sun to gild the fog, and just enough fog to give the bricks and mortar, and stone, and stucco the insubstantial glamour which Turner loved and painted. Nice to be going to meet Henry. Nice to be off on an adventure without knowing where she was going — because Montague Mansions was only an address to her, and not a place. She got quite a thrill out of thinking that if this was happening in a book and not in real life, the voice on the telephone would turn out not to be Henry's voice at all, and the minute she entered No. 15 she would be gagged, and drugged, and hypodermicked. She immediately made up her mind that she wasn't entering any house or any flat without Henry. She had always thought how unpleasant it would be to be gagged. So if Henry wasn't on the doorstep, there wasn't going to be anything doing here either. Better an Infant Bib bazaar than a Lair of Villains complete with drugs and lethal hypodermics. Besides, Henry had promised to pay the taxi.

Henry was on the doorstep. They went up in a lift to No. 15 and both talked all the time, because Henry was trying to explain Miss Maud Silver, and Hilary was telling him what she would have done if it had been a Den of Murderers.

'I didn't want to go to a woman, but Charles Moray says —'

'I'd absolutely made up my mind —'

'There's something about her that impresses you. She found out —'

'Suppose it hadn't been you —'

'That the Mercers weren't married —'

'But someone imitating your voice —'

'Until the day after James Everton's death.' The superior resonance of Henry's voice got through with this.

Hilary pinched him hard and said,

'*What?*'

'If you'd been listening instead of talking all the time —'

'Henry, I like that! You've never stopped — I haven't been able to get in a word!'

'Then why didn't you hear what I said?'

'I did.'

'Then why did you say "*What?*"'

Hilary extricated herself nimbly.

'Well, darling, what did you expect me to say? I mean — Mrs. *Mercer!* Say it again!'

'The Mercers weren't married till the day after James Everton's death.'

The lift had been stationary for some time. Hilary

opened the door and walked out on to the landing.

Mrs. Mercer — how incredible! Respectable, middle-aged Mrs. Mercer! There was something quite horrifying about it. She felt shocked and a little frightened. Her dream, which she had forgotten, came vividly up in her mind. It came up so vividly that it made Henry, and the lift-shaft, and the bare, cold landing outside Miss Silver's flat all seem rather unreal. She heard her own voice say in the dream, 'What did you sell it for?' And she heard Mrs. Mercer say, 'Something I'd have given my soul to get.' They were talking about Mrs. Mercer's evidence — the evidence which she had sold — and what she had sold it for —

Henry's hand fell on her shoulder, and she blinked up at him.

'What's the matter?'

'Nothing. I remembered something.'

He put his arm round her for a moment. Then he rang the bell and they went in.

Miss Silver sat at her desk with the file of the Everton Case open before her. An infant's pale blue coatee had been relegated to the edge of the table, and the ball of wool attached to it had fallen unnoticed on to the floor and rolled away. Hilary picked it up as she came in.

'Thank you,' said Miss Silver. 'Wool becomes so very easily soiled. If you would just spike it on one of the knitting-needles — thank you very much.'

She had not appeared to be looking at anything except the file. Now she lifted a slightly frowning gaze, inclined her head towards Hilary, and indicated a chair.

'This is Miss Carew? . . . Will you please sit down? Captain Cunningham has explained why I wish to see you?'

'No, he hasn't,' said Hilary. 'He just rang me up, and I came.' She contrived a reproachful look at Henry out of the corner of her eye, but it did not appear to get anywhere.

Miss Silver continued:

'Captain Cunningham rang me up at a very early hour. He seemed a good deal perturbed — ' she paused, coughed slightly, and added — 'about you, Miss Carew. He desired my advice without delay, and he informed me that he had in his possession the entire file of the Everton Case. I asked him to bring it round to me, and he did so. When he had told me about your experiences yesterday I suggested that he should ask you to join us. In the meanwhile I could run through the file and find out whether it contained any evidence with which I was not familiar. I have not, of course, had time to read all the documents. The accounts of the inquest and the trial are taken from the public press, and I am quite *au fait* with them. The statement made by the chambermaid at the Caledonian Hotel is new to me, and so is the statement of the Glasgow solicitor with regard to Mr. Francis Everton. They are both typed copies, and I imagine that the originals were obtained by the police. Do you know if that is so, Miss Carew?'

'No, I don't. I was abroad in July — I didn't come home until the inquest was over.'

Miss Silver said, 'I see. Captain Cunningham was abroad too, and he tells me that Mrs. Grey is exceedingly disinclined to answer questions.'

'She simply won't,' said Hilary.

Miss Silver primmed her lips.

'Decidedly foolish,' she said. 'Relatives almost invariably hamper investigation by an unwillingness to be frank. They are afraid of disclosing some point which will tell against the person in whom they are interested. Yet if Mr. Grey is really innocent, the more light that is thrown upon every point the better for his case. If Mrs. Grey is concealing something which she fears may tell against her husband — '

Henry struck in, frowning:

'We haven't any reason to suppose she's doing anything of the sort.'

But Miss Silver's small pale eyes were fixed not on him, but on Hilary.

'Miss Silver, why do you say that?'

'It is true, is it not? Why else should she refuse to answer questions — to aid in an investigation? She is afraid of what may be brought to light — something damaging — something she has knowledge of — something — Miss Carew, I think you know what it is.'

Henry looked with astonishment at Hilary, and saw the red distressed colour run up to the roots of her little brown curls. Her eyes swam with tears. She said in a startled voice, 'How did you know?'

Miss Silver looked down at the file again. She gave a deprecating cough.

'There is nothing wonderful about seeing what is in front of one. Will you tell me what Mrs. Grey is afraid of?'

'I don't see how I can.'

Miss Silver looked at her in a different way. She had the air of a kind aunt — of Aunt Emmeline when she was about to give you five pounds at Christmas. She said in a voice that was nice as well as prim.

'I am a great admirer of Lord Tennyson's. The *mot juste* — how often one comes across it in his writings. "Oh, trust me all in all, or not at all." I find I often have to quote that to my clients. The most complete frankness is necessary.'

Hilary looked at Henry, and Henry nodded. After all he didn't see that anything Hilary said could do any harm. They wouldn't hang Grey now whatever came out, and he was prepared to bank on the discretion of this respectable little spinster.

Hilary put her hand to her cheek and began to tell Miss Silver about going to see Mrs. Ashley.

'She was the daily help at Solway Lodge, and nobody thought of calling her, because she went away at six o'clock and she told the police she didn't know anything.'

Henry took her by the arm.

'What's all this?'

'I didn't tell you, Henry—I couldn't.'

'Go on,' said Maud Silver.

Hilary went on between quick breaths.

'I went to see her—she's a frightened little thing. She cried, and said she'd promised Marion not to tell.' Henry began to regret his nod. His hand tightened on Hilary's arm. 'I made her tell me. She did leave at six, but she went back. She had dropped a letter, and she thought it might be in the study—and she thought she could get in through the open window—but when she got near she heard voices—quarrelling. And she heard Mr. Everton say "My own nephew!" And then she heard a shot, and she ran away and never stopped running till she got home.'

'I see,' said Miss Silver. 'Yes, I see. And what time was this?'

Hilary caught her breath.

'That's the worst part of it—for Geoff, I mean. She heard a church clock strike as she came by Oakley Road. It struck eight, and at first when she said that, I thought it was going to be all right, because the outside of what it would take her to get to Solway Lodge from Oakley Road would be ten minutes. Geoff did it in five, and I don't think anyone could really take more than seven or eight, so I'm saying ten as an absolute limit. Well, if she heard that shot at ten minutes past eight, it clears Geoff, because the very earliest he could have got there was a quarter past, so I thought it was all right.' Her voice very plainly indicated that it had turned out all wrong.

Henry said, 'Why wasn't it all right?' and Miss Silver gazed at her expectantly.

'Oh, it wasn't, because she said, and stuck to it like a leech, that that blighted clock was a good ten minutes out, and that it must have been "getting on for the half hour" when she reached the house.'

'She said the clock was slow?' said Miss Silver.

'She said everyone in the house knew it was slow.'

'Clocks,' said Miss Silver, 'are extremely unreliable as evidence. You are quite, quite sure that she said the clock was slow?'

'I asked her, and asked her, and asked her,' said Hilary in a wretched voice. 'She said she was always talking about it to Mrs. Mercer. She said it used to give her a turn coming in the morning.'

'Why?' Miss Silver shot the word out short and sharp.

'It made her think she was late when she wasn't.' Hilary's eyes widened suddenly. 'Oh!'

'But then it was *fast*,' said Henry. He took her by the arm and shook her. 'I say, Hilary, wake up! Use the head — it's meant to think with! The clock would have to be fast to make her afraid she was late, not slow.'

Hilary's eyes got rounder and rounder. She said 'Golly!' in a hushed whisper.

Miss Silver said, 'Exactly.'

'How could you be such an ass?' said Henry Cunningham.

'Golly!' said Hilary again. 'She said it just like I told you, and I just gulped it down! And she must have said it to Marion, and Marion swallowed it too, and made her promise not to tell. And if she had told, — Miss Silver, it would have cleared Geoff — oh, it *would*!'

Miss Silver coughed.

'Do not build on it too much. The facts must be verified — and fifteen months have elapsed. But if it can be proved that this church clock was ten minutes fast in the July of last year, it would seem that the shot which killed Mr. Everton was fired at somewhere very near to eight o'clock.'

'Oh, Miss Silver!'

Miss Silver nodded.

'Then with regard to the words which Mrs. Ashley overheard, they are' — she gave her little dry cough — 'well, they are certainly capable of more than one construction. She appears to have considered, and Mrs. Grey appears to have considered, that those words "My own nephew!" indicated that Mr. Everton was at that moment addressing his nephew Geoffrey Grey. You appear to have taken the same view. But it really doesn't follow, you know. He may have been addressing Mr. Geoffrey Grey, but the words which you have quoted by no means prove that he was doing so. For instance, he may have been replying to some accusation or slander against Mr. Grey, and the words 'My own nephew!' might be construed as an indignant denial. Further, Mr. Everton had three nephews. The words may have had no reference at all to Geoffrey Grey.'

'It's the time that matters,' said Hilary. 'If we can only prove that the clock was fast — oh, Miss Silver, we *must* be able to prove it! Because if James was shot at eight, Geoff couldn't possibly have done it.'

CHAPTER TWENTY-SEVEN

Miss Silver produced a copybook and wrote down Mrs. Ashley's address, after which she wrote, 'Church clock, Oakley Road.' Under this she put the word 'Nephew'. Then she turned back to the file.

'There are a number of points on which I should like a little more information. Do you know either of Mr. Everton's other two nephews, Captain Cunningham?'

'I met Bertie Everton the other day for the first time,' said Henry.

'An accidental meeting?'

'No — he came to my shop. I told you I'd had an antique shop left me. Well, he came in there and talked about china.'

Hilary sat up bright-eyed.

'Henry, he came there on purpose to tell you Mrs. Mercer was mad. You know he did!'

'Well, I don't know it,' said Henry. 'He did talk about china.'

'And he did say Mrs. Mercer was mad — and that's what he came there for. And that's what Mercer followed me for, tagging after me all round Putney and telling me his poor wife wasn't right in her head till I was ready to scream. And if you can believe it all happened by accident the very morning after Mrs. Mercer talked to me in the train, well, I can't, and that's all about it!'

Miss Silver coughed.

'Will you tell me the whole thing from the beginning? I have heard Captain Cunningham's version of it, and I would like to hear it from yourself.'

Hilary began at the beginning and went right through to the end. She told about Mrs. Mercer in the train, and she told about everything that had happened since. She enjoyed telling it, and she told it very well. She made Miss Silver see the people. When she had finished she said, 'There!' and Miss Silver wrote in her copybook for a minute or two.

'And now,' she said — 'now, Captain Cunningham, I would like to know what impression Mr. Bertie Everton made on you.'

Henry looked puzzled.

'I've heard such a lot about him — over the case, I mean. If I hadn't, I don't know that I should have thought anything about him at all. He's not my sort of chap, you know— a bit finicky, a bit mincing in his talk.'

'He's got red hair and foxy eyes,' said Hilary in a tone of warm dislike.

'Thank you, Miss Carew,' said Maud Silver. She wrote in her copybook. 'And the other nephew, Francis Everton — what about him?'

'Bad hat,' said Henry. 'Remittance man. Old Everton paid him to keep away. Glasgow was a safe distance — he could soak quietly in the cheaper brands of alcohol without any danger of getting into the London papers. That was about the size of it, wasn't it, Hilary?'

Hilary nodded.

'Very interesting,' said Miss Silver — 'very, very interesting. And has he also got red hair?'

'I've never set eyes on him,' said Henry.

'Nor have I,' said Hilary. 'But he hasn't, Miss Silver, because I remember Marion and Geoff talking about him. At least what they were really talking about was red hair. Marion said she hated it, and that she'd never have married Geoff if she'd known it was in the family — because of not having gingery babies, you know. They were chaffing, of course. And Geoff said she needn't worry, because Bertie was the only one, and he got it from his mother. And she said hadn't Frank got it too, and he said no, he hadn't, he'd come out black, and that all his Aunt Henrietta's family were either black or red. So you see — '

'Yes,' said Miss Silver, in rather an abstracted tone, 'I see.' She turned the pages of the file and read in them here and there. Then she said, 'Would you care to go to Edinburgh, Captain Cunningham?'

'No,' said Henry, with the utmost decision.

'May I enquire why?'

'I think Hilary wants someone to look after her.' The fact that he used the Christian name was a tribute to Miss Silver's success in creating the impression that she was some kind of semi-professional aunt.

'Quite so. I was thinking that it might be as well if Miss Hilary could go, too. So many people have relations in Edinburgh. It occurred to me to wonder whether a short visit — '

'There's Cousin Selina,' said Hilary in rather a gloomy voice.

'Yes?' said Miss Silver brightly. 'That sounds very suitable.

Hilary made a face.

'She's Marion's cousin as well as mine. And she thinks Geoffrey did it, so Marion won't go near her, but she *has* asked Henry and me to stay — at least she did before we broke off our engagement.'

'It's on again,' said Henry firmly. After a moment's pause he added, 'It wasn't ever off.'

Hilary cocked an eyebrow, and Miss Silver said,

'Nothing could be better. You have a most admirable excuse for going to Edinburgh — a delightful city, and one of the most beautiful in Europe, so I am told. I think it very advisable indeed that Miss Carew should not be exposed to the risk of any more motor accidents. Edinburgh has an exceedingly good record in that respect, I believe — the Scotch are a careful people. It will be an excellent place for you to visit, and while you are there you can interview Annie Robertson whose statement we have here, and Captain Cunningham can make some enquiries at the local garages. I should be glad also if he would run over to Glasgow. You could accompany him if your cousin did not object. Some enquiries about Mr. Francis Everton. I will make a few notes which will indicate the line I should advise you to take in each case.'

Hilary leaned forward.

'What about the Mercers?'

'Yes,' said Henry, 'what about the Mercers?'

CHAPTER TWENTY-EIGHT

Miss Silver looked up from her copybook with an air of bright helpfulness.

'Ah yes — to be sure. I have some information for you, Captain Cunningham. I have not seen you since it came in.'

'Yes?' said Henry.

Miss Silver leaned across the table and picked up the half finished infant's coatee and the ball of pale blue wool. Then she sat back in her chair and began to knit.

'Yes,' she said. 'I put a small advertisement in the paper. It is so fortunate that Mrs. Mercer should have had an uncommon name like Anketell. One could feel practically sure that there would not be more than one Louisa Kezia Anketell, or at least not more than one in the same generation. These peculiar names generally run in a family. My own second name is Hephzibah — most unsuitable with Maud, but there has been a Hephzibah in our family for at least two hundred years.' She coughed. 'I have wandered from the point — I apologise.' She clicked a needle out and clicked it in again. 'To resume — I interviewed a woman yesterday who says she is a cousin of Mrs. Mercer's. She wrote in answer to the advertisement, and I called upon her in Wood Green. Her name was Sarah Anketell — not a very pleasant person, but, I think, truthful. She seemed to have some kind of grudge against her cousin, but I can see no reason to doubt what she told me.'

'And what did she tell you?' said Hilary.

'Well, to begin with she said that Louie, as she called her, had always thought more of herself than there was any need for — I give you the vulgarism, as it conveys the woman's frame of mind. Louie, she said, was very high in her notions, and thought herself better than those that were every bit as good as herself — a good deal of animus here, and a good deal of pleasure in informing me that pride had gone before a fall, and that Louie, with all her fine ways and her fine talk, had got herself into trouble. There was a baby, but Mrs. Akers said it did not live.'

'Oh,' said Hilary, 'that's why she minded so much about Marion losing her baby.'

Miss Silver looked up, and down again — an odd fleeting look. 'The man's Christian name was Alfred. Mrs. Akers did not know his surname. He may have been Alfred Mercer or he may not. Well, thirty years ago a young woman who had lost her character had very little hope indeed of ever getting another place. Louisa Anketell was considered very fortunate in attracting the sympathy and interest of a lady who was willing to give her a second chance. This lady heard Louisa's story whilst visiting in the neighbourhood. She had a kind heart and considerable means, and when she went away she took the girl with her to be trained under her cook. Sarah Anketell saw no more of her cousin, and knew nothing except by hearsay. She believed that Louie rose to be cook, and stayed on in the same service for a number of years, in fact until the lady's death. This may not seem very important to you, Captain Cunningham. I myself was inclined to be disappointed, but just at the end it occurred to me to ask Mrs. Akers whether she knew the lady's name. She did, and when she repeated it to me I felt very amply rewarded.'

Hilary said, 'Oh — ' and Henry said quickly, 'What was the name?'

Miss Silver allowed her knitting to fall into her lap.

'The name was Everton — Mrs. Bertram Everton.'

'*What!*' said Henry. Then, after a moment of stupefaction, 'Who — I mean what? I mean, Bertie Everton isn't married.'

'Thirty years ago!' gasped Hilary — 'Bertie's mother — Aunt Henrietta — the one that brought the red hair into the family!'

'Exactly,' said Miss Silver.

'Was anything known about this?' said Henry after a pause spent in dotting I's and crossing T's. 'Hilary, did Marion know that this Mercer woman had been in service with the Everton family before she came to James Everton?'

Hilary looked bewildered.

'She never said.'

Miss Silver glanced from one to the other.

'A connection between Mrs. Mercer and Bertie Everton's family, especially one of old and long standing, must surely have been mentioned at the time of the trial — if it had been acknowledged. If it was not mentioned, it must have been because it was not known.'

'But look here, Miss Silver,' said Henry — 'how could it have not been known? If this Louisa Anketell Mercer woman was his brother's cook for years, James Everton must have known her by sight.'

'That is a point, Captain Cunningham. But a cook in a big house might never be seen by a visitor.'

'But he wasn't!' cried Hilary. 'I mean he wasn't a visitor — I mean James Everton wasn't! Marion told me. He had a frightful row with his brother Bertram because they both wanted to marry Henrietta, and James never went there, or saw them, or anything.'

'That certainly makes things easier,' said Miss Silver. 'I

think we may assume that Mrs. Mercer concealed her previous connection with the Everton family. She may have done so because she felt that it would be no recommendation, or – there may have been a more sinister reason. We are bound to give weight to the fact that her employer's nephew Bertie Everton instead of being a complete stranger to her was someone whom she had seen grow up from childhood and to whose mother she owed a deep debt of gratitude.'

'That's all very well,' said Henry. 'But debt of gratitude or no debt of gratitude, are you going to tell me that Mrs. Mercer perjured herself and swore away a perfectly innocent man's life just because she'd once been cook to the real murderer's mother? I take it that you are now casting Bertie Everton for the part of the murderer. Hilary, of course, is quite sure he did it, but then she doesn't bother about evidence — I suppose you do.'

'A good deal of evidence will be necessary, Captain Cunningham, if Mr. Geoffrey Grey is to be got out of prison. I am not assuming that Mr. Bertie Everton was the murderer. I have merely suggested that you and Miss Hilary should check up that very useful alibi of his.'

'You *say* you are not assuming that Bertie Everton was the murderer — and unless his alibi breaks down he couldn't have been, because he simply wasn't within four hundred miles of Putney when James Everton was shot. But suppose his alibi was a fake and he did shoot his uncle, do you mean to say that a poor frightened creature like Mrs. Mercer would instantly on the spur of the moment invent a story which incriminates Geoffrey Grey and, what's more, stick to it under cross-examination?'

'I didn't say anything about the spur of the moment,' said Miss Silver gravely. 'The murder of Mr. Everton was very carefully planned. Observe that Alfred Mercer married Louisa Anketell the following day. Notice must have been given of that marriage. I believe it was part of the plan, and was at once a bribe and a safeguard. Observe also the deaf woman who was invited to supper. Her evidence cleared the Mercers as, I believe, it was intended to do, and her deafness made it certain that she would not know at what hour the shot was really fired. Everything about this case points to systematic timing, and a very careful consideration of detail. The person who planned this murder is extremely ruthless, ingenious, and cunning. I shall be very glad to feel that Miss Carew is at a safe distance during the next few critical days.'

'You really think she is in danger?' said Henry.

'What is your own opinion, Captain Cunningham?'

Hilary shivered, and quite suddenly Henry's opinion was that he would like to fly away with her in an aeroplane to the Mountains of the Moon. And on the top of that he remembered the foggy Ledstow road and his feet were cold. He said nothing, and Miss Silver said.

'Exactly, Captain Cunningham.'

Hilary shivered again.

'I keep thinking about Mrs. Mercer,' she said. 'She's afraid — she's awfully afraid of him. That's why she wouldn't speak to me last night. Do you think it's safe for her — in that cottage — all alone with him?'

'I think she is in very great danger,' said Miss Silver.

CHAPTER TWENTY-NINE

'If I'd had to keep my temper for another second I should have burst!' said Hilary.

Henry slipped a hand inside her arm.

'If you're going to develop a temper, the engagement's off again,' he said firmly.

Hilary wrinkled her nose at him.

'I never said it was on. Oh, Henry, isn't Cousin Selina grim? Much, much, *much* worse than I remembered.'

They had just emerged from Mrs. McAlister's house in Murrayfield Avenue and were walking away from it as rapidly as possible. Mrs. McAlister was Cousin Selina, and the visit, which had only begun over night, had not so far added very greatly to the gaiety of anyone concerned.

'Her husband was a pet,' said Hilary. 'He was a professor or something. He used to give me sweets, and she always said they were bad for me. And she's got worse since he died, and the horrid part of it is that *she* is our relation, not *him*. She's Marion's and my grandfather's first cousin twice removed, and her name was Selina Carew, so it's no good pretending she doesn't belong. Fancy starting in about Geoff practically the first minute we got off the train! And when you got her off that she had a go at lipstick and nail-polish, and then skidded back to Geoff again? I don't know how I'm going to stick it out. How long do you think it's going to take us to dig up all this stuff Miss Silver wants?'

'That depends,' said Henry.

'Henry, do stop being monosyllabic and non-committal! What are we going to do first — garages, or Annie

Robertson? Or shall we make a sort of sandwich and put her in the middle?'

'We'll do her first. She oughtn't to take any time.'

But at the Caledonian Hotel it emerged that Annie Robertson was no longer there. She had left to be married. After some pressure and some delay a girl was produced who said that Annie was a friend of hers, and her married name was Jamieson, and she was living out at Gorgie in a 'nice wee flat'. She obliged with the address, and to Gorgie Henry and Hilary proceeded on the top of a tram.

There were a great many stairs up to Mrs. Annie Robertson Jamieson's flat. They were clean but they were steep. Mrs. Jamieson opened her door and stood waiting for them to explain themselves. She was a large, fair young woman with rosy cheeks and a pair of buxom arms which were bare to the elbow.

Hilary explained.

'We've come on from the Caledonian Hotel, Mrs. Jamieson. If it wouldn't be too much trouble, we should so very much like to talk to you for a few minutes. It's about something that happened in the hotel last year, and we think you might be able to help us.'

Annie Jamieson's round blue eyes became even rounder.

'Will it be a divorce? Because my man's real strict about divorce.'

'Oh *no*,' said Hilary as quickly as possible.

'Will you come in then?'

They came in. The flat smelt of kippers and soft soap. The sitting-room had bright red curtains and a red and green linoleum. There were two chairs and a sofa upholstered in crimson plush, the produce of Annie Robertson's savings and the pride of her heart. They sat down and there was one of those silences. Hilary had forgotten every single thing she had meant to say, and

Henry had never meant to say anything at all. Garages might be his job, but ex-chambermaids were Hilary's.

'Mrs. Jamieson —' said Hilary at last. Perhaps if she broke the silence, something would come. But how awful if it didn't. She felt desperate, and all she could find to say was the woman's name, 'Mrs. Jamieson —'

Annie took pity on her.

'It was something that happened in the hotel you were saying.'

'Last year,' said Hilary, and then she was off with a rush. 'Oh, Mrs. Jamieson, do you remember signing a statement about the Everton murder?'

This wasn't in the least how she had meant to begin. Henry was making a most awful face at her.

Annie Jamieson said 'Ay,' her voice lifting on the word, her blue eyes steady and dependable. Hilary liked her, and all at once it wasn't difficult any longer. She felt as if she was talking to a friend.

'I'll tell you just why we've come,' she said. 'I've got your statement here, and I want to go through it and just ask one or two questions if you'd be so very kind, because we think that perhaps there's been some terrible mistake, and it's my cousin's husband who's been sent to prison for life. She's like my sister really, and she's so dreadfully, dreadfully unhappy — so I thought if you could help us —'

'It's all true that I put my name to — every word of it's true. I can't say any different.'

'I don't want you to. I only want to ask you some questions.'

Hilary rummaged in her bag and produced a sheet of paper on which she had copied Annie Robertson's statement. The things she was to ask were quite fresh and bright in her mind now. She read the statement through.

Annie Robertson said Mr. Bertram Everton had been staying in the hotel for three or four days before July

16th. He might have come on the 11th, or the 10th, or the 12th. She couldn't say for certain, but they would know in the office. He had room No. 35. She remembered Tuesday, July 16th — she remembered Mr. Everton complaining about the bell in his room. He said it was out of order, but it seemed all right. She said she would have it looked at, because Mr. Everton said sometimes it rang and sometimes it didn't. It was at about three o'clock in the afternoon that Mr. Everton complained about the bell. He was writing letters at the time. Later that evening at about half past eight his bell rang and she answered it. Mr. Everton told her he wanted some biscuits. He said he didn't feel well and was going to bed. She brought him the biscuits. She thought he was the worse for drink. She brought him his tea next morning, Wednesday, July 17th, at nine o'clock. He seemed all right then and quite himself.

'That was what you signed, Mrs. Jamieson.'

'Ay, that's just the way it was. I'd not put my name to anything that wasn't true.'

'Well then, I want to ask you about Mr. Everton and the bell. You said he complained about it.'

'Ay.'

'Did you come to the room for something, or did he ring for you?'

'He rang.'

'He rang to say the bell wouldn't ring?'

'Ay. I didn't think it was just very sensible, but he said whiles it rang and whiles it didn't ring.'

'You said he was writing letters. How was he sitting when you went into the room?'

'He was by the window. There's a wee table there.'

'Did he have his back to you then?'

'Ay — he was writing.'

'But he turned round when he spoke to you?'

'No, he didn't. He just said, "Yon bell's out of

order — whiles it rings and whiles it doesn't," and kept on with his writing all the time.'

'Then he didn't turn round at all?'

'No.'

'Then you didn't see his face?'

'No, I can't just say that I did.'

'Then how do you know that it was Mr. Everton?'

Annie stared.

'It was Mr. Everton all right — you couldn't mistake yon red hair.'

'It was just the hair you saw and not the face?'

'Ay — but you couldn't mistake it.'

Hilary leaned forward.

'Lots of people have red hair.'

Annie plaited her skirt in her fingers. She went on staring at Hilary. She said in a surprised voice,

'No that kind o' red hair.'

'What kind?'

'Gey long on his neck for a gentleman. You couldn't mistake it.'

Hilary remembered Bertie Everton's hair — 'Gey long for a gentleman,' as Annie said. She nodded.

'Yes — he does wear it long.'

And Annie nodded too, and said, 'Ay.'

Hilary went back to the statement.

'Well, that's all about the bell. You didn't see his face then, but only the back of his head and his red hair. And in the evening he rang for you again?'

'Ay.'

'At half past eight?'

'Ay.'

'He said he wanted some biscuits, and he told you he didn't feel well and was going to bed, and you brought him the biscuits.'

'Ay.'

'Now, Mrs. Jamieson, did you see his face that time?'

Hilary's heart was beating as she asked the question, because everything hung on it — *everything* — for Geoff, and for Marion.

A deep, straight furrow appeared between Annie Jamieson's brows.

'He rang his bell,' she said, speaking slowly, 'and I knocked and went in.'

'How did you get in?' said Henry suddenly.

She looked round at him, puzzled.

'The door was a wee thing open like.'

'And was it open in the afternoon when he rang about the bell?'

'Ay, sir.'

'It was open both times? You're quite sure of that?'

'Ay, I'm sure of that.'

'All right — carry on.'

She turned back to Hilary.

'You knocked and went in,' said Hilary.

'Ay. And Mr. Everton was looking out of the window, and he said without turning round, "I'm not at all well — I'm going to bed. Get me some biscuits, will you?"'

'And when you came back with the biscuits, what was he doing then?'

'He was washing his face,' said Annie Jamieson.

'Washing his face?'

'Ay — he'd the towel to it, drying it.'

Hilary's heart leapt.

'Then you didn't see his face that time either?'

Annie looked puzzled.

'He'd the wee towel up to it, drying it like.'

'Did he speak?'

'Ay — he said, "Put them down." So I put them down and come away.'

Hilary looked down at the statement again.

'You said you thought he was the worse for drink.'

'Ay — he was that.'

'Why did you think so?'

Annie stared.

'I didn't think — I was sure.'

'Why? I mean you didn't see his face.'

'There was an awful strong smell of spirits. And there was the way he spoke — it wasn't like his own voice at all.'

Hilary said, 'I see.' She tried not to think what this might mean. She looked just once again at the paper in her hand.

'And when you took him his tea at nine o'clock next morning, he was all right then and quite himself?'

'Ay — he was all right then.'

'And you saw his face that time?'

'Oh ay — he was quite himself.'

Henry struck in.

'Then it comes to this, Mrs. Jamieson — you did not actually see Mr. Everton's face at any time on Tuesday, July 16th. Your statement only mentions the afternoon, but I take it you didn't see him in the morning.'

'No, I didn't see him — he had his door locked.'

'So there was no time on Tuesday, July 16th, when you actually saw Mr. Everton's face?'

'No.' She began to say something, and stopped herself, looking from one to the other in a bewildered manner. 'If it wasna Mr. Everton, who was it?' she said.

CHAPTER THIRTY

They drew three garages blank, and were late for lunch. Cousin Selina was not at all pleased. She said it didn't matter in the tone of one who holds fast to politeness in face of overwhelming temptation. She bit her lip and feared the joint would be overdone, and having tasted her portion, sighed and cast her eyes up and then down again. After which she partook of beef and Brussels sprouts with the air of a martyr.

When the tablemaid was in the room Henry and Hilary supplied a little difficult conversation, but as soon as they were alone Mrs. McAlister found a mournful voice.

'It is a great pity that Marion does not change her name,' was the text upon which a considerable sermon could be preached. Cousin Selina preached it with vigour. It had always been her opinion that Geoffrey Grey was an unsuitable husband for Marion.

'Very good-looking young men never make good husbands. My own dear husband — ' A long excursus on the virtues of the late Professor, who had certainly not been renowned for his beauty. As Hilary put it afterwards — 'A pet lamb, darling, but exactly like a ginger monkey.'

Leaving the Professor, his widow rehearsed the advice she had given to Marion on more than one occasion — 'And if she had taken it she would not be in her present painful position. There was a young man whom I would have been very glad to see her married to. But no, she insisted on having her own way. And what is the result — will you have any more beef, Captain Cunning-

210

ham? . . . Then perhaps you will kindly ring the bell for Jeannie.'

'Henry, I *shall* burst!' said Hilary when they got away again. 'What do we do now — Glasgow, or garages? She rests till tea-time.'

'If it's Glasgow, we can't get back to tea.'

'We could ring up and say we'd got stuck — important business — any old thing.'

'Or I could go, and you could stay here,' suggested Henry.

Hilary stamped on the pavement.

'Look here, my lad, you say that again, and you'll see what happens! If you think that I'm going to stay here and talk to Cousin Selina while you go off sleuthing by yourself, well, you've made a mistake, that's all!'

'All right, all right — you needn't get worked up about it. We'll go to Glasgow tomorrow. We'd better get on with the garage business this afternoon, though how in the world Miss Silver expects anyone to remember anything about any car in the world after more than a year. It's a wild-goose chase, but I suppose we'd better get on with it.'

'We might find a wild goose in a mare's nest,' said Hilary.

They found nothing. It was a most cold, discouraging quest. Snow began to fall in the Pentlands, and the streets of Edinburgh ran with a chilly rain. Later there were six hours of Cousin Selina's conversation before it was decently possible to go to bed.

Next day Glasgow, under one of those dark skies which appear ready to discharge every conceivable type of bad weather — rain, snow, sleet, hail or thunder. It hung low, it bulged, it threatened, but for the moment nothing happened.

From the firm of Johnstone, Johnstone and McCand-lish they obtained Frank Everton's address, and presently found themselves in a poorish quarter, from which they arrived rather suddenly at a very authentic slum.

Henry frowned at the place. It was very much worse than he had expected. There were some ill-looking hooligans about. The tenement houses reared up gaunt and dirty. He looked at the stair up which they would have to go, and took Hilary firmly by the elbow.

'Look here, you can't come up. I oughtn't to have let you come. I'd no idea the fellow was living in a slum.'

'I'm not going to wait here,' said Hilary. She felt no enthusiasm for the stair, but even less for this cold slummy street.

'No, you'll have to go back.'

'Back where?'

'I'll come with you as far as the corner. There's quite a decent street beyond. You can just walk up and down there till I come.'

A frightfully dull occupation walking up and down and waiting for someone to come. The street might have been a street in any town. Its flat, ugly houses were as drably dull as they could be. Hilary got tired of walking between them. She thought she would go a little way round the corner to see if Henry was coming. There was no sign of him. The street was much emptier than it had been. She walked a dozen paces, and then a dozen more.

And then she wasn't sure which of those big crowded tenement houses Henry had gone into. A little thin, strange voice spoke inside her mind. It said, 'Suppose he doesn't ever come back.' And with that a sort of horror came up amongst her thoughts like a fog. She was cold with it, through and through to her very heart. But it was nonsense. What could happen to Henry in that big crowded house? It was swarming with people. It was the safest place in the world. It was full of chattering, scolding women and noisy children. *And who would take any notice if anyone shouted or cried out?* The horror came again. She stared up at the rows and rows of windows on those great reared-up blocks, and suddenly high up at one of the windows, she saw Mrs. Mercer's face.

CHAPTER THIRTY-ONE

The face stayed there for the time it took to miss a ⏉reath and then take two with a gasp between. Then it was gone, moving back from the pane and lost in the room behind.

Hilary went on staring up at the window. It was a fifth-floor window on the left of the common stair. Mrs. Mercer's face had certainly been there a moment ago. She couldn't doubt that, because even if she had imagined the face, she couldn't possibly have imagined its ghastly look of fear. She had never seen such a look on any human face before, and she hoped she would never see it again. At the thought of those desperate, staring eyes, that mouth loose with terror, Hilary knew that she couldn't wait — she must do something at once. She didn't even think about Henry. She ran across the street and plunged into the darkness of the stair.

At the second floor she stopped, breathless. You can't run up five flights of stairs, and there's no sense in trying to.

> Here we go up, up, up.
> Here we go down, down, down.

'No, not down — up. And you've got to keep your head, and your breath, or you won't be any good when you get there.'

All the way up she passed no one except perhaps a dozen children by twos and threes on the landings. They were all very small, because the older ones were at school. They took no notice of Hilary, and she took no notice of them. She reached the fifth floor and knocked on the first door on her left, and it wasn't until the sound of her knocking came on the air that she began to wonder what she would do if Alfred Mercer answered it. It was a most horrid thought, and what was the good of thinking it — now when it was too late? *She could run away* . . . She wasn't going to run away.

There wasn't any answer to her knocking. She raised her hand to knock again, but it stayed there, an inch away from the door, without the power to move forward or make any sound. A sort of frozen terror was gaining on her. To break it she made a sudden effort, bringing her hand down upon the door knob. Her hand turned, and the knob with it. The door opened inwards with a click.

Hilary stood on the threshold, and saw a bare passage with three doors opening off it. Funny to say *opening* when all the doors were shut. It would be the left-hand one behind which Mrs. Mercer had stood and looked out of the window. She closed the outer door and went towards it, and as she did so a cold, cold shiver ran down her spine. The other rooms were behind her now. Suppose Alfred Mercer came out of one of them and caught her by the throat and choked her dead . . . He wouldn't. Why should he? One voice said that. And another, 'He would if he thought you knew too much.'

Now she was listening at the door and could hear nothing. Outside the tenement hummed with noise, but here in this flat there was an empty silence. If she let herself stop to think she would run away from it into the noise again. She struck her hands sharply together, put a tingling palm to the cold door knob, and went in.

It was a bare, wretched room, with a dirty rag of curtain looped back from the window where she had seen the face. A ramshackle double bed stood facing the light, and there was some kind of press or cupboard against the right-hand wall. There was a rickety table in the middle of the room with a couple of chairs beside it. The door hid the head of the bed as Hilary came in, and at first she thought the room was empty.

She came farther in, and saw Mrs. Mercer standing against the wall. She had gone back as far as she could go. One hand clutched the rail of the bed, the other was pressed against her side. Hilary thought she would have sunk down if she had been less stiff with terror. Her face showed the same extremity of fear which had brought Hilary up five flights of stairs to find out what was wrong. And then, before her eyes, the tension broke. Mrs. Mercer let go of the rail, slumped down on the side of the bed, and began to cry.

Hilary shut the door. She said, 'What's the matter? What's frightened you?'

There were choking sobs, and a rain of tears.

'Mrs. Mercer —'

'I thought you was him — oh lord, I did! What shall I do? Oh lord! What shall I do?'

Hilary put a hand on her shoulder and kept it there.

'You thought I was Mercer? Is he in the flat, or is he out?'

The terrified pale eyes looked up at her.

'He'll be coming back — any time now — to finish me. That's what he's brought me here for — to finish me off!' She caught Hilary's other hand in a cold, damp grip. 'I darsn't sleep, and I darsn't eat! He's left the gas tap on once already — and there was a bitter taste in the tea — but he said it was nothing — but he didn't drink the cup I poured him out — and when I said to him, "Aren't you going to drink your tea, Alfred?" he took and pushed the saucer so that half of it spilled — and he said, "Drink it yourself, and a good riddance!" — and he called me a name he didn't ought to a-done — because I'm his wife and got my lines to show — whatever may have happened in the past — and not for him to throw it up at me neither — lord knows it isn't!'

Hilary pressed hard on the thin shoulder.

'Why do you stay with him, Mrs. Mercer? Why don't you come away? What's to stop you? Come away with me now — at once, before he gets back!'

Mrs. Mercer twisted away from her with a sort of desperate strength.

'Do you think he'd let me go? There isn't nowhere he wouldn't follow me and do me in. Oh lord — I wish it was over — I wish I was dead!'

'Why does he want to kill you?' said Hilary slowly.

Mrs. Mercer shuddered and was silent.

Hilary went on.

'Shall I tell you? I know, and you know. That's the trouble — you know too much. He wants to kill you because you know too much about the Everton murder. He wants to kill you because you know that Geoffrey Grey is innocent. And I don't *care* whether he kills us both or not — you're going to tell me what you know — *now!*'

Mrs. Mercer stopped crying. She drooped there on the bed, quiet and limp in her respectable black. With her faded eyes fixed on Hilary's face, she said with a heart-rending simplicity,

'They'd hang me.'

Hilary's pulses jumped. Hope flared in her. She said in a hurried undertone,

'I don't think they would. You're ill. You didn't do it yourself — did you?'

The pale eyes winced from hers.

'Mrs. Mercer — you didn't shoot Mr. Everton, did you? You must tell — you *must!*'

Mrs. Mercer's tongue came out and wetted her dry lips. She said 'No,' and forced her voice and said it again a little louder — 'No.'

'Who did?' said Hilary, and with that there came to them both the click of the outer door.

Mrs. Mercer got to her feet with a jerk that was not like any natural movement. She pushed Hilary, and pointed at the press. Her voice made a sound in her throat, and failed.

But there was neither time nor need for words. Alfred Mercer had come back, and in all that bare room the press offered the only possibility of a hiding-place. There was not even time for thought. Sheer primitive instinct took its place. Without any conscious interval Hilary found herself in the dark, ill-smelling cupboard with the door shut close. There was very little room. Her shoulder touched rough wood. Her back was against the wall. Something swung and dangled against her in the darkness. Mrs. Mercer's words started into her mind, and the sweat of terror broke upon her lip, her temples. 'They'll *hang* me.' Something was hanging here —

She wrenched herself back to sanity. Of course there was something hanging there — that was what cupboards were for. Mrs. Mercer had hung her coat in this one. It hung and dangled and swung against Hilary's cheek. The sweat broke again. She heard Alfred Mercer speak in the room beyond. He said roughly,

'Sulking again?'

'No, Alfred.'

Hilary wondered at the way the woman had regained control of herself. The words sounded almost as they were meant to sound — almost, but not quite.

'*No, Alfred!*' said Mercer, mimicking her. 'That's what you keep on saying — isn't it? Have you been leaking to that damned girl? *No, Alfred!* Have you seen her? Did you speak to her? Did she come nosing round the cottage? *No, Alfred!* And all the time — all the time it was yes — yes — yes — you damned sniveller!'

Hilary had to guess at the shuddering effort with which Mrs. Mercer answered him.

'I don't know what you mean — I'm sure I don't.'

'Oh, no — you wouldn't! You didn't speak to her in the train, I suppose?'

'I only asked after Mrs. Grey — I told you, Alfred.' She was breaking again. The effort had spent itself. Her voice dragged.

'And what call had you got to speak to her at all? It's you that's stirred the whole thing up. The case was closed, wasn't it? Mr. Geoffrey Grey was in prison. If you'd kept your tongue between your teeth we were in clover. Do you think I can trust you after that?'

'I never said nothing — I swear I didn't.'

Alfred Mercer's voice dropped to an ugly whisper.

'Then what brought her down to Ledlington? And what brought her nosing along the Ledstow road? And what brought her to the cottage if it wasn't that you'd as good as told her you knew something that'd get Mr. Geoffrey out of prison?'

'I never, Alfred — I *never!*'

'Oh, no — you never do nothing! If it hadn't been for me finding the marks of her shoes up against the scullery window, you wouldn't never have told me she'd come nosing round. And how am I going to know what you told her then? And how am I going to know you haven't set the police on us?'

'I'll take my Bible oath —' said Mrs. Mercer in a wild, shaken voice. It broke upon a sob — upon a torrent of sobs.

'Chuck it!' said Mercer. 'You don't do yourself no good that way. This door's shut and the outside door's shut, and there's no one to hear if you scream your head off. There's a sight too much noise outside for anyone to notice—I've told you that before. That's why we've come here, Louie. There's a man in the flat across the landing that gets drunk regular three times in the week and most Sundays, and when he's drunk he beats his wife, and when he beats her she screams something horrid, so they tell me. I was talking about him to a man on the stair last night. Something horrid, she screams. And when I said to the man I was talking to, "Don't the neighbours come in?" he laughed and said, "No fear — they're used to it." And when I said, "Don't they fetch the police?" he said, "The police know better than to come interfering between man and wife, and if they didn't they'd get a lesson they'd be sorry for." So it won't do no good screaming, Louie.'

There was a pause, and a shuffling sound. In her mind Hilary saw again what she had seen when she came into the room, Mrs. Mercer backed up against the wall and clutching at the bed rail. She thought if the cupboard door were open, that she would see her just like that, with the frantic terror in her face.

There wasn't any sound after the shuffle. There wasn't any sound until Alfred Mercer spoke again. He said harshly,

'That's enough of that, my girl! You come and sit down to the table and write what I tell you!'

Hilary heard Mrs. Mercer's gasp of relief. Whatever she had expected, it wasn't this. It was some horror of violence which she had stiffened herself to meet. At this demand that she should sit down and write, her breath came again with a sob.

'What do you want me to write, Alfred?'

'You come and sit down and I'll tell you.'

Hilary heard the shuffling sound again, the sound of unwilling, dragging feet upon the boarded floor. A chair scraped. There was a rustle of paper. And then Mercer's voice.

'You take and write what I tell you, and don't be all day over it! You're a good enough scholar when you choose. And don't you leave nothing out nor yet put nothing in, or it'll be the worse for you. Now! You put the date at the top of the paper, November 27th, and then you start writing, "I can't stand it any longer . . . I've been a very wicked woman, and I've got to tell what happened so that Mr. Geoffrey Grey can go free." '

The chair scraped again as if it had been pushed back. In a faint agitated whisper Mrs. Mercer said,

'What do you want? You said you'd cut my heart out if I told.'

'You write what I tell you!' said Alfred Mercer. 'If you don't — you see this knife, Louie — d'you see it? It's sharp. Do you want me to show you how sharp it is? All right, then, you write down what I said!'

She wrote. The room was so still that Hilary could hear the sound of the pen as it hurried across the paper — a tiny rustling sound. And then Alfred Mercer's voice. And then the pen again — and the voice again — and a long, shuddering breath.

'Got that lot down? All right, go on — "I didn't mean to kill Mr. Everton . . . Alfred and me had been sweethearts long ago . . . He said if I'd go with him as man and wife to Mr. Everton he'd marry me, so I went . . . And he kept putting me off, and one day Mr. Everton found out — " '

Hilary heard a slow breath taken.

'What's this I'm writing?' said Mrs. Mercer's whispering voice.

'You'll know when you've written it, my girl,' said Alfred Mercer. 'Have you got that down — "One day he found out"? All right, go on — "It was the day Mr. Bertie Everton come to see him from Scotland . . . He didn't have time to talk about it . . . He was very angry . . . Alfred said he'd make it all right, and he give notice for us to be married ... but it wasn't any good ... Mr. Everton said we'd got to go ... and he said it was his duty to expose us ... So I took Mr Geoffrey's pistol as he'd left in his bottom drawer ... It was the sixteenth of July ... Mrs. Thompson from next door was having a bit of supper with us ... I went through to the dining-room ... and as I passed the study door ... I heard Mr. Everton telephoning to Mr. Geoffrey Grey ... He wanted him to come round at once ... I thought he was going to tell him about Alfred and me ... It was eight o'clock ... I made up my mind what I would do ... I knew when Mr. Geoffrey would get there ... A little before the time I said I must go and turn the bed down ... I went and got Mr. Geoffrey's pistol — " '

'Alfred!' It was less of a word than a gasp. A faint, frightened scream followed it.

'You'll get more than that, if you go asking for it! You get on! Ready? "Mr. Geoffrey's pistol" — you've got that down? ... Now! "I put it under my apron and went into the study ... I asked Mr. Everton to have mercy on me and not tell no one ... He called me a bad name ... and I shot him — " '

Hilary heard a rustle, as if the paper had suddenly been pushed away.

'I won't — I won't write it — they'd hang me!' The whisper was wild with fear.

'You've written enough to hang yourself already,' said Alfred Mercer. 'But they won't hang you, Louie — you needn't be afraid of that. They won't get a chance to hang you, because as soon as you've written this and signed it, you're going to drink what I've got in this bottle, and when you've drunk it you'll go off asleep and you won't know nothing more.'

'I won't,' said the whispering voice — 'I won't!'

'You won't, won't you? Then — ' His voice dropped until Hilary could hear no words, only rough sound — harsh, rasping sound like an animal snarling.

Mrs. Mercer screamed again and gasped out, shuddering,

'No — no! I'll do anything?'

'You'd better. Here get on! I don't want to be all day. It's a good job a blot or two don't matter, for you've made a fair mess of the paper. "I shot him" — you just write that down! And mind it's clear enough to read! Come along now!'

The paper moved again. The pen moved. Mrs. Mercer groaned. Mercer's voice went on, cool and hard.

' "I locked the door . . . and I wiped the key and the handle . . . I wiped the pistol too . . . and I put it on the mat in front of the garden door . . . Then I ran round and got in by one of the drawing-room windows and shut it after me . . . They were all latched when the police came . . . but I'd left one open on purpose so that I could get in quick . . . I waited till I saw Mr. Geoffrey come past the window and go into the study . . . Then I ran into the hall and screamed . . . and Alfred came running, and Mrs. Thompson . . . and banged on the door . . . And everyone thought he done it . . . and I let them think so . . . I didn't tell my husband nor anyone . . . Alfred never knew nothing, only what I told him . . . He thought Mr. Geoffrey done it same as everyone did . . . And I swore false at the inquest and at the trial . . . but now I can't bear it no longer . . . Alfred and me got married like he promised . . . and he's been good to me. But I can't bear it no longer . . . I'm a wicked woman and I ought to die" . . . And now you sign your name nice and clear underneath — your lawful married name, Louisa Kezia Mercer!'

Hilary's hair was wet against her temples. A cold drop ran trickling between her shoulder-blades. It was like the most dreadful nightmare with every sense an avenue for horror — the unclean smell of the place, sight lost in darkness, a violent threat in her ears. What had she been listening to? What was this story which Alfred Mercer had dictated? Was it a lie that he was forcing on this poor broken creature at the point of the knife — or was it true? It might very easily be true. It fitted everywhere, and it explained everything. No, it didn't explain why James Everton had changed his will. That didn't matter. Nothing mattered if only Geoff was cleared.

These thoughts floated in the terror and confusion of her mind, while at the same time she heard Mrs. Mercer raise her voice in a frantic appeal.

'Alfred — for the Lord's sake! I can't sign that! Alfred, I'll never say a word — I swear I won't! I'll go where no one won't ever find me, and I'll never say a word — I'll take my Bible oath I won't!'

On the other side of the door Alfred Mercer wrenched away from the grovelling woman who clutched his knees. He let out an agry oath, and then controlled himself. Whatever happened, she'd got to sign the statement, she'd *got* to sign it. He said, in a deadly quiet voice —

'Get up, Louie! Get up off the floor!'

Mrs. Mercer looked up stupidly. She was so much afraid that she could no longer think. She was afraid of being hanged, and she was afraid to die, and she was afraid of the knife in Alfred's hand — but she was most afraid of the knife. She got up, and when he told her to sit she sat, and when he told her to sign her name she took the pen in her cold shaking hand.

'Put your name to it!' said Alfred Mercer. He came close and showed her the knife.

Hilary strained against her own terror, and strained to hear. She listened for the faint small sound of the pen on the paper as it moved in the loops and curls of Louisa Kezia Mercer's signature. 'If she signs it, he'll kill her — he'll kill her at once. I can't stop here and let her be killed. He's got a knife. He'll kill me too. Nobody knows where I am. Henry doesn't know — *Henry* —'

'Are you going to sign that paper, or have I got to make you?' said Alfred Mercer.

Mrs. Mercer signed her name.

CHAPTER THIRTY-TWO

Hilary caught at her courage with all her might. If the worst came to the worst, she must run out and get to the door and scream. 'There's a woman over the way who screams three times a week when her husband beats her, and no one takes any notice. It's no good screaming.' No good thinking of that. Think — think hard about the room — about where the furniture is. He'll be taken by surprise. Think where the table is, and the chairs. *The chairs*. Pick one up if you can — yes, pick one up and drive at him with a leg — at his knees — or his head. A good deal could be done with a chair, and his knife would be no good to him.

She put her hand on the latch of the cupboard door and lifted it. The door moved outwards a shade, a thread, a crack — a crack to look through. She could see a long streak of daylight, and in the daylight Mrs. Mercer leaning back with her hands in her lap. Her face was drained of all expression. The terror had gone from it to her eyes. They were fixed on Alfred Mercer, who faced her across the table. Hilary couldn't see his face. She didn't dare open the door any wider. She held on to the latch to prevent it swinging out. She could only see Mercer's hands. One of them held the knife. He put it down on the far side of the table. Hilary could just see as far as where it lay with the blade catching the light — a horn handle, a bright blade, and a fine, keen edge. The sheet of paper upon which Mrs. Mercer had been writing just failed to touch this edge. The pen had rolled against the inkpot, a cheap twopenny bottle, with the cork lying beside it.

She forced her eyes away. There had been two chairs. Mrs. Mercer was sitting on one of them. Where was the other? It must be on the far side of the table, behind Alfred Mercer. His hands went out of the picture and came back again with a little packet done up in white paper. Hilary watched him undo the paper and let it fall. There came out a small glass bottle with a screw top, a little thing not more than three inches long. Mrs. Mercer's pale, terrified eyes stared at it fixedly. Hilary stared, too.

Alfred Mercer held the bottle in his left hand, un-screwed the top, and cupping his palm, tilted out into it a dozen round white pellets. Hilary's heart began to beat very fast indeed. He was going to poison that poor dreep, right there in front of her eyes, and if he began she would simply have to burst out of the cupboard and do what she could to stop him. She tried to think, but it wasn't easy. He would have to dissolve those things in water — you couldn't make anyone swallow a dozen pellets dry. The question was, had he got any water here or hadn't he? There wasn't any on the table. If he had to go to the kitchen for it, there would be just one lightning chance to make a dash for safety.

Alfred Mercer's right hand put the bottle down and dropped the little screw cap carelessly beside the blotted sheet of paper upon which Louisa Mercer had written her confession. His left hand closed on the pellets.

'Damn it — I've forgotten the water!' he said, and picked up the knife and was gone from Hilary's field of vision. He crossed it again on his way to the door, and this time she saw his face going past her quickly in profile. It gave her a thrill of horror to see how ordinary he looked, how entirely the respectable butler. He might have been fetching the water for one of his master's guests.

As he passed, Hilary was giving herself orders — urgent, insistent orders — 'Count three when he's gone through the door — let him go out of the door and count three. Then run. Make her run too. You must — you've got to. It's the only chance.'

He went past the foot of the bed and out of the door. Hilary let the cupboard door swing wide and counted three. Then she ran to Mrs. Mercer, taking her by the shoulders, shaking her, and saying breathlessly,

'Run — run! Quick — it's your only chance!'

It was a chance that was lost already. There was no life, no movement, no response. The head had fallen back. The eyes stared glassily at the ceiling. The arms hung limp.

'No good,' said Hilary to herself — 'no good.'

She snatched the inkpot from the table and ran out of the room. The kitchen door was open, and the outer door was shut. They faced each other with no more than a yard between. From the kitchen came the sound of running water. It stopped. Hilary snatched at the knob of the outer door, but before she could turn it Alfred Mercer's hand came down on her shoulder and swung her round. They stared at each other for a long, intolerable moment. He must have put the knife in his pocket, for there was no sign of it. One hand gripped her, the other held a glass half full of water with the little pile of dissolving pellets sending up air bubbles through it. The respectable butler's face was a snarling mask.

Hilary screamed at the top of her voice and struck hard at his face with the bottle of ink.

CHAPTER THIRTY-THREE

Henry Cunningham came down the dirty tenement stair and emerged upon the street. He wore a puzzled frown, and he carried a small parcel done up in an extremely crumpled piece of brown paper. A yard from the step he walked into the last person he was expecting to meet — Miss Maud Silver, in a black coat with a shabby fur collar, and a black felt hat enlivened by a bunch of purple velvet pansies. Henry exclaimed, and Miss Silver exclaimed. What she actually said was, 'Dear me!' After which she put a hand on Henry's arm and began to walk briskly up the street beside him.

'We will not, perhaps, talk here. I was on my way to interview Francis Everton, but I see you have already done so. I have another appointment, so we must not lose time. I should prefer to hear your report before proceeding any farther myself.'

'You can't proceed any farther,' said Henry, casting an odd look at her. He was thinking that she would pass very well as a district visitor, but that he himself was rather conspicuous, and that the sooner they collected Hilary and went somewhere where they could talk the better.

'And just what do you mean by that?' said Miss Maud Silver.

They turned into a side street.

'Frank Everton is dead,' said Henry.

'When?'

'Buried yesterday.'

'How?'

'They say he was drunk and fell downstairs.'

'I wonder if he was pushed,' said Miss Silver in a quiet, meditative voice.

Henry jerked an impatient shoulder.

'He's not much loss anyhow.'

'On the contrary.' Miss Silver's tone was prim. 'An invaluable witness if he could have been induced to speak.'

'Well, he can't now,' said Henry in a brutally matter-of-fact way. 'But, look here, Miss Silver, did you know he was married?'

'No, Captain Cunningham.'

'Well, he was. Factory girl out of a job. Quite young. Fond of him. *Not* fond of his brother — that's putting it mildly. She hates Bertie Everton like poison. Says he got Frank to do his dirty work, and didn't ever pay him properly for it.'

'Good,' said Miss Silver. 'Good work, Captain Cunningham. Go on.'

Henry was warming to his story. It sorted itself out as he proceeded. He was conscious of a very definite excitement.

'The girl's decent. She didn't know anything — that is, she guessed there had been dirty work, but she wouldn't have stood for it herself. She married Frank Everton about six months ago, but she seems to have been friendly with him for some time before that. When she said Bertie got Frank to do his dirty work for him, I encouraged her to talk along those lines. She was only too pleased to get it off her chest.'

'Very good work,' said Miss Silver.

They turned into the street where Henry had left Hilary. The houses stood in their close rows, a few people went up and down, but there was no girl in a brown tweed coat and cap.

'I left Hilary here —'

'She must have gone round the next corner. She would walk to keep herself warm,' said Miss Silver.

Henry felt an odd relief. He had expected to see Hilary. In some obscure way he felt as if he had missed a step in the dark. He was jarred, and a little angry. Miss Silver's reasonable explanation was reassuring.

'If we wait here, she'll come back,' he said.

He went on telling her about Frank Everton's wife — 'She says Bertie Everton's been promising them money. He kept putting Frank off because he said he couldn't do anything till the will was proved. Then they found out that it had been proved, and Bertie put them off with promises. He said he wanted Frank to go abroad, and Frank wouldn't because of her. That was before they were married, and afterwards he said Glasgow was good enough for him, and he wouldn't budge. He said all he wanted was a nice little flat and plenty of money to pay for drinks all round, and he wasn't going overseas to please anyone.'

'That,' said Miss Silver, 'is very interesting.'

Henry nodded.

'I thought so. Of course you can't say he was a credi-table relation to have around — I mean, nothing very compromising about Bertie feeling that a good stretch of the Atlantic or the Pacific between them would make Frank less of a handicap. But there was something about the way she said it, if you know what I mean. Bertie had been very pressing, and Frank had been cocking snooks when he'd had one over the odd, and hinting at what he could say if Bertie pushed him too far.'

Miss Silver put her head a little on one side with the air of a bird who sees a plump and juicy worm.

'Did he say what he would do, Captain Cunningham?'

'He hinted that he could make it hot for Bertie. He said he'd done dirty work for him once too often, and that he wouldn't have done it if he'd known what Bertie was up to — said he'd got evidence that would hang Bertie if he took it to the police. The girl Phemie says he showed her the evidence and then made her promise she wouldn't tell anyone, because, he said, they might hang him, too, and he never meant the old man any harm.'

Miss Silver faced him on the narrow pavement, her eyes bright and alert.

'This evidence, Captain Cunningham — did she tell you what it was?'

'I've got it here,' said Henry. He gave his limp paper parcel a bang and produced it with the air of a conjuror bringing something out of a hat.

A curious change came over Miss Silver's expression. She put out her hand for the parcel and she opened her mouth to speak, but she neither spoke, nor did she touch the crumpled brown paper. Her hand fell to her side, her lips stayed open, and her eyes lost their brightness whilst remaining even more alert than before. She said in a quick, restless voice,

'Captain Cunningham, where is Miss Carew?'

At once Henry was jarred again.

'I left her here.'

'Then where is she?'

'She must have gone round the corner. You said so, — you said she would walk to keep herself warm.'

'She wouldn't go far. She ought to be here. I don't like it, Captain Cunningham.'

Henry was off before she had finished speaking. The street ran straight for about a quarter of a mile without a side turning. His long legs took him to the end of it in a very short time. He went out of Miss Silver's view round the left-hand corner. After an interval he crossed the head of the street again and disappeared in the opposite direction. Then he came sprinting back.

Miss Silver turned before he reached her and hurried back along the way by which they had walked together. Henry came up with her, panting. His heart thumped, 'Hilary — Hilary — Hilary — ' and he was afraid with that unreasoning fear which is the hardest of all to control.

'She isn't anywhere — Miss Silver — '

Miss Silver began to run in an odd hen-like manner.

'I think I ought — to tell you that — the Mercers are — in Glasgow — Captain Cunningham. In — point of fact — I — followed them — here. A police-constable is — meeting me at — their lodging — immediately. I am very apprehensive on — Mrs. Mercer's account. If — by any chance — Miss Carew — ' The words popped out in jerks, but she ran gamely.

They came into the street where the tenement houses were, and she caught Henry by the arm and pointed.

'That door — where the policeman is — fifth floor — on the left — ' This took the last of her breath, but as he broke from her she snatched the brown paper parcel and tucked it under her arm.

Henry went pounding across the street, shouted to the policeman, and flung himself at the stair.

After a moment's hesitation the policeman followed him.

Miss Silver followed the policeman.

A little while before, Hilary had been quite sure that no one could run up five flights of stairs. Henry now proceeded to smash this theory. From the moment Miss Silver mentioned her name a most devastating conviction that Hilary was in danger had driven him. It took him up the five flights at a record-breaking pace, and on the third step from the landing he heard her scream. He took those three steps in a stride and rushed the door. For a moment it held. He had the idea that someone was holding it against him, and thrust with such violence that the sudden inward swing shot Hilary and Alfred Mercer across the passage and into the kitchen. Hilary fetched up against the kitchen table gasping for breath, and Mercer, stumbling, blinded, with blood and ink running down his face clutched at his eyes with one hand

and with the other lugged an ugly horn-handled knife from his pocket. A steady stream of curses poured from his lips. There was ink on the floor, there was ink on Hilary, there was ink everywhere. It seemed impossible that so much ink should have come out of one small bottle.

Henry stood for a moment stupefied, and in that moment Alfred Mercer put his other hand to the knife and got it open. Hilary tried to scream, but she couldn't get her voice to do anything. It stayed shut up in her throat and choked her. She saw Henry take a step forward. She heard the sound of breaking glass as his heel came down on the bottle neck, and she saw Alfred Mercer gather himself up and spring. The knife flew out of his hand as Henry caught his wrist and banged his elbow against the door. And then there was a wild free fight, and a chair went down and Mercer tripped over it and Henry tripped over him. After which the Scotch policeman arrived and took charge.

Miss Silver walked in a moment later. She looked at the ink, the blood, the knife. She looked at Alfred Mercer in the big policeman's grip. She looked at Hilary, very pale and holding on very tightly to Captain Henry Cunningham. And she said in a gentle, enquiring voice,

'Pray, what about Mrs. Mercer?'

Hilary shuddered.

'I think she's dead. He — He — '

'I never touched her!' said Alfred Mercer. 'I never laid a finger on her — I swear I didn't!'

Henry put his arm round Hilary and held her up. She was shaking from head to foot.

'He was going — to poison her. He made her sign — a — confession — '

'Shut up, you!' said the policeman, and put a hand over Alfred Mercer's mouth.

'He made her — write it. I saw her — at the window —

232

she looked terrified — so I came up. She told me he — was — trying to — kill her. I wanted her — to come away. Then he came — and I hid — in the cupboard. He had that knife — and he made her write — what he said — and sign it. Then he — was going to give her something — to make her sleep — and she wouldn't have waked up again — ever —'

'I see,' said Miss Silver. She turned and went into the bedroom.

They waited in a dead silence. Hilary wished that she could stop shaking. She was so cold — that was it, she was shaking because she was cold. Nothing made you so cold as being afraid. It was horrible to be in the room with Alfred Mercer, even though he was quiet now and dabbing at his eyes with a stained handkerchief and the policeman's hand was heavy on his shoulder.

Miss Silver came back, walking briskly.

'Mrs. Mercer is not dead,' she said — 'oh, dear, no. She has fainted. She will certainly recover and be able to make a statement. Constable, I think you had better take that man to the police-station. I will see that nothing is interfered with here. Captain Cunningham, I should like your help in getting Mrs. Mercer on to the bed — I cannot manage her alone. And if you, Miss Hilary, will blow up that fire and put on a kettle, we will make her a nice cup of tea. In fact, I think we should all be the better of a nice cup of tea.'

CHAPTER THIRTY-FOUR

'We shall have to telephone to Cousin Selina,' said Hilary. She pushed back her hair and gazed rather wanly at Henry.

It was actually only about two hours since she had smashed the ink-bottle in Alfred Mercer's face, but it felt like a long and sordid week. The large Scotch policeman had taken his prisoner away. A detective had arrived to take charge of the flat. Mrs. Mercer had come out of her swoon only to go from one weeping fit into another until she was taken away in a taxi with a policeman and Miss Silver in attendance. Henry had then removed Hilary to an hotel, where she had got the worst of the ink off her hands and resigned herself to the fact that it would never quite come off her coat. They had just had lunch.

'Henry, we shall have to telephone to Cousin Selina,' she said.

'I don't see why. She wasn't expecting us back to lunch, anyhow.'

'It feels like months,' said Hilary with a shudder. 'Henry, can't you get married in Scotland just by saying you're married? I mean could we just do it, and then we needn't go back at all? I mean, I don't *feel* like Cousin Selina.'

Henry hugged her.

'Darling, I wish we could! But you've got to have a Scottish domicile nowadays.'

'How do you get one?'

'Three weeks' residence, I believe. You see, I've never lived in Scotland, though my name is Scotch. But we can get married a lot quicker than that in England.'

'That's no good,' said Hilary in a forlorn sort of voice. She rubbed her cheek against his coat sleeve. 'It's all rather beastly — isn't it? I mean about Mrs. Mercer. She — she cried so. Henry, they won't *do* anything to her? Because whatever she did, he made her do it. She wouldn't dare to go against him. Whatever she did, he *made* her do it — like he did with that confession.'

'H'm — ' said Henry. 'I wonder if she did shoot James Everton. It's possible, you know.'

'I know it is. That's what's making me feel so bad. I do hope she *didn't*.'

'If she did, I don't see where Bertie Everton comes in — and he does come in, he must come in. Hullo — I've only just thought of it — where's that parcel I had?' He jumped up from the sofa corner where he and Hilary had been sitting very close together and began to feel in all his pockets.

Hilary looked bewildered.

'What are you talking about darling? You hadn't any parcel.'

'It wasn't a parcel, it was evidence, with a capital E — and I've lost it!' He ran both hands distractedly through his hair. 'Hang it all, I can't have lost it! I had it in the street when I was talking to Miss Silver. We were talking about it, and then we got the wind up about you and I forgot all about it. You know, Hilary, I don't want to rub it in, but if you'd done what you were told and stayed where you were put — '

She gazed meekly at him through her eyelashes.

'I know, darling — Mrs. Mercer would have been dead.' The meekness vanished. 'She would — *wouldn't* she?'

Henry threw her a look of frowning dislike.

'Anyhow, I've lost that dashed parcel, and if you hadn't — '

'*Not* quarrelling,' said Hilary with a quiver in her

235

voice — '*please* not.' And all at once nothing mattered to Henry in the world except that she shouldn't cry, and nothing mattered in the world to Henry except that he should love her, and hold her close, and make her feel safe again.

Miss Silver entered upon a very touching scene. She stood just inside the door and coughed gently, and then neither of them took any notice of that she waited for a moment and thought it was pleasant to see two young people so much in love, and then coughed again a good deal louder than before.

Hilary lifted her head from Henry's shoulder with a start. Henry jumped up. Miss Silver spoke in her ladylike voice.

'I was afraid you might be worrying about your parcel, Captain Cunningham. I took charge of it, as I thought it would be safer with me.' She held it out, a shabby, disreputable parcel tied with a raffish piece of string.

Henry took it from her with considerable relief.

'You've opened it?'

Miss Silver appeared surprised and pained.

'Oh, dear me, no — though I confess that I have felt curious. You were telling me that Mrs. Francis Everton gave it to you, and that it contained a very important piece of evidence.

'It contains a red wig,' said Henry. He slipped off the string and dropped the paper to the floor. A most authentic red wig emerged.

Hilary said 'Oh!' and Miss Silver said, 'Dear me.' They all looked at it — red hair of a peculiar shade, red hair worn longer than is usual for a man, red hair of the exact shade of Bertie Everton's hair, and worn as he wore his.

Miss Silver drew a long satisfied breath.

'This is indeed an important piece of evidence. I congratulate you with all my heart, Captain Cunningham.'

Hilary's eyes were bright and frightened.

'What does it mean?' she said in a troubled whisper.

'That,' said Miss Silver, 'I am now in a position to explain. Will you both sit down? There is really no need for us to stand. No, Captain Cunningham, I prefer an upright chair.'

Hilary was glad enough to get back into the sofa corner. She slipped her hand inside Henry's arm and looked expectantly at Miss Silver sitting bolt upright in an imitation Sheraton chair with a bright yellow shell on the back. Miss Silver's mousy grey hair was smooth and unruffled, and her voice was prim and calm. The pansies bloomed serenely in her tidy dowdy hat. She removed her black kid gloves, folded them neatly, and put them inside her bag.

'Mrs. Mercer has made a statement. I think that what she has said this time is the real truth. The wig which enabled Francis Everton to impersonate his brother and thus provide him with an alibi on the day of the murder is a strongly corroborative piece of evidence.'

'It was Frank Everton at the hotel — *Frank*?' said Hilary.

'I was sure of it from the first,' said Miss Silver.

'But he was here — he drew his allowance here in Glasgow that afternoon.'

Miss Silver nodded.

'At a quarter to six. Let me run over the details, and you will see how it all fits in. Bertie Everton's alibi depends on the evidence of the people who saw him in the Caledonian Hotel on Tuesday, July 16th, the day of the murder. His own account is that after dining with his uncle on the evening of the fifteenth he caught the 1.5 from King's Cross, arriving in Edinburgh at 9.36 on the morning of the sixteenth, that he went straight to the Caledonian Hotel, where he had a late breakfast and put in some arrears of sleep. He lunched in the hotel at half-past one, and then wrote letters in his room. In the course of the afternoon he complained to the chambermaid that his bell was out of order. He went out some time after four, enquiring at the office if there had been any telephone message for him. He did not return to the hotel until getting on for half-past eight, when he rang and asked the chambermaid to bring him some biscuits as he did not feel well and intended to go to bed. In her statement she says that she thought he was the worse for drink, but when she brought him his tea at nine o'clock next morning he seemed all right *and quite himself*.'

Miss Silver paused, coughed in a refined manner, and proceeded.

'There were several points that struck me in this statement and in the evidence as to Bertie Everton's movements. To begin with, why, when he was staying at the Caledonian Hotel, did he take a train from King's Cross? The King's Cross trains arrive at the Waverley Station, which is a mile from that hotel. If he had taken a train from Euston, he would have got out at the Caledonian Station, where he would only have had to walk through a swing-door. Why, then, did he choose the King's Cross-Waverley route? It occurred to me at once that he must have had some strong motive. The point was unnoticed at the inquest, and it does not seem to have emerged at all at the trial.'

'Why *did* he arrive at the Waverley?' said Hilary.

Henry said, 'He didn't,' and Miss Silver nodded.

'Exactly, Captain Cunningham. It was Francis Everton who arrived at the Waverley Station, having come over from Glasgow, probably on a motor-bicycle. You were not able to get any information on this point?'

'No — no luck — too long afterwards.'

'I was afraid so. But I feel sure that he came on a motor-bicycle. The head-dress and goggles make a perfect disguise. Having garaged his machine, he had only to go down into the station, present the cloakroom ticket with which, I feel sure, his brother must have furnished him, and take out a suit-case containing a suit of Bertie Everton's clothes and this wig. The change would be easily effected in a lavatory. With his own clothes in the suit-case, he could then take a taxi to the Caledonian Hotel, and be seen breakfasting there.'

'How much alike were they?' said Henry. 'It was a bit of a risk, wasn't it?'

Miss Silver shook her head.

'No risk at all. The first thing I did was to secure photographs of the brothers. There is a decided family likeness, but Frank had short dark hair growing well back from the temples, whereas Bertie Everton's shock of red hair is easily the most noticeable thing about him. In this wig Frank would deceive any hotel servant. It would be so easy to avoid being seen full face. He had only to rest his head on his hand, to be busy with a newspaper, to be blowing his nose — there are half a dozen expedients.'

'The chambermaid never saw his face,' said Hilary in an excited tone. 'We found her, and she said so — didn't she, Henry? She said no one could mistake that red head of his, and when he complained about the bell he was writing letters with his back to the door, and he ordered his biscuits standing over by the window looking out, and when she brought them he'd been washing and had the towel up to his face drying it. I got it all out of her — didn't I, Henry?'

Henry put his arm round her.

'You'll get wind in the head if you're not careful,' he said.

'You did very well,' said Miss Silver. 'That was how it was done. And you see there was very little risk. Everyone in the hotel knew that noticeable head of red hair, and when they saw it they were quite sure that they were seeing Bertie Everton. At a little after four Frank left the hotel, asking about a telephone call at the office as he went out. He must have taken the suit-case with him and changed back into his own clothes. He could have done it in the station. He had then to pick up his motor-bicycle, ride over to Glasgow, and present himself at Mr. Johnstone's office by a quarter to six. The distance is about forty-two miles, I believe. He could do it easily. He was in the office till a quarter past six. At half-past six he was, I feel sure, upon the road again. But he made one big mistake — he stopped on the way for refreshment. Drink, as you know, was his enemy, and he was unable to resist the temptation. The moment I read in the chambermaid's statement that she thought Bertie Everton was the worse for drink when she answered his bell at half-past eight that Tuesday evening, I had the feeling that here was a very important clue. I was right. Enquiry quickly informed me that drink was not one of Bertie Everton's vices — I could not find anyone who had ever seen him the worse for it — whereas his brother's weakness was notorious. At that moment I felt sure that Bertie Everton's alibi was fraudulent and the result of a cleverly contrived impersonation. We shall never know all the details. Having got rid of the chambermaid, Frank would have had to watch his opportunity and leave the hotel. He most probably changed back into his own clothes up there in his brother's room. There would not be many servants about at that hour in the evening. He had only to get out of the room without being seen, after which no one would notice him. He could proceed to wherever he had left his motor-bicycle and return to Glasgow. But he did one thing which I feel sure was not in his brother's plan — he kept the wig. I have a strong conviction that he was never intended to keep the wig.'

'And it's the wig that's going to smash Bertie Everton's alibi,' said Henry in a tone of great satisfaction.

Miss Silver nodded.

'That, and Mrs. Mercer's statement,' she said.

Hilary leaned forward.

'The one Mercer dictated to her? Oh, Miss Silver!'

'Not that one. She kept on saying that it wasn't true, poor creature, and when I told her you could testify that it had been written in fear of her life she said she had put down what really happened a bit at a time when her husband was out of the way, and that it was pinned inside her stays. And there it was, done up in an old pocket handkerchief. It was very blurred and ill written, poor thing, but the Superintendent had it typed out and read over to her, and she signed it. We are old acquaintances, and he has allowed me to bring away a copy. Bertie Everton will be arrested without delay. I think that Mrs. Grey should be communicated with at once and advised to place Mr. Grey's interests in the hands of a first-rate solicitor. I will now read Mrs. Mercer's statement.'

CHAPTER THIRTY-FIVE

MRS. MERCER'S STATEMENT

'I want to say what I know. I can't go on any longer and not tell. He said he'd kill me if I didn't do what he said. I've wished and wished I'd let him kill me then and not swore false and let Mr. Geoffrey go to prison. I've not had one happy moment since, thinking about him and about Mrs. Grey.

'I've got to go back to explain. Alfred and me was sweethearts when I was a girl, and he let me down and lost me my character. And when I was out of a place Mrs.

Bertram Everton that was Mr. Bertie's mother heard about me. She was staying near my home, and she took me away to give me another chance, and had me trained under her cook, and by and by when the cook left I got the place. It's all a matter of twenty-five years ago. Mr. Bertie was five years old, and Mr. Frank was the baby. Mr. Bertie was the loveliest child I ever did see, though you wouldn't think it now. He'd the wonderfullest head of hair, for all the world like a new-minted penny, and he'd the sort of way with him you couldn't stand out against, and I suppose that was his ruin — everything come easy to him. He liked pictures and music, and he liked money, oh, something terrible. That's where it all began. He got into disgrace taking money that belonged to the other children, and then it come out that some of them had give it to him so he shouldn't tell on them for things they'd done, and it seemed that was worse than stealing. It fair broke his mother's heart, and she was never the same again. They sent him to be educated somewhere foreign after that, and he come home a very gay young gentleman and got into a fast set in London. And presently his mother died and the house was broke up, and I was in other places for years and didn't hear nothing about the Evertons.

'Well, then one day I come across Alfred Mercer again. I was in a place in London, and it was my afternoon out, so I had a cup of tea with him and we got talking about old times. We went on seeing each other after that, and he began to get the same sort of hold over me he had before. It seemed as if he could make me do anything he liked, so when he said I was to give in my notice I done it. He said we was to get married and take up a job with Mr. James Everton that was brother-in-law to my Mrs. Bertram. Solway Lodge, Putney, was the address, and we went and applied for it as man and wife, because that was what he was wanting. Alfred he said we'd get married before we went in, but he kept putting of it off. I had my references and Alfred had his, and he told Mr. Everton we'd got married, but we never, not till afterwards. Alfred he kept putting of me off, and come the last, I darsn't talk. He'd always made me do what he wanted, but now he'd got so as I was right down afraid to death of him.

'Well, then I got to know that Alfred was seeing Mr. Bertie on the quiet. We met him once when we was out together, and he stopped and spoke, and called me Louie same as he used to when he was a boy and come into my kitchen coaxing for titbits. I thought to myself "He wants something now," but I didn't know what it was. I said so to Alfred, and he told me to shut my mouth.

'Mr. James Everton didn't like Mr. Bertie. He was all for his other nephew Mr. Geoffrey Grey that was in the business — chartered accountants they called themselves. I don't know how it come about, but Mr. Bertie found out something his uncle done wrong in the way of his business. I don't know the ins and outs, but from what Alfred told me he'd obliged a friend over his accounts, and it would have got him into trouble with the law if so be it had come out. Mr. Geoffrey didn't know nothing about it, and his uncle was mortal afraid in case he'd get to know, because he thought the world of Mr. Geoff.

'It came so that Mr. Everton agreed to see Mr. Bertie and talk it over. Mr. Bertie come down from Scotland on purpose. That was the fifteenth of July, the day before Mr. Everton was killed. Mr. Bertie come to dinner, and afterwards they went into the study and talked. I knew there was something up, but I didn't know what it was, not then. I went upstairs, and when I come across the hall I could hear Mr. Everton shouting as if he was clean out of his senses. And all Alfred would say was that we'd be made for life, and he kissed me, which he hadn't done for

243

a long time, and said he'd given in our notice to be married, and told me to buy a new bonnet and make myself smart. I didn't know nothing then — I swear I didn't.'

'Blackmail!' said Henry suddenly. 'By gum! That's why he altered his will! He was in the soup, and Bertie blackmailed him into making a will in his favour!'

'Let her go on,' said Hilary in a whisper — 'let her go on.'

Miss Silver nodded, and went on reading.

'Next day Mr. Everton wasn't well. Alfred told me he'd gone to alter his will, and he was to let Mr. Bertie know as soon as it was done. "And that's a bit of luck for us all," he said. And then he told me he'd asked Mrs. Thompson in to supper that night. It was the sixteenth of July and a hot sunny day. Mr. Everton stayed shut up in the study. There was to be cold supper in the dining-room, and he'd go in when he wanted to. At a quarter to seven Alfred had me up into our room and told me Mr. Everton had shot himself. He said nobody mustn't know till after Mrs. Thompson had been in the house long enough to clear us of having a hand in it. He said they'd put it on us if we were alone in the house when he done it. He said Mrs. Thompson being deaf wouldn't know whether there was a shot or not, and he told me what I was to do and what I was to say. He swore if I went from it he'd cut my heart out, and he took out his knife and showed it to me, and said all the police in the world couldn't save me, and he made me go down on my knees and swear. And I was to tell Mrs. Thompson I'd got the toothache to cover up the way I was — after what he'd said. Mrs. Thompson come in at half-past seven. I don't know how I got through. Alfred told her I was near off my head with the pain, and she never doubted nothing. At eight o'clock I went through with some plates. I put them in the dining-room and come back. Half-way across the hall I could have dropped, for I heard Mr. Everton talking in the study. He was talking on the telephone — and I'd been thinking him dead this hour past! I didn't seem I could move. He said, "Come as soon as you can, Geoff," and he rang off.

'The door was the least thing ajar, and I could hear quite plain. I heard him go across the room, and I heard him scrape his chair like he always done pulling it up to the desk. And then he called out sharp, "Who are you? What do you want?" And so true as I'm a sinful woman I heard Mr. Bertie say, "Well, you see I've come back," and Mr. Everton said, "What are you doing in those clothes, you mountebank?" Mr. Bertie laughed and said, "Private business," and Mr. Everton said, "What business?" I was right by the door, and I looked through the crack. Mr. Everton was sitting at his desk very pale and angry, and Mr. Bertie was over by the window. He'd got overalls on like they wear on their motor-bikes, and a leather cap, and the goggles pushed up out of the way. I wouldn't hardly have known him if it hadn't been for his voice, but it was him all right. Mr. Everton he said, "What business?" and Mr. Bertie put his hand in his pocket and said "This". I didn't see what was in his hand, but it was Mr. Geoffrey's pistol that he left here when he got married, like he swore at the trial. I couldn't see what it was, but Mr. Everton seen it, and he started to get up, and he called out loud and said, "My own nephew!" and Mr. Bertie shot him.

'I didn't seem I could move. Mr. Bertie come over and shut the door and I heard the key turn in the lock, and then there was a kind of a soft sound that was him wiping the handle and wiping the key. And he must have wiped the pistol, too, because they didn't find any fingermarks on it, only poor Mr. Geoffrey's later on.

'I come over so frightened I couldn't stay no longer. I got back to the kitchen and sat down by the table and put my head in my hands. I hadn't been gone no time to speak of. Alfred was there with Mrs. Thompson. He'd heard the shot, but she hadn't heard nothing along of being so deaf. He shouted in her ear that I was pretty near off my head with the toothache, and then he come over to me and we spoke together quiet. I said, "He's killed him — Mr. Bertie's killed him." And he said, "That's where you're wrong, Louie. It's Mr. Geoffrey that's a-going to kill him in a quarter of an hour's time from now, and don't you forget it." '

Miss Silver looked up from the neatly typed copy of Mrs. Mercer's scrappy, blotted confession.

'You will notice the discrepancies in the poor creature's statement. She says Mercer led her to believe that Mr. Everton had committed suicide, but it is obvious that she had been primed beforehand with the evidence which she gave to the police on their arrival. Two such careful conspirators as Bertie Everton and Alfred Mercer would never have risked taking her by surprise in the manner she describes here. It is quite certain that she must have known that Mr. Everton was to be murdered, and that she had been well rehearsed in the part she was to play — she admits it with one breath and denies it with the next. There is of course no doubt that she acted under extreme intimidation.

'Yes,' said Henry. 'What I don't see is how they would have got Geoffrey Grey there if Mr. Everton hadn't telephoned for him.'

Miss Silver nodded.

'An interesting point, Captain Cunningham. I think it is clear that Mr. Everton was beginning to repent of having given way to blackmail. He intended to confide in Mr. Grey and enlist his help. He had been thrown off his balance by a sudden shock, but he was making a struggle to regain it.'

'Yes, I suppose it was like that. But that's not what I meant. The plan was to implicate Geoffrey Grey. Mr.

Everton played into their hands by telephoning for him, but how did they know he had telephoned, and what would they have done if he hadn't sent for Geoffrey?'

'Exactly,' said Miss Silver. 'The Superintendent raised those very points. Mrs. Mercer says that Bertie Everton overheard his uncle's conversation on the telephone. It was a piece of luck for them and reduced the risks they were running. Bertie Everton, who is an excellent mimic, had intended to ring Mr. Grey up after the murder. He would have imitated his uncle's voice and have said very much what his uncle did actually say. It was essential to the plot that Geoffrey Grey should find the body and handle the pistol.'

'They couldn't be sure that he would pick it up,' said Hilary. (Poor Geoff — walking into a trap! Poor Geoff! Poor Marion!)

'Nine hundred and ninety-nine men out of a thousand would have picked it up,' said Henry. 'I should for one. Any man who'd ever had a pistol of his own would.'

'Yes?' said Miss Silver. 'The Superintendent thought so, too. He is a very intelligent man.' She coughed. 'I think that disposes of those two points. I will continue.'

The paper rustled. She went on reading the anguished sentences in her cool, precise voice.

' "It's Mr. Geoffrey that's a-going to kill him in a quarter of an hour's time from now." That's what he said. I don't know how I kept from screaming. Such a wicked plot. And Mr. Geoffrey that never done them any harm — only his uncle was fond of him, and Mr. Bertie had set himself to get the money. He done murder for it and put it on Mr. Geoffrey, and that's the gospel truth if I never wrote another word.

'Mrs. Thompson she never noticed nothing. She thought I'd come over bad and she thought what a kind husband Alfred was, patting me on the shoulder and talking to me comforting like. If she'd heard what he said she'd have thought different, but she couldn't hear nothing. Alfred said, "Did he ring Mr. Geoffrey up?" — meaning Mr. Bertie — and I told him Mr. Everton done it himself. And he said, "When?" and I remembered as the clock struck eight when I was in the dining-room. Alfred turns round and shouts to Mrs. Thompson that I'll be better soon and a pity I didn't have the tooth out like he said. Then he goes into the pantry and he says to me, speaking quiet, "It's seven minutes past now, and you've got to pull yourself together. At a minute short of the quarter you go upstairs and turn down the bed and look slippy about it, and then you come down and stand by the study door till you hear Mr. Geoffrey, and then you scream just as loud as you can. And remember, you've just heard the shot, and if so be there's any mistake about it, it's the last mistake you'll ever make, my girl." And he picks up one of the knives he was cleaning, and he looks at it and he looks at me. Mrs. Thompson couldn't see nothing from where she sat, but I could, and I knew well enough that he'd kill me if I didn't do what he said.

'So I done it. I swore false to the police, and I swore false at the inquest and at the trial. I swore I heard voices in the study quarrelling, and a shot, and then I screamed and Alfred come running and Mr. Geoffrey opened the door with the pistol in his hand. And so he did, but it was Mr. Bertie shot his uncle and put the pistol there by the garden door for Mr. Geoffrey to find, knowing he'd be sure to come in that way like he always done. And Mr. Geoffrey picked it up, that's all he done, and come over and tried the door, and when he found it was locked he turned the key same as they reckoned he would. So there was his finger-marks for the police. But he never done it, and I've never had a happy moment since. Alfred and me got married next day, but he only done it to shut my mouth, and what's the good of that?

'Mr. Bertie he's come in for the money, and there's talk of our going to America with what he promised Alfred. It's a lot of money, but I'll be dead first. It wasn't any use my doing what I done, because Alfred'll kill me just the same. He's afraid of my talking — ever since I saw Miss Hilary Carew, in the train. I'm writing it down, because he'll kill me and I want Mr. Geoffrey to get free.'

Miss Silver laid the last sheet down on her knee.

'She signed it as a statement after it had been read through to her. I think there is no doubt that it is true as far as it goes.'

Hilary sat up. She still held Henry's arm. You need something to hold on to when the world swings round.

'I ought to be so frightfully glad — about Geoff and about Marion — but I can't — not yet. She's so unhappy, that poor thing!'

Miss Silver's expression changed. She looked very kindly at Hilary, and said in a gentle voice,

'It's better to be unhappy when you've done wrong, my dear. The worst thing that can happen to anyone is to be able to hurt other people without being hurt oneself.'

Hilary didn't answer. She understood that, and it comforted her. She waited a moment, and began to talk about something else.

'I don't understand about the time — I don't understand when Mr. Everton was shot.'

'It would be just after eight. He telephoned to Mr. Grey at eight. Mrs. Mercer corroborates that — she says the clock struck when she was in the dining-room. It would have been only a minute or two after that.'

'But, Miss Silver —' Hilary's eyes had a bewildered look — 'Mrs. Ashley said — you know, that daily help woman I went to see, the one that went back for her letter and heard the shot and all — she said the church clock in Oakley Road struck eight as she came past and it would take her anything from seven to ten minutes from there to Solway Lodge. I thought that helped Geoffrey, but she says the clock was wrong — a good ten minutes out — and that it would be getting on for the half-hour when she got up to the house.'

'Yes — so you told me,' said Miss Silver. She sniffed gently. 'And I told you that clocks were very unreliable as evidence. I think we really cleared this up.

'We went into it before. Mrs. Ashley did not tell you that the clock was slow — did she? She said she was afraid she was late. But if she thought she was going to be late, the clock was fast, not slow. You know, people find it very difficult to keep their heads about clocks. Hardly anyone would know whether to put their clock on or back for Summer Time if the newspapers did not tell them what to do. Mrs. Ashley is a very muddle-headed person. She used the same expression to me as she did to Miss Hilary, and when I pressed her she became exceedingly confused. I hope it will not be necessary to call her as a witness.'

'It must be possible to find out whether the clock is fast or slow,' said Henry in an exasperated voice.

Miss Silver looked decorously competent.

'Certainly, Captain Cunningham. I interviewed the verger, and found him most obliging. The clock was most undoubtedly fast fifteen months ago — quite ten minutes fast. It has a tendency to gain, and the late Vicar preferred it to be on the fast side, but the present incumbent has it regulated monthly. There is no doubt at all that it was fast on the day of the murder. When Mrs. Ashley heard it strike eight it was really only ten minutes to. She was then at the far end of the road, and she says it would take her a good ten minutes to reach Solway Lodge. She arrived, as she told you, in time to hear Mr. Everton exclaim, "My own nephew!" and when the shot followed she ran away.'

'Silly ass of me!' said Hilary.

Henry agreed.

CHAPTER THIRTY-SIX

Harriet St. Just looked across her showroom and thought she was doing well. These small, intimate dress shows were very good business. People clamoured for tickets, asked if they might bring their friends, and having come, they bought, and went away under a pleasant illusion of recaptured youth. They too would glide unearthly slim, they too would move in grace and beauty, as Vania did.

Marion was certainly well worth her salary. All the same, she mustn't get any thinner. She was a marvel at showing clothes, but if she went on losing weight they would be liable to drop off her. Harriet's mouth twisted. Outside business hours she often felt sorry for Marion Grey.

Just at the moment there was no Marion Grey — only Vania who was showing a black afternoon dress high to the throat, with long tight sleeves which came down over the hand. It was called *Triste Journée*. The heavy crepe took a simple yet tragic line. Marion wore it with a curious inward satisfaction, because Geoffrey was truly dead and it consoled her to wear this mourning robe, as if she wore it for him. She walked slowly round the circle of interested women, her head a little bent, her eyes cast down, her thoughts a long way off. Snatches of comment came to her ears without really reaching her mind. She had to stand, turn, walk round a second time.

Harriet gave her a nod, and she went out as Celia entered in a daring orange tweed, the gayest possible contrast to Vania's *Sad Day*.

As the door of the showroom closed behind her, she was aware of Flora in some excitement.

'Oh, my dear, you're *wanted* — on the telephone! A long-distance call — from Glasgow — that little cousin of yours, I think! And I told her you were showing, but she said it was more important than all the dress shows in the world, so perhaps — ' Flora continued to be informative even whilst Marion was saying 'Hullo — hullo — hullo!' with the receiver at her ear. She heard her say 'Hilary!' and then, 'What is it?' For some reason she found it impossible to go away. She had got as far as the door, but no farther. She remained there upon the threshold, and saw Marion put out a hand and feel for Harriet's desk and lean on it. She had not said a word after speaking Hilary's name. She listened, and she leaned upon the desk.

Flora felt unable to go, and unable to look away. She saw Marion's face change before her eyes. It was like watching ice melt, it was like watching the sunrise. There was a melting, and a softness, and a lovely surge of colour. She knew quite well that she ought not to be looking on, but she was thrilled to the bottom of a very warm, kind heart. She hadn't the slightest idea how long it was before Marion hung up the receiver and came to her with tears running down her face — tears from eyes that were young and soft again. She took Flora's plump, busy hands and held them as if they were the hands of her dearest friend. There are moments when everyone in the world is the friend of your heart and must share its joy. She said in the voice of a child who has waked from a dream of terror,

'It's all right — it's all right, Flora.'

Flora found her own eyes beginning to fill with tears. She never could help crying when anyone else cried.

'My dear, what is it — what's happened?'

But Marion could only repeat, 'It's all right, Flora — it's all right. Hilary says so.'

252

At the other end of the line Hilary clutched Henry in the horrid publicity of the hotel call-box.

'Henry — she didn't say anything — she didn't speak! Henry, I'm going to cry!'

'You can't cry here.'

'I can — I'm going to.'

'You can't!'

There were people in the lounge. There were two old ladies knitting on either side of the drawing-room fire. By the time they reached an empty writing-room Hilary no longer wanted to cry. She threw herself into Henry's arms, and rubbed the top of her head against his chin.

'Love me! Love me a lot! Heaps, and heaps, and heaps! You do — don't you?

Henry's reply was satisfactory.

'Because if it had happened to us — oh, darling, it couldn't happen to us — could it?'

'I'm not likely to be tried for murder,' said Henry.

'But we might get separated — we might quarrel and get separated — we nearly did — I thought we'd lost each other — I *did*! My heart was all squeezed up with misery!'

'Silly!' said Henry with his arms round her.

'Not!'

'*Very* silly.'

'Why?'

Henry had the last word.

'We belong,' he said.

THE END

By the year 2000, 2 out of 3 Americans could be illiterate.

It's true.

Today, 75 million adults... about one American in three, can't read adequately. And by the year 2000, U.S. News & World Report envisions an America with a literacy rate of only 30%.

Before that America comes to be, you can stop it... by joining the fight against illiteracy today.

Call the Coalition for Literacy at toll-free **1-800-228-8813** and volunteer.

Volunteer Against Illiteracy. The only degree you need is a degree of caring.

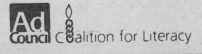

Ad Council Coalition for Literacy

Warner Books is proud to be an active supporter of the Coalition for Literacy.